The Danish Scheme

D1526569

Other Titles from Ring of Fire Press

Fiction:

Second Chance Bird
Essen Steel
Joseph Hanauer
No Ship for Tranquebar
Turn Your Radio On

Non-Fiction

Airships and Flight
Medicine and Disease
Railroads and Steam
Roads and Transportation
Ships and Sailing

These titles are available through Amazon CreateSpace, Amazon Kindle and other booksellers.

The Danish Scheme

by

Herbert Sakalaucks

Ring of Fire Press
East Chicago, IN
2013

The Danish Scheme
by
Herbert Sakalaucks

The Danish Scheme Copyright © 2013 by Herbert Sakalaucks
Brave New World Copyright © 2013 by Eric Flint

All rights reserved, including the right to reproduce this book or portions thereof in any form.

Published by Ring of Fire Press
East Chicago, IN, U.S.A.
http://www.1632.org

An earlier version of this story was serialized in the Grantville Gazette.

Publisher: Eric Flint

Editor: Paula Goodlett

Cover art by: Garrett W. Vance

Production supervisor: Rick Boatright

This is a work of fiction. Any resemblance to any person living or dead is entirely coincidental.

A Ring of Fire Press Original.

Introduction

This book is the first example of a new project we're launching in the 1632 series. We're publishing e-books under the imprint of Ring of Fire Press, consisting of two kinds of materials.

The first are reissues -- sometimes expanded and/or re-written -- of stories which were originally serialized in the Grantville Gazette. These stories were simply too long to be included in any of the paper anthologies published by Baen Books. At the same time, we felt it would be useful (and hopefully popular) to put them together in unitary volumes so that people who want to re-read them, or read them for the first time, don't have to hunt for them scattered over a number of separate issues of the magazine.

The second type are also reissues taken from the Grantville Gazette; in this case, compilations of fact articles on the same (or similar) subjects. We used to reissue fact articles along with stories in the paper editions published by Baen Books. But beginning with the change in format with Grantville Gazette V, where we switched from a direct one-to-one reprint of magazine issues to anthology-style "best of" collections taken from half a dozen issues, we stopped reissuing fact articles altogether. Again, we felt it would be useful (and hopefully popular) to put together unitary e-book volumes devoted to a single topic or closely related set of topics. That way, people interested in the subject matter don't have to hunt for the separate articles scattered across many issues of the magazine.

This is being done in consultation and with the agreement of Baen Books. As before, Baen will continue to publish the paper editions of the Ring of Fire series, as well as the e-book formats of those volumes. The material we will be publishing as Ring of Fire Press is material that Baen would not be publishing.

As evidenced by this volume, the Ring of Fire Press books will be available as e-books, and as paper volumes available from Amazon.com, CreateSpace.com and other retail outlets.

We hope you enjoy them.

Eric Flint
June 2013

Prologue

The Grantville Public Library was doing a land office business. Ever since the library had been opened to outside researchers all sorts of interesting individuals had shown up, with even more interesting results.

Today was no exception. Closing time had been half an hour ago and the researchers were *supposed* to all be out. Cecelia Calafano, the head librarian, heard the outside door close and glanced up to make sure someone wasn't trying to sneak in after hours. The researcher's most common excuse was that it was a matter of life or death, usually theirs at their employer's hands. This time it was a late departure. She heaved a sigh of relief, until she noticed her assistant holding a book in her hand, staring at the door and pale as a sheet. "Nancy, are you alright? You look like you've just seen a ghost!"

Nancy shook her head and turned around. "Maybe I have. Do you recall the name of the gentleman that just left? He's had me digging into all sorts of topics the past few weeks. He started on sailing and coastal maps and then moved on to farming and then mining earlier this week. Today he finished with investment prospectuses and North American history."

Cecelia paused for a moment, trying to recall the visitor. "I believe he said his name was Foxe. Luke Foxe, if my memory serves me correctly. Or at least that's what the letter of introduction from the Abrabanel's said it was. Why?"

"That's what I thought too." Nancy held up the last book the visitor had read. "Well, it says here he's going to die soon." She showed the book to Cecelia. It was a

1

simple children's book on early North American explorers. It said that Captain Luke Foxe died in 1635, after a brief illness. "The last thing he asked for, before he left, was this book. He read the entry and went white, but then started to laugh. I was curious and checked to see what was so funny. I almost wish I hadn't."

Cecelia gave a brief shrug. "Well, we've seen this before and probably should be prepared for it to happen again. You remember those Russians a while back? They were worried when they saw the dates on the czar. I must say though, it's the first time someone's laughed at their own death notice. We brought a lot of changes through the Ring; people change too. Maybe he'll find a way to beat his fate." They both turned as a late arriving customer rang for their attention, the incident quickly forgotten.

Meanwhile, the object of their attention was outside, tying down a trunk on his two wheel cart. It contained a wealth of coastal maps, synopses on nutrition and medical treatments, drawings of nautical and farming gear, and notes on mineral deposits throughout North America. Even without seeing the materials, the casual observer would have known Luke Foxe was a sailor. From his salt stained boots and his boat cape smelling slightly of distant shores, to his stance and walk, the years at sea had molded the man.

He finished tying the knots on the trunk and then shook his head in amazement as he thought again about the article. It wasn't often that one got to read their own obituary. The doctor he'd seen when he first came to Grantville had told him he needed to change his diet to help his stomach. Otherwise, the pain he'd been feeling would become a full blown ulcer and eventually kill him. The doctor evidently knew what he was talking about! He'd definitely have to follow the diet he'd prescribed. Maybe now the story would be different. He'd sure try to prove it wrong!

His luck seemed to be changing. He looked again at the old sailor's trunk, picturing the dreams it contained.

One final expedition to the New World! He sighed. It would have to wait until he finished the sailing charter for the Spaniard. He wasn't looking forward to that voyage now. He'd been contacted by them right after he had returned from his last exploration voyage. His usual patrons had been unavailable. King Charles had refused to see him and Sir Thomas had been sent out of the country and couldn't be reached. That had left him short of funds and starving. Otherwise he would have refused the Spaniard's commission. But a man had to eat, so he'd signed on and accepted his pay.

A week later, a letter from his patron, Sir Thomas Roe, had arrived from Copenhagen, with funds. It asked that Luke to go to Grantville and do some research for an enterprise for which Sir Thomas was trying to raise funds. The Spaniard had also asked him to go to Grantville to research sailing maps. Two payments for the same work finally put some weight in his money belt and food in his stomach. Hopefully, things should work out. The Spanish charter shouldn't take too long. After that, maybe Sir Thomas would make his dreams possible. He swung up on the cart with a practiced ease from climbing ship's rigging his entire life. He reached for a whip from under the seat and headed the horse and cart west.

September 1633, the Dutch and Spanish fleets off Dunkirk

"Fire as your guns bear, Mister Huetjens! I want each shot to count." Captain de Groot was determined to follow Admiral Tromp's order to engage the Spanish closely. The *Friesland* rocked to a steady beat as the gunners mate walked down the deck training and firing each gun individually.

It was less than an hour since the opening shots between the fleets. Cloud banks of gun smoke wreathed the ships and cut visibility to a few yards. Beyond sight in the smoke, the Dutch *fregatte Rotterdam* added her fire to the action. The *Friesland* had cut off the straggling Spanish galleon as soon as the fleets had met and the *Rotterdam* had joined her. The Spaniard was now paying for his poor seamanship. His main and mizzen masts were gone and only a stump of the foremast up to the foresail yard remained. Why he didn't surrender was a mystery. From the aftercastle, de Groot surveyed what little damage his ship had taken. The Spaniard's aim had been miserable, only a dozen or so shots through his canvas and two spars shot away. Tjaert called to his First Lieutenant, who was stationed near the tiller. "If this is the best the Spanish have, I'm not sure we'll need our allies."

Pieter de Beers smiled back. "Speaking of our allies, I wonder where they are?"

Tjaert shook his head in disgust, "Late as usual. The French commanders never can get started on time and I'm not sure if our English allies really have their heart in this fight. You'd think that they couldn't wait to finish off the Spanish threat. All these years we've been fighting and finally a chance to end the Spanish menace once and for all. They'll probably get lost in the smoke and end up shooting each other." He motioned toward the mastheads hidden in the smoke, "I've sent lookouts aloft to watch them and call out when they're close." He stopped before he added on his real fear. There was no need to worry the crewmen nearby, standing at their guns. *I just hope they don't blunder in and shoot us instead of the Spanish! This battle has all the signs that could happen.*

During a lull between broadsides, the *Friesland'*s mainmast lookout hailed the deck, "Many ships to starboard!" De Groot waved his broad brimmed hat to signal that he had heard the call. He turned to de Beers at the tiller, "Bring her up into the wind Pieter, clear of the gun smoke. I want to see what our allies have brought to the fight and make sure they know we're here." As the light sea breeze slowly cleared the deck of smoke, a mass of spray stained sails was clearly visible stretching across the horizon to starboard. The ragged formation of the combined French and English fleets had *finally* arrived.

The vanguard of the fleet was just about in cannon shot range of the fighting. The French were in some semblance of order, while the English were spread throughout the fleet, like a gaggle of geese going to market. In the slow motion action typical of fleet actions, the French columns spread out to sail into the ongoing battle. Stripped down to fighting sails, they were lucky if they were making three knots. Their strategy seemed to be to wait on firing and engage the entire Spanish fleet simultaneously. De Groot climbed into the lower shrouds to get a better view of the impending Spanish defeat. The Spanish fleet seemed oblivious to the approaching doom.

The reinforcements held their fire until they were well into the engagement area. *So they do plan to hold fire until they can deliver a decisive broadside! Maybe they do have someone in command that can fight.* A fluke wind cleared the smoke from the nearest English ship. Through his telescope Tjaert could even see its captain raise his arm and point out a target for his gunners. He tried to focus the glass in better. Somehow the direction he'd pointed didn't seem right. The captain snapped his arm down and a coordinated broadside was fired. A heartbeat later, the entire French fleet opened fire; into their Dutch allies.

Cloud banks of gunpowder smoke mercifully hid the shattered Dutch fleet from view. Captain Tjaert de Groot stood in the shrouds, dumbfounded, as the combined French and English fleets fired a second broadside into their former allies. He was helpless to intervene. Chasing down the Spanish straggler had taken them over a mile away from the main engagement. Only that quirk of fate had saved them from the disaster developing off their starboard quarter.

As the rumble of the second broadside subsided, de Groot shouted down to his officers near the tiller, "It's no mistake! The bastards have betrayed us!" A huge flash of light wrenched his attention back to the battle. An expanding cloud of debris was all that remained of Admiral de With's flagship. The entire ship's magazine had gone up at once. Ten seconds later, the concussion from the blast nearly shook Tjaert loose from the shrouds.

After he regained a firm grip on the tarred rigging, he again scanned the oncoming combined fleets. That simple action gave him time to think. Why the Spaniard he'd caught had been shooting high was clear now. They just needed to hold the Dutch fleet until the French and English could stab their former allies in the back. What wasn't clear was why, after all the years of support against the Spanish, they would choose the exact moment when a Spanish defeat was within their grasp to turn against the Dutch. A movement at the rear of the English fleet caught his attention. Three English ships had broken off from their ragged formation, shaken out their topsails, and appeared to be heading in the direction of *the Friesland*. De Groot swung down to the deck and casually walked aft to the group of officers at the tiller. Any appearance of concern could start a panic in the nearby gun crews. "*Mijnheer*, I believe it's time to break off and retire. Bring her about Mr. de Beers! I'll have one more broadside into the Spaniard's stern. Then we'll hail the *Rotterdam* and decide on a course home. The Prince will need to know about this betrayal." The nearby gun crews raised a ragged cheer.

The short respite from fighting had allowed the light breeze to clear most of the smoke bank away. The Spanish ship, the *San Pedro de la Fortuna,* was now visibly settling by the bow, but still firing back with her few remaining guns. As the *Friesland* prepared to fire a final broadside, de Groot shouted to the gunners, "Make it count men! This may be our last chance at a Spaniard for a long time!" As the broadside struck home, the Spanish ship visibly staggered. A lone shot from a stern chaser answered in reply. De Groot followed the shot as it sailed high. In a stroke of bad luck, it struck the *Friesland's* fore topsail yard and shattered it. Pieces of the mast, yard, sail, and rigging came down in a tangled mass over the starboard side. It acted like an anchor and slowed the ship down instantly. Even before the sail had settled over the side, Tjaert was shouting orders to clear the mess. Idlers on deck seized axes and immediately started to chop away at the tangled lines.

Meanwhile, off the port quarter, the *Rotterdam's* captain seemed to have divined Tjaert's original intent and was bringing his ship within hailing distance.

A corpulent figure appeared at the railing of her aftercastle with a speaking trumpet. Captain Joris van den Broecke hailed the *Friesland.* "Captain de Groot, do you need assistance?"

De Groot snatched up a nearby trumpet from the side rail and answered. "Joris, the day I need help from you will be the day you stop drinking schnapps!" He pointed to the English ships that were now definitely heading in their direction. "I think it's time to head for home." A final thud from an axe and the whip snap of parted cordage signaled that the wreckage over the side was cleared. "Let's head nor'east and try to lose the pursuit. If we can't, just follow my lead." Van den Broecke waived an acknowledgment and turned to pass orders to his crew. Tjaert set the trumpet down and walked to the opposite rail, where Lieutenant de Beers joined him to stare at the shattered Dutch fleet. "Remember this day well Pieter! Someday you can tell your grandchildren you were there when our country died." He paused and wiped a solitary tear away. If anyone had been brave enough to ask, he would have insisted it was from the gun smoke. His face went grim from a silent vow. *Those bastards will pay for this treachery, if it's the last thing I do!* In the meantime, he had three enemy ships to out sail! He started shouting orders across the deck to bring them to a nor'east heading, away from the English, and hopefully, home with a warning.

Chapter 1

Late September 1633, Copenhagen

The anteroom for the main audience chamber of Rosenborg Castle was bustling with servants and visitors. Sir Thomas Roe, the English ambassador to the Danish court, stood quietly contemplating a newly hung portrait of Princess Margaret, waiting for his audience with the Danish king. A rather splendid painting of the harbor had previously hung there and he wondered briefly about the reason for the change. The new painting made the room seem dreary.

He stole a quick glance around. All of the nearby servants were obviously concentrating on appearing invisible. By the sounds coming through the door, that wasn't a bad strategy. Either the king's current visitor was being royally reamed or the king was in his cups again. In either case, the prospects for this audience seemed bleak. To make matters worse, the summons gave no indication as to why his presence was requested. The recent arrival of news on the Dutch defeat off Dunkirk, which had been aided by the French and English fleets, seemed a likely reason for the summons, but the Ambassador had mentioned nothing about that particular tidbit of news.

Sir Thomas sighed in frustration. Since the signing of the treaty that created the League of Ostend, Roe had received no correspondence from court. Nothing like this had happened on his previous assignment to the Moghul's court. There, he had received regular, monthly guidance. His appointment as plenipotentiary for the Ostend treaty had left him with broad negotiating powers, but the recent lack of instructions left him very concerned about his position at court. Court intrigue had been on the rise even before he left on this assignment. What little English gossip arrived in Copenhagen indicated Charles was becoming increasingly difficult to deal with and Wentworth's faction appeared to be on the rise. Wentworth had once been a friend, but his recent silence was even more troubling. *Something* had to be changing at court. In addition, his requests for royal approval of a New World trading company had also been completely ignored.

A courtier came into the anteroom from a side door. Roe had met him before but couldn't recall his name.

"The king is ready to see you now, Sir Thomas." He turned back the way he had come.

Winding through the palace halls, they finally came to a stout, wooden door, guarded by two soldiers armed with swords. They simply nodded to the courtier and opened the door. Inside, Christian was seated with the Danish chancellor, Christen Scheel, while the king's oldest son, Prince-Elect Christian, stood near the fireplace. The king motioned for Roe to take a seat across the table from the chancellor.

"Sir Thomas, I suspect you are somewhat at a loss for what's happening in London, seeing as no instructions from your king have arrived in some time." Sir Thomas started to answer but the king continued, stifling the perfunctory denial. "It seems Charles is more concerned about the future loyalty and trustworthiness of his nobility, based on information he received from 'Grantville'. This may be a fine time for you to be out of sight and mind." He smiled sympathetically, but then assumed a look of displeasure. "Cardinal Richelieu seems to be using this fear to reap some valuable advantages. That's the main reason why I asked for this meeting. The less the French know, the better. I have a matter that needs to be presented personally by you to Charles."

The king gestured and Chancellor Scheel pushed a document across the table to Sir Thomas. "Since

Charles is in such a generous mood with his territories," Christian continued, "I feel that it is in Denmark's best interests to redeem its outstanding dowry pledge, before Charles sells those lands to someone else as well."

Sir Thomas was struck by the brevity of the document. The proposal was very straight forward. It simply stated that Denmark was paying the sixty thousand florins that it still owed on the dowry for Princess Margaret. In exchange for the payment, England would return the Shetland and Orkney Islands to Denmark, which had been the original guarantee for the dowry payment. Since the dowry agreement didn't have an expiration date, nor interest terms, the sum was the original amount.

Sir Thomas' eyes widen slightly. *Charles was sure to complain about that! In that regard, he was worse than the London moneylenders.* The reason for this personal meeting still was not completely clear. The document was simple and could have been handled by a Danish emissary. He set the document down. "I assume that Your Majesty has some additional points to add. The document itself is very straightforward. I'm just not sure how receptive my king will be to an amount agreed to over one hundred years ago."

Scheel leaned forward. "His Majesty and I had that very same discussion. As His Majesty rightly pointed out to me, the incomes the English Crown received from the property while they held it would more than satisfy any interest amounts owed. You simply need to present that to Charles, in your usual elegant manner."

Christian nodded, like a school master confirming the performance of a prize student and then continued the explanation. "I want you to make the presentation, because reports I've received seem to indicate that foreign visitors have not been well received by the officials surrounding Charles." He paused to let those implications sink in. "I realize this trip will involve some personal expense and hardship on your part, Sir Thomas, and I am prepared to provide the necessary funds."

Scheel reached down, brought up a leather bag that contained a significant amount of coinage, and pushed it across to Sir Thomas. The king continued, "My sources also tell me that you have expended a large sum in promoting a New World exploration company. I hope Captain Foxe's information is as valuable as he thinks it is." Without blinking an eye, Sir Thomas managed to digest the fact that Christian was *too* well informed and must have a source among his associates. "Unless I'm mistaken, though, this land sale by Charles to the French is a serious setback to your efforts. When you return with the signed agreement, we will speak further about your expedition. It may be that we have some mutual interests in that area"

The reason for the meeting was now clear. The king wanted his personal ties at court to smooth the transaction. Just how good his current ties were was a question that might involve his personal safety. The implied help for the exploration company outweighed the possible safety issue. With most of his wealth already tied up in the adventure, he needed it to succeed or he would be bankrupt. But could he,*emotionally,* handle returning to England? Since his wife's death there last year, he had simply let his affairs there linger, without thought. If he returned, he'd have to face her loss. In the end, he simply nodded his acquiescence.

The chancellor rose and motioned for Sir Thomas to accompany him. The meeting was over. Once they left the room, Scheel proceeded to supply further details on the trip. "I will accompany you on the trip, with two guards for the gold. The funds will be turned over only after the agreement is signed. It's not that the king doesn't trust you; he's concerned what Charles might do to you if the gold were in your possession. The stories we hear about the English court concern us."

"You're not the only one!' Sir Thomas thought. "I'll appreciate your company. Hopefully the voyage will be swift and uneventful." They continued down the hall, discussing details for the voyage.

As soon as the door shut, Prince-Elect Christian reached for a tankard from a nearby servant and then resumed his earlier argument. "Father, why spend this much money on some worthless islands? And what does Denmark need with barren lands across the seas?"

As soon as he finished, Prince Christian realized he'd overstepped himself. The king took a deep breath but before he could burst out angrily, his son hastened to add: "Did you find something in the books from Grantville, Father? Or is it just something the French let slip?"

That mollified the king. He took a swallow from his flagon and said: "As a matter of fact, both. Undoubtedly, Richelieu has read about the future of France and wants to create a new French Empire, second to none. He needs resources to do that and the Grantville books confirm that the New World can provide those. I foresee nothing but problems if that transpires. What will happen to a Lutheran Denmark if a Catholic France becomes the strongest country in the world after the Swede is finished?"

He slammed a fist on the table. "Our faith and our country would cease to exist! There is a future saying that to stay the same means stagnation and eventual death. We must grow to survive. If we can hold off the Swede and stymie the French plans, the New World offers us an opportunity. I can't build a large enough army, but a navy may be within our means. The Dutch and Spanish are shattered and the English are turning inward. We can be a naval power. In the future, the books show that the North Sea will play a vital role. The price I'm paying is a pittance compared to what will come."

Looking at the map on the wall, the prince saw a pattern and realized what the acquisitions would do. "You'll make the North Sea a Danish lake! And provide stopping points to the New World. We can expand west, but where will we find the people to settle the land?"

Christian simply smiled. "That's what I need the Englishman for." He drained the flagon and held it out to the servant. "Bring me another!"

Chapter 2

October 1633, London

Sir Thomas waited, alone, to present the Danish proposal to King Charles. The debate with Scheel had been long and vocal during the voyage, whether he should do it alone or with the Danish Chancellor. They hadn't resolved the issue until they had arrived at their lodgings in London. A heated discussion in the inn's taproom between two patrons had convinced Scheel that Charles would not *appreciate* a foreigner at the meeting. The Chancellor had nearly choked on his drink when the nearby discussion was ended with one patron slamming his tankard down and roaring out, "I don't care what you think! My cousin's a guard at Court and I tell you, he's seen Charles have foreigners thrown out who presume to petition the Crown. The only ones who get a hearing are Englishmen who are in favor with Wentworth or mercenaries with companies for hire!" Once he could speak coherently, Scheel turned to Sir Thomas, "You're right. If even commoners are privy to such details on the King's attitude, it must be true. You present it to Charles alone." Sir Thomas smiled. The two shillings he'd paid the actors had been well spent!

When Sir Thomas and Chancellor Scheel presented the Danish request for a meeting with the King, Thomas Wentworth had demanded that they simply tell him about the proposal and he would make the presentation. Wentworth had once been a friend, but the changes in Court had changed him, for the worse. Rumor said that his relationship with Charles was rocky and other factions were using that to advance themselves. As far as Sir Thomas could tell, Wentworth had been too nice to handle the intrigues of court. Before he could phrase an appropriate reply, Chancellor Scheel had simply stared Wentworth down, informing him that, "King Christian directed that Sir Thomas, *and only Sir Thomas*, was to present his proposal to Charles. You may attend. It makes no difference to me. But if you try to interfere, I will return to Denmark and Charles will not be pleased when word finally reaches him why I was here!" Wentworth acquiesced, but the look he gave Sir Thomas promised a payback in the future.

Two days later, Sir Thomas waited outside the audience chamber, alone, to present the treaty. The door to the audience chamber opened. Sir Thomas picked up the leather case containing the proposed treaty and was ushered in. As he entered, he was struck by the differences between the Danish and English courts. Where Christian had simply his council present, Charles was surrounded by a host of court favorites. Two small dogs sat at his feet and another was in his lap. Wentworth stood beside the throne, twisting his moustache in boredom, ready to offer advice. Charles looked irritated and waved Sir Thomas to come forward.

The King wasted no time getting to the point. "Sir Thomas, I understand that Christian has sent you here to make a proposal. What does the old drunkard want now?" Two of the nearby courtiers tittered at the implied insult.

Bowing low, Sir Thomas opened the case and withdrew the proposed treaty. "Your Majesty, King Christian requested that I present this proposal to you." He handed the treaty to the King. "He has been informed by the French of your need for funds and wishes to provide what assistance he can. He proposes to settle a long outstanding debt between our countries."

Avarice and confusion were both evident on the King's face. "And what is this *debt* that he has sent you here to settle? And how much is it?" Avarice had won out.

"Sixty thousand florins, in gold, to settle the dowry for Princess Margaret. His Chancellor accompanied me on my voyage and brought the funds with him. He awaits your Majesty's direction where to deliver the funds."

"And what does he expect in return? I know he's too tight to do this just from the goodness of his heart!" The crowd of courtiers laughed at the King's jest.

"He wants to redeem the islands that were pledged as earnest for the debt, the Shetland and Orkneys." Sir Thomas had closely watched the King as he made the presentation. At the mention of gold, Charles had taken the bait. Now he had to seal the deal.

Wentworth whispered a long explanation to the King. Charles scowled at Wentworth like he'd bitten into a lemon. He finally gave a grudging nod of dismissal and turned back to Sir Thomas. "We're familiar with that agreement. Why should I settle for the same amount as was pledged all those years ago? Surely I deserve interest on the funds pledged!"

Sir Thomas had been waiting for that question. "Your Majesty, you have received interest on those funds. The rents and incomes from those lands have inured to the Crown all these years. That was the reason why the lands were pledged, so that you wouldn't have to deal with something as degrading as usury while the funds were owed."

Charles still looked like he'd bitten into something sour, but the thoughts of what an extra sixty thousand florins *in gold* would buy won out. Wentworth started to say something, but Charles waved him off with his lace handkerchief, his contempt apparent to all in the room. "Very well, I'll agree." A page stepped up with a writing table. Charles dipped a quill in an ink stand and signed with an angry flourish. "Just make sure the funds are delivered to the palace today!" The page heated a wax stick over the document and then Charles smashed his ring in the pool of hot wax, sealing the agreement.

16

Sir Thomas bowed, but remained. "I have one more request, Your Majesty, if I might?" Charles gave a brief wave of the kerchief to indicate he continue. "I have sent a number of requests to court to confirm whether the exploration company I had proposed chartering had been approved. To date I have heard nothing. I had hoped this was due simply to replies being lost between London and Copenhagen."

Wentworth smiled and leaned forward again to say something to Charles. This time the advice seemed to please Charles. The King smirked and then answered. "Your requests were not misplaced. They were ignored! My treaty with France has placed those lands beyond my authority to give." From behind the throne, Wentworth beamed. "If you persist in pursuing this effort beyond this date, the Crown will view that as treason and deal with it accordingly!" Throughout the crowd, there was a scattering of feral smiles from those that saw a possible rival squashed before he could even become a remote threat.

Sir Thomas maintained a straight face. He had anticipated the answer. There was no reason to give Wentworth and his faction something more to gloat about. It simply was time to get out of England and return to Denmark. At least there was a possibility there for his plans. Still, returning to his estate in Woodford before the return voyage filled him with pain.

* * *

The ride to Woodford, just outside London, was brief. As the carriage approached the parish church, he rapped on the ceiling to signal the driver to stop. The cold, bitter wind blowing the low clouds across the sky were a perfect reflection of his emotions. It seemed just like yesterday that he'd received word from his attorneys' that his wife had died from one of the fevers that had swept through London last winter. They had laid Eleanor to rest at St. Mary's in the family's plot.

Theirs had been a marriage that had grown through the years. She'd always been there for him in their nearly twenty years of marriage whenever he returned from travels. She'd even gone with him to Constantinople, but this last trip, she'd wanted to stay home. The posting was supposed to have been short and she wanted to have the house ready for him when he returned from this last assignment from the King. Now he had one last duty.

He entered the graveyard next to the church and walked slowly to the family plot. A freshly carved stone immediately caught his eye. "*Here lies Lady Eleanor Roe, Much Beloved Wife of Sir Thomas Roe*". An urn, with faded flowers from summer stood nearby. A blank space next to the stone's inscription was left for his final resting place. As he stood there, Sir Thomas reminisced on all the wonderful times he and Eleanor had shared. Quietly sobbing, he said softly, "Ellie, I have to leave England for a time. I don't know when I'll return. Most likely 'twil be to join you. Forgive me for not being here when you needed me the most. May God keep you in the Grace and Peace you deserve." After a short, silent prayer, Sir Thomas made his way slowly back to the carriage to finish the trip to his home.

As the carriage pulled up in front of the manor, he noticed that the staff had maintained the house in good order. Michael, the doorman, hurried to open the door. "Welcome home Sir Thomas! We've been expecting you. It's just Matilda and me here now, but if you're planning to stay, I know how to reach the rest of the staff that's still in the village." He noticed Sir Thomas' red rimmed eyes. "I see you've already stopped by the church. I've made sure her favorite flowers were there during the summer. I knew you'd want that. We all miss Lady Eleanor deeply." He bowed his head in sympathy.

"Thank you Thomas, I know Ellie would have welcomed the flowers. As to your other question, I don't plan on staying. I'll be closing up the house and moving out of the country. If you and Matilda are willing, I'd like you to accompany me when I return to Copenhagen. There will always be a job for the two of you."

"We suspected this from the tone of your message, Sir, and we do want to stay with you. There is one thing though that we're not sure you know about. The letter probably crossed paths with you on your trip here." He turned toward the front door and motioned, as if calling someone. The door opened and a slim dark haired young girl stepped out. "This is Agnes Roe, your cousin's child. She arrived last month. Both of her parents died in the plague and she had nowhere else to go. She's been a big help since she arrived and we hoped you might find it in your heart to let her stay." The look of fear and concern on his face was mirrored by the young girl.

Sir Thomas stared at the young lady he hadn't seen in years. The last time had been when her parents came for Eleanor's thirty fifth birthday celebration. All he remembered was a little girl that was fascinated with his books. Now, she was a scared young lady waiting for her fate to be spoken. His heart caught in his throat. He and Eleanor had so wanted children, but what was a widower to do with a nearly grown child? His emotions must have been evident as Agnes' wan smile seemed to fade. *Well, this surely must be God's answer to my prayer!* He quickly took a deep breath and answered, "Welcome child! I may not have much experience as a parent, but I'm sure you can help me learn!" Extending his hand, he let her lead him into the manor. For a brief moment, the sun broke through the clouds.

Chapter 3

November 1633, New Amsterdam Harbor

The two Dutch *fregätten* floated quietly, wrapped in a white shroud, waiting for answers. The dense fog that had settled over the New Amsterdam harbor was both a blessing and a curse. It hid them from potential enemies but made navigation hazardous and obscured what was happening onshore. That something *was* happening was evident to the ships' captains. The muffled cries and the reflection of flames in the night fog were noticeable, even out in the harbor off Fort Amsterdam. The *Friesland* and the *Rotterdam* had used the full moon to approach the coast and then used the cover of the harbor fog to sail unobserved into the anchorage. When the disturbance on shore became evident, they had quietly sent their crews to quarters, with their guns loaded but not run out.

Captain de Groot strained to make some sense out of the lights from shore. Ever since the decision to try and reach New Amsterdam after the defeat at Dunkirk, he'd worried that they might not reach the colony before their enemies. It appeared that the worst had happened. After a hurried discussion with Captain van den Broecke, he used the fog and darkness as cover to send his last remaining boat ashore with his first officer to scout the situation. The boat was now overdue and he was worried.

Visibility was down to ten yards. Every swirl of the fog brought visions of a French or English ship bearing down with guns run out. Finally, he could wait no longer. He picked up a speaking trumpet, and stepped to the railing. He made sure the trumpet was directed at the *Rotterdam*'s aftercastle, away from shore and possible foes, and hailed the ship. "Joris, my boat is overdue and I have no others left to send. Can you send one? We must know what's happening." He placed the trumpet to his ear to catch the reply. Instead of the expected answer, a laugh could be heard close by on the water. He reversed the trumpet and hailed the *Rotterdam* again. "Hold off, we've heard something." Slowly a lantern became visible through the fog. It came roughly from the direction the ship's boat had taken earlier when it headed toward shore.

"Ahoy, the *Friesland!* Where the hell are you?" The shout was loud enough to carry across the harbor. It was the first officer, Pieter de Beers, and he was obviously drunk.

De Groot raced to the opposite rail, fear for his ship making a cold knot in his gut. A drunken sailor revealing their presence to possible enemies was the last thing he needed. If the French or English had somehow beaten them to New Amsterdam, they could be facing serious opposition. Surprise would be their only hope if they were outnumbered. The boat bumped alongside and he hissed down at it, "Quiet you fool! You'll give us away. Come aboard and make your report." Oars creaked loudly as they were shipped and stored. Tjaert silently gnashed his teeth in frustration at the commotion.

De Beers boarded slowly, holding onto a rum bottle. When he reached the deck, he swayed more than the wave motion would account for and there was a broad smile on his face. Tjaert could smell the rum half way across the deck. De Beers gave an exaggerated salute, still holding the bottle. "Everything is fine, sir. The town is just celebrating a successful harvest. The director general extends his greetings ... " He raised the rum bottle. " ... and an invitation to both crews to join the celebration." He extended the bottle to his captain.

"Very well, Mr. de Beers." In his relief at the news, Tjaert reflexively accepted the bottle and took a small taste, and then a longer swallow. The rum sent a warmth to his stomach that drove away the chills of the night fog and his fears. "It seems you've already received your share of the invitation. You'll be staying on board." He turned to the watch officer by the companionway. "Have the men secure from quarters and pass the word over to the *Rotterdam* that everything's fine. Then tell off some men for an anchor watch. Everyone else can go ashore. After what we've gone through the past months, they deserve it. We'll see about fresh provisions and water in the morning."

Word of the invitation spread quickly and sailors appeared on the deck ready to disembark, as if by magic. They ended up milling about for some time. The battle damage from Dunkirk had left the Friesland with only one usable boat. The captain went ashore in the first trip. It took nearly an hour after he left to finish rowing the remainder of his crew ashore.

De Groot intended to seek out the Director General, Wouter van Twiller, to learn the latest local news and pass on what had happened at Dunkirk. The director general apparently had the same intention and was waiting for him on the dock. Van Twiller was short, stout, and very well off, judging by the cut of his clothing. "Captain de Groot, to what do we owe this pleasure? It isn't often that two ships of our fleet come to call. I want to assure you our fullest cooperation to make your stay enjoyable. Your men are welcome to join our harvest celebration." He gestured toward the crowd around the fires. "Your first officer mentioned that you have news, but he said I had best talk to you."

Other well wishers started to drift toward the dock. Tjaert took van Twiller aside. "Is there someplace I could speak to you and your other leaders in private?"

The look on Tjaert's face sobered up von Twiller quickly. "The church is just up the street. I'm sure no one's there at this time of night." He grabbed a young man who had been hanging back. "Go and fetch Krol, my uncle, Schuyler, and de Vries. Tell them I said for you to fetch them and don't take no for an answer. Bring them to the church! Do you understand?"

"Yes, Uncle." The youth ran off to the partiers by the bonfire.

Wouter asked de Groot quietly, "How bad is the news?"

All voyage-long Tjaert and Joris had debated this very question. The fleet had undoubtedly been defeated at Dunkirk. What remained of it was unknown. They had been in the best position to carry a warning home and had been driven off. Most likely, any survivors had gathered at Batavia or Recife. In any case, what remained of the fleet would need an extensive refit before it go do anything to hinder the Spanish. Tjaert answered, "It's long and involved and I'd rather go through it just once. Suffice it to say that there won't be many Dutch ships calling here for some time." His face took on a nasty scowl. "I can't say the same about others."

Van Twiller pulled on his moustache as the words sank in. The colony was in danger of attack! By the time they reached the church, his stomach was twisted up in knots. The company's money meant for the city's defenses had gone to other, more profitable, personal ventures. When he had spent those funds, he never dreamed that someday the defenses would actually be necessary.

It took nearly half an hour to locate and bring the leaders to the meeting. Others had also drifted in and Van Twiller had agreed they might be needed, so they too had stayed. As soon as Captain van den Broecke arrived in the company of the last two members, Tjaert started in with his news. "There's no way to make this easier to hear. Our fleet has suffered a major defeat."

The New Amsterdam leaders all started to ask questions at once, but Tjaert cut them off with a wave of his hand. "Let me finish first. We met the Spaniards off Dunkirk in September. The action initially began very well for us. "When the French and English fleets arrived,

I watched as they passed through our fleet to attack the Spaniards. Without warning, they fired into our fleet instead. It was a slaughter."

He paused to let that fact sink in, and then continued. "That's when I noticed that three Englishmen were definitely heading to engage us. I intended to try and head to port and warn our countrymen of the defeat, but the English had the weather gauge and kept forcing us to the north. They kept coming, but their pursuit seemed halfhearted at best. Eventually we were able to lose them in a fog bank, but by then our only choice was to head here."

Joris van den Broecke stood up with a beer in hand and slapped Tjaert on the back. "He's too modest. The ploy he used to make our escape was brilliant. As we approached a fog bank, he had a brazier set up in a hatchway and lit off some old, damp gunpowder and rags to smoke like there was a fire below decks. Then he started his men pumping water like they were fighting the fire. As soon as we reached the fog bank, he doused his running lights and launched his long boat with a spar holding decoy lights. The long boat held four casks of old spoiled gunpowder and a slow fuse. When the powder went off, the English must have thought he'd blown up. They broke off the pursuit. I guess they didn't think *my Rotterdam* was worth any further effort."

Tjaert was blushing from the praise but added, "I'm not sure their hearts were in it from the beginning. Their fleet seemed more than willing to let the French have the lead from the brief observation we had before the chase. I just gave them an honorable excuse to break off." The scowl reappeared on his face as he growled, "We may have escaped, but they kept us from carrying a warning home!"

"But what of our fleet? What happened to it?" Kiliaen van Rensselaer, von Twiller's uncle, had cut straight to the crux of the matter.

"I don't know." Tjaert answered and Joris just shrugged his shoulders in agreement. "The French treachery destroyed or heavily damaged most of the ships not already closely engaged with the Spaniards. We'd been pounding the Spanish, but had gotten almost as much damage in return. I'd guess only a dozen, at best, were still fit enough to try to escape. In any case, the fleet has ceased to exist as a force to hold off the Spanish and their new allies. What advantage the Spanish take from their victory depends on their leadership. The best we can hope for is that they only close off our ports. Or we may have lost the war. In any case, we're on our own here."

"But what do we do here in the colony?" Van Twiller had started as a West Indies Company clerk years before and realized the implications from the loss of the fleet. The Spanish were a long-time enemy, but were more concerned with retaking Holland. The English were fierce trade rivals at sea and the French, rivals in the fur trade. Trade and money were powerful motivators. "Without the fleet, we're at the mercy of any fleet that arrives here. The French and English both have reasons to wish us gone and the means to hurt us here."

Tjaert paused to ponder his answer. If he phrased it properly, they might follow his lead and he had a vow he wanted to keep. Van Twiller appeared to be a weak leader and might be easily manipulated. "You probably have some time before you have to worry about an attack. We didn't go down without inflicting heavy losses. They'll need to refit before anyone can show up here. We need to ourselves. We both suffered damage to our masts and rigging in the fight and on our voyage. Our bottoms need to be careened and shot holes repaired. Do you have a yard that can handle those types of repairs?"

"Only if we do it one ship at a time." A slender, elderly man in the back answered. From his weathered appearance, he had once served at sea. De Vries owned the local shipyard and understood the tasks involved.

"It doesn't sound like you've suffered any damage we can't handle. Your size may complicate matters. How fast we have to finish will be the biggest concern."

Tjaert's spirits rose. "I'd hoped you'd say that. In that case, I'll keep one ship on patrol. We may have been badly hurt at Dunkirk, but we can still take the fight to our enemies. We plan on trolling the Grand Banks for prizes. I intend to hurt the French and English as much as I can. It may be only a pinprick now, but who knows what the future will bring." All of the heads seemed to nod in unison. They hadn't the faintest idea what they were agreeing to, but at least someone was offering a plan they could follow. Tjaert felt a warm glow inside. *I can keep my vow! France and England will pay!*

Tjaert sat quietly, off to the side, as the meeting slowly wound down. He tried to size up who the real leaders were in the colony. Van Twiller might be the Director General, but his earlier impression was confirmed. He certainly was no leader in a crisis. As long as they didn't seem to be drifting from where he wanted them to end up, he kept quiet.

During the discussion, De Vries added an extra two weeks to his estimate for repairs when he realized that both ships were *fregätten*. He announced he would have to extend the slipway to handle the larger size of the ships. In the end, the consensus was that repairs on both ships would last about two months after the slips in the yard were extended.

By the time the meeting had broken up, Tjaert was relieved that at least the local leaders seemed to grasp the severity of the situation. They would do what needed to be done to get his ships battle worthy again. If only the French and English would cooperate. As they left the church, everyone wanted to get them aside for a private talk. Van Rensselaer's prestige won out.

Chapter 4

November 1633, Copenhagen

The Chancellor was waiting to greet him as the carriage arrived. Sir Thomas was mildly amused. *A successful mission has its advantages! Suddenly, everyone's your friend. I hope it carries over to this meeting with the King.* It was only two days since their return from England with the signed treaty. He instinctively reached down to insure the seals were still intact on the pouch. It was in a lot better condition than he was. The return voyage had been swift, due to an autumn storm. Throughout the voyage, he and the Chancellor had both remained below decks, suffering from seasickness. His stomach still refused to keep down anything with even a hint of grease. Scheel, on the other hand, looked disgustingly cheerful. *Maybe the good news has put his master in a good mood too. For our sakes, I hope so.* The message summoning him had included a pointed request that his partners also come along. His two passengers were in answer to that request.

Saul and Reuben Abrabanel had contacted him shortly after he first started putting out feelers to various investors about a planned expedition to the New World. They were younger members of the far flung Abrabanel banking family. They represented a number of interested parties from Germany that were interested in developing resources in the New World. Besides money, they had brought an even more valuable resources, information and access, to the partnership. They had eased the way for his explorer, Captain Luke Foxe, to investigate the records in Grantville. Most people were still not aware of the vast treasure trove of information that had been brought back through the Ring of Fire when Grantville was transported from the future. Where most looked to technology and politics, Sir Thomas recognized that the mining and sailing information available was by far more valuable. But it still took money to develop the opportunities presented by that information.

Now, if he could just get them to keep their mouths shut and let him make the presentation to King Christian, they might have a chance to get the financing they needed. Their family had money, but not enough, and definitely not the power that would be needed to protect the new settlements. They were young, and brimming over with schemes to make more. Just the combination that would not endear them to royalty. On the carriage ride to the palace, he'd already had to shoot down two hare brained schemes by Reuben. He couldn't imagine getting Christian to give them money to transport settlers! Simply getting him to invest would be difficult. Their schemes would just scare the King off.

As they exited the carriage, he made introductions all around. Scheel's attitude was immediately apparent, *two Jews*. Even with all their hair brained schemes, Sir Thomas had taken a liking to the Abrabanels and Scheel's attitude stuck in his craw. Maybe the King *should* pay for the settlers. It would definitely be a thorn to Scheel, who seemed to feel that all the King's money was really his. Their host motioned for them to follow him into the castle.

The Chancellor appeared in a hurry and spoke over his shoulder as they walked. "His Majesty will see you right away. He is short for time today but insisted that your business be included on his schedule. He's having to deal with some issues on the navy yard in Bremerholm that have arisen." They followed Scheel, who maintained a brisk pace, until they arrived at the audience chamber. The guards came to port arms, but Scheel stepped around them and opened the door. Inside, King Christian was seated next to a fireplace that was struggling mightily to keep the large room a few degrees above the outside temperature. He waved them in, to sit in the chairs around the walls. Two of his sons were also in attendance, standing near the fire, warming their backsides. By the look of the servants bustling around the room, it had only been opened and a fire laid in the hearth a few minutes before their arrival.

The King motioned impatiently for the presentation to begin. "Well Christen, You know I'm expected in the main audience chamber in an hour. You insisted that I squeeze that meeting in. We'll have to be quick about this!"

"Yes, your Majesty!" Chancellor Scheel nodded for Sir Thomas to start. The two Abrabanels stood quietly in the background.

Sir Thomas broke the seal on the pouch and presented the signed treaty to the King. "As you suspected your Majesty, the scent of gold convinced Charles to ratify the treaty. He objected to the lack of interest, but finally acquiesced when I pointed out the income he'd received in the meantime. Your analysis of his temperament was brilliant." *It never hurt to acknowledge royalty's brilliance, especially on the rare occasion it was true.* "As you can see, it's signed and sealed with the royal seal. Shetland and the Orkneys are again Danish lands." Sir Thomas stepped back with the bearing of someone who had successfully accomplished a difficult task.

King Christian contemplated the treaty for a moment, with a slight smile, and then got down to business. "You've done all I asked Sir Thomas. Indeed, from what I understand from Christen, at some risk to yourself. Your efforts will be rewarded. I remember our previous discussion on your enterprise and that's why I asked you to bring your associates. I have some plans for that area, but I would like to hear what you have to propose before I proceed further."

Sir Thomas took a deep breath before starting. He was an Englishman to his very soul, and King Charles had made it clear that any attempt to explore the Americas would be viewed as treason. On the other hand, the chance to open up new lands would secure his place in history, not to mention the profits that would result He'd left no hostages for Charles to threaten him with. In a way, he was like Charles; greed had won out.

"Your Majesty, when I learned of the Ring of Fire and the knowledge that had come from the future, I took a chance. I realized that a man who took advantage of the lessons written in those books and the information they contained could change the world. I sent someone I trusted to research the trade that evolved from the settling of the new lands. I believe you mentioned you knew of Captain Foxe the last time we spoke. He returned with a treasure trove of information. He has already undertaken one successful voyage of discovery and learned the hard lessons that exploiting these new resources will involve. What I propose is an expedition to settle the lands in and around Hudson's Bay and places between here and there. The wealth of gold, steel, furs and fish that these lands hold is beyond comprehension. My associates," he pointed to Saul and Reuben, "represent the House of Abrabanel and are the main investors so far in this endeavor. What we intend to do is avoid the mistakes so many others made and insure the settlers are well supplied and numerous enough to survive their first two years. We are seeking support to insure that success." He paused to let the King ask questions.

Instead, Christian surprised him. "I am well acquainted with Grantville. I too have received information on what the future holds. My efforts were more toward what would benefit Denmark in the future. It seems that France, too, has obtained knowledge of the future and is taking steps to strengthen herself, I fear, at the expense of the rest of Europe." He fixed Sir Thomas with a stare. "You do realize that where you're proposing to go is now all part of New France? Even as an ally of France, I doubt the Cardinal would approve of my officially sending an expedition there."

Sir Thomas smiled. "It's been *claimed* by many parties. Even Denmark has some history in this area in the past. So far, no one has bothered to do anything about this area. France's record so far has been abysmal in protecting her interests. She couldn't even stop two freebooters from capturing New France for England. She had to depend on English charity to get it back. If we successfully plant a settlement there, we would control the area. We're not asking for Danish military support, simply funds to do the job ourselves and a port to ship our goods to when we are ready to start trading."

Christian looked unconvinced. "How do you plan on coaxing people to such a desolate region? As you've said yourself, Richelieu can't even settle the lands south of there."

Reuben stepped forward, an animated smile on his face. Sir Thomas froze, praying Reuben wouldn't sink all their hopes. Reuben bowed, "If I may Your Majesty?" He pulled out a broadside from the case he'd brought and passed it to the King. It was a copy of a recruiting broadside Captain Foxe had found to bring settlers to Canada. "We intend to repeat what worked extremely well in the future. These regions would be known for the gold they held and we intend to spread that message far and wide. In the future, gold rushes brought thousands to hunt for gold. In the end, they settled down to work the land when the gold ran out. We will take anyone interested and charge them for the privilege of passage. As long as they have food and tools, they can work the land. We know where the minerals are and will control the wealth by controlling the valuable land." He bowed again and sat down. Sir Thomas let out a silent sigh. Reuben had been listening to some of what he'd said. He'd just added a little embellishment.

The King looked toward the two princes. "You see, I was right. They do have a plan!"

Turning back to Sir Thomas, his demeanor became grave. "Our plans seem to be compatible. I am interested in supporting your endeavor, but not as the Crown. As a current ally of France, I cannot afford to offend the Cardinal too much. Neither can I tolerate a France that grows too powerful. The alliance is already strained. If you can live with that, then we can proceed further."

Sir Thomas looked from Saul to Reuben. They both nodded agreement. "We can accept that Your Majesty. But if France should intervene militarily, what would Denmark's reaction be?" Christian just smiled and admired the warm glow from the fireplace.

"I understand. As someone said, we would have look out for ourselves" Sir Thomas returned a standard diplomatic response.

King Christian stirred and added, "Non-involvement also extends to anything Charles should do, too. I cannot protect you if he recalls you and formally asks for your return. However, if I can't find you, I can't return you. Do you understand?"

Sir Thomas understood, since it was a game he'd been playing most of his adult life. "I've always enjoyed new sights. I'm sure this enterprise would have some to offer."

"Very good. What I propose is that, in exchange for investing twenty thousand florins, all trade comes back through Denmark and pays the usual customs and We receive an annual income of five thousand florins. Your company will administer the new territories, to include collecting taxes in the Shetlands and Orkneys. You will receive a third of those funds for your expenses. The rest shall come back to pay back the dowry funds."

Again, Sir Thomas looked to his partners, who both nodded. "Agreed! Who shall we send the proposed charter to for review?"

"My Chancellor will be our coordinator, to reduce the visibility. You need to expedite your preparations. It appears that the war may be heating up in the spring. My

French allies are pressing for further attacks on the Swede. I haven't committed yet, but somehow word has leaked. My next meeting is to address the problem of the refugees that are already in the city."

Sir Thomas saw the scowl on Scheel's face and just managed to hold back a laugh. He could hear behind his back that someone was already stepping forward. He didn't even need to turn to know that it was Reuben, taking advantage of the opening.

"Your Majesty, if I might make a suggestion?" Christian made a hurry up motion to proceed. "I know that the refugees are costing the crown to keep them quiet and peaceful. Why not let one problem solve another. I'm sure the Company could transport the refugees to the New World for less than what they will cost to maintain here. We would get extra settlers, and you clear out the riff raff."

Christian rose to leave. "I'll consider it. Send me a proposal with the charter. I'll have Christen work out the details for both." The door opened and a servant entered, a worried look on his face.

"Your Majesty, word just arrived from Bramstedt that Lady Kruse has given birth. You have another daughter, Elisabeth Sophia."

After twenty three previous children, the King merely shrugged. "Now, I must be off!" He reached for his forehead, in evident pain. A nearby servant quickly handed him a drink that he knocked back in a long draught. He paused a moment to savor the taste and then set the tankard down. After a prodigious belch, his demeanor improved. He stood up, and motioned for both princes to accompany him. Everyone then rose and bowed, until the door shut behind the King and his entourage. Sir Thomas then looked at Reuben and slowly shook his head in amazement.

* * *

A bright, warm sun and a cool breeze made Copenhagen the best place in the world as far as Sergeant Karl Andersen was concerned. He strolled with the three young members of his city watch patrol through the open air market. They paused occasionally to gossip with the shopkeepers. There was an undercurrent of tension in the market, but all the patrol got for their questions were dry throats. Karl anticipated stopping for a large stein of beer with his men when their shift ended in an hour. Otherwise, the day had been relatively peaceful, with only the one pickpocket breaking the calm. The thief had literally fallen into their arms as he rounded a corner to escape from his victim. Karl's years on the city watch and in the army had taught him to enjoy days like today, since they usually meant the other shoe would drop soon.

He was jolted out of his daydream of beer by an unusual noise. A faint commotion could be heard from ahead of them. "Come on, men," he said and headed toward the noise.

When they reached the next corner, there was a definite commotion off to their right. "Sounds like a fight!" The most junior member, Jens, nearly squeaked in his excitement. Everything recently had been blissfully quiet and Jens was anxious for action. Muffled cries sounded, coming from the section of the city where the recent influx of refugees had congregated. Trouble had been brewing there for some time.

As they got nearer, Karl spread his arms and brought them to a halt. "Seems like our afternoon's peace is over, boys. Check your gear; it sounds like the refugees have started to riot." He shook his head in disgust. "Third time this month. They're getting hungry and the council does nothing, as usual." Karl glanced back to check his men. Gunnar and Jakob were ready, but Jens' scabbard threatened to trip him again. "I thought I told you to get a new strap for that scabbard! Serves you right if it trips you and you get stuck."

The sounds of a major riot were now plainly audible from the square ahead. "Jens, be prepared to go for help if I tell you." Karl didn't need a green recruit in a riot. He'd be just as likely to stick one of the patrol with his sword as a rioter. "Now, draw swords and cudgels and follow me. Wait for my signal before you do anything drastic!"

They charged around the corner, buff coats flapping and boot nails sparking on the cobblestones, only to halt, completely dumbfounded. A crowd of men, women, and children were laughing, cheering and dancing in the street. A number of people waved copies of a broadside. Extra copies were posted on the wall of the nearby church.

Karl grabbed a youngster who had a broadside in his hand. "What's going on here? We thought there was a riot!"

The boy grinned and held up the sheet. "Says here they're giving free land to all able-bodied men; two hundred rods square!" Father says now we won't have to beg the city council for a meal." He twisted free and raced off into the mob.

Karl shook his head in amazement. "Put 'em away, boys. It looks like we aren't needed here now. I just wonder what will happen when these fools wake up and find out this was a lie. There'll be hell to pay then!"

The watchmen sheathed their swords and cudgels. Karl watched the crowd for a few minutes and then announced, "Let's call it a day! I don't know about the rest of you, but a beer sounds good right now." The run had worked up a powerful thirst for all of them and their watch was over. As they started out, Karl bent over and picked up a broadside that someone had dropped and jammed it in his tunic.

* * *

The door slammed shut and nearly shook the painting off the wall. The logs in the fireplace settled, giving off a shower of sparks. Sir Thomas stalked into the room, looking like he was ready to spit nails. "What the hell were you thinking, Reuben? We agreed to post broadsides announcing the new company, not tell all of Copenhagen that we're giving away free land. The King hasn't signed the charter yet! What's he going to say if he sees a broadside?" He paused to catch his breath, and then turned to the other of the pair. "Or was this your idea, Saul?"

The Abrabanel brothers started to laugh.

This only set Sir Thomas off again. "Your uncles may have put up funds for the expedition to Hudson's Bay, but my friends and I have our fortunes tied up in it, too!" Normally a very mild-mannered English diplomat, Sir Thomas Roe appeared ready to strangle the younger men.

Saul attempted to calm Sir Thomas down. "Yes, Reuben was the one who had the broadsides printed and distributed. According to the discussions you and Captain Foxe had with us, recruiting colonists is the biggest task facing us if the expedition is going to sail on time." He poured a glass of wine, handed it to Sir Thomas and then continued. "We've already had fifteen families stop by the office to sign up. Another week or two and we should have all the soldiers, fishermen, and farmers we need. Then all we'll need are the miners and craftsmen you said you would locate."

Sir Thomas stared at the glass and then downed it in one long swallow. "Just how do you plan to pay for their passage? You're giving away thousands of acres."

Reuben said, "Remember, the king said he wants the refugees and all the riffraff cleared out? If he keeps his promise that the crown will pay for every refugee family and prisoner we send, we should cover all the charter costs for the first fleet." With a cocky grin he continued, "We've made sure that everyone we've signed up is listed as a refugee. I've also made arrangements with the city jailer to have all prisoners with craft or military experience turned over to us. We may not have to cover any passage expenses ourselves. The king will cover it all!

"Besides, what are a few thousand acres, compared to the millions that the Company will still own."

His calm manner stopped Sir Thomas as he was working up to another outburst. Slowly, the impact of what the brothers had done dawned on him. "Well, I'll be damned. You boys may actually put one over on Christian with that charter. Now, I just have to get him to decide to sign it!" With a firm goal to accomplish, Sir Thomas visibly relaxed. "And you're right, only settlers will make our lands valuable. It looks like I'll have to get the miners and craftsmen moved here as soon as Christian signs the company's charter." His demeanor brightened visibly as another thought struck him. "Captain Foxe will need to get his ships ready to sail sooner than I thought, too. I'll notify him that he needs to proceed with his part of the enterprise immediately."

Chapter 5

Captain Luke Foxe reread the note from Sir Thomas. He chuckled when he read the part about Reuben's ploy to recruit colonists. In the flickering lamp light, his features still showed a hint of the experiences from his last discovery voyage to Hudson's Bay and the recent voyage to Greenland. The privations he suffered as he waited for the audience with King Charles that never came, and the poor food the Spaniards had for their sailors on the voyage to Greenland, had aged him. The last month, though, had done wonders for his health. The small inn, where he was currently lodged, had some of the best food he'd eaten since he first went to sea. He'd finally been able to follow the Grantville doctor's advice on changing his eating habits. His stomach no longer bothered him. The only problem was that his trousers were starting to get a little snug. *A month back at sea and that problem should take care of itself.* He waved the letter at his young clerk.

"Svend, I want you to prepare the letter to Sir Thomas that we discussed earlier, on the four captains I met with today. They are all interested in charters for the expedition and their ships meet our needs. I'll meet at his convenience tomorrow to go over the details."

"I'll get to it immediately, Captain." At fifteen years of age, Svend McDermott had all the eagerness of youth for a great adventure. Ever since Captain Foxe had first sought lodging at his mother's inn, Svend had been like a young puppy trying to please its master. Captain Foxe's tales of exploration had fired Svend's longing for adventure. Luke had finally surrendered to the inevitable. As his share of the work to prepare the expedition to Hudson's Bay increased, Luke hired Svend as a messenger. Surprisingly, Svend had turned out to be well-educated, with a clear hand for writing. He now served as Luke's temporary clerk.

"As soon as you have a clear copy ready, I'll sign it and you can take it to Sir Thomas' house. Wait for his answer, if he's there. I'll ask Mette to keep a meal warm for you."

* * *

With the signed letter in a leather pouch, Svend set off for Sir Thomas' house. Supper tonight was to be chicken with dumplings. Svend could almost taste his mother's cooking as he raced out the door and rounded the corner. With his mind on dumplings, he barreled right into one of the four watchmen heading toward the inn. Svend knocked the youngest man over in a tangle of limbs and scabbard.

The older watchman, who was evidently the leader, grabbed Svend by his collar and lifted him clear. He roared at the man on the ground, "I told you Jens, get that strap fixed! If this had been a real brawl, you'd be dead." Then he growled at Svend, "And where are you off to in such a hurry, lad? Or are you running from someone?" He set Svend down but still held onto his collar. If Svend was a thief, he was too agile for the older man to run down.

Svend opened the flap of his pouch to show the letter. "I'm carrying a letter from Captain Foxe to Sir Thomas Roe. I apologize for my inattentiveness, Sergeant."

Karl finally got a good look at his captive's face and grinned. "You're from the inn, aren't you?" Svend just nodded vigorously. "I thought you looked familiar. Be on your way, but watch where you're going!" He let go of the collar, then gave Svend a smack on the backside that propelled him off. He opened the door to the inn and motioned his men in. "Let's get that beer before anything else interrupts us."

As befitted the status of the ambassador from the English court to Denmark, Sir Thomas' house was in the Hovermarken neighborhood and was solidly built of gray, faced stone. Before he climbed the steps to the door, Svend paused to straighten his tunic and run his fingers through his hair. *The Captain would really dress me down if I showed up looking like a street urchin,* he thought, as he reached for the bell pull. This was the first time he'd been to Sir Thomas' house since the ambassador's family and staff had arrived from England. The door opened and Svend was surprised to be greeted by a petite, dark-haired young lady.

"May I help you?"

Tongue-tied, Svend finally managed to blurt out, "I have a letter for Sir Foxe from Captain Thomas, I mean Sir Thomas from Captain Foxe."

She smiled at his mix-up, but then opened the door wide and invited him in. "My uncle is in the study. Please have a seat and I'll get him."

As she walked down the hall, Svend noticed that the dress she was wearing was a recut hand-me-down from a larger woman's wardrobe. He also noted that it still set off her slim figure.

A few minutes later, Sir Thomas appeared. "Agnes said you've a message from Captain Foxe?"

"Yes, sir." As he handed over the letter, Svend continued, "Captain Foxe asked me to wait for your answer, if it was convenient."

Reading the note, Sir Thomas started back down the hall. He motioned for Svend to follow. As they entered the study, Sir Thomas pointed to a set of hardback chairs along the wall. "Have a seat. I do have an answer and I won't be a moment composing it." He opened the desk drawer, took out a sheet of writing paper and a quill and quickly penned a reply. He then blotted the sheet to dry the ink. He passed the note across to Svend. "Take this back to the Captain. If he should ask, you may tell him that I'm very pleased with his choices."

Svend placed the note in the pouch and headed for the door. The young lady watched his departure from behind a partially shut door at the end of the hall.

* * *

"I must be getting old," Karl thought, trudging through the gathering dusk to his home. "Only two beers, and Magda won't even be surprised I'm early and sober. I've been home early every night the past two weeks." He sighed. "Just an old married man." He opened the door to the small house he and his wife, Magda, shared with their son, Johann and his family.

"*Farfar!*" He was instantly mobbed by his four oldest grandchildren. The youngest sat in a cradle near the fireplace just watching the scene. Magda looked up from her cooking. "Children, let your grandfather get in the door before you pester him." She kissed Karl with a full spoon in her hand, "Dinner will be ready as soon as Johann finishes at the shop." She tasted the stew and then continued to stir the pot. The stew's aroma had Karl's mouth watering. She gave Karl the look every wife had when she knew something was up. "I hear there was some excitement this afternoon among the refugees. Anything important happen?"

"No, just someone posted broadsides about free land. Can you imagine, the fools actually thought someone would give them free land?" He reached into his tunic and pulled out a rumpled paper. "Here's a copy. Some people will believe anything."

Magda read the broadside and frowned. "Too bad you're too old to start farming and the land is so far away. We could turn the house over to Johann." Karl looked at her like she had lost her mind, but Magda continued with a twinkle in her eye. "Then they would have enough room, especially since Bergitte just found out she's expecting again!"

Karl's jaw dropped, "Does Johann know yet?"

"No. Bergitte plans to tell him when he gets home tonight. And don't you dare let the cat out of the bag beforehand!"

"This calls for a celebration. I'll get the akvavit from the cabinet."

Karl headed to the storage closet, and Magda turned to toss the broadside into the fire. She paused instead, folded the paper and tucked it into her apron, a thoughtful expression on her face.

* * *

The next day dawned cold and cloudy with a hint of precipitation to come. Winter was not far off. Luke finished the last of his breakfast, then sighed, contented. "Mette McDermott, I can't remember when I've eaten so well!"

"You must be getting old, Captain. You've already forgotten you said the same thing yesterday." Smiling, Mette picked up Luke's dishes and headed toward the kitchen.

While the buxom, blonde widow retreated into the kitchen, Luke realized that he felt better than he had in years. Ever since his trip to Grantville, where he saw his "obituary" in the history books, his attitude on life had changed. Knowing when and how one was supposed to die tended to change one's focus on life. If he could cheat death, anything seemed possible, even starting a family. *Now where did that idea come from?*

Muttering to himself about crazy old men who should know better, Luke looked up when Svend entered the room. "Are you ready? We have a busy day. We'll head to the ship and get my books and papers for the meeting. I want you and Mr. Barrow to come with me." Luke picked up his boat cape. He needed to concentrate on the upcoming meeting, but the retreating image of Mette McDermott stayed with him.

As they walked to his ship, the familiar sea smells on the morning air set Luke to thinking about the planned voyage. There were still serious questions to resolve for the planned expedition. He had heard from other sea captains about the problems that had beset the Roanoke, Jamestown, and Plymouth expeditions and he wanted to avoid their disasters. Those expeditions had tried to get by on half measures and, inevitably, ended up on half rations. If investors could be convinced to actually start a colony on a firm footing, the long term payoff should justify the cost. Four or five seaworthy vessels of at least eighty tons each should meet the initial shipping needs. They would carry not only settlers, but adequate food supplies, tools and trade goods. His ship, the *Köbenhavn*, would serve as one of two main ships to carry colonists. He wanted two other ships to carry the soldiers, equipment, and enough food to last until a harvest could be brought in. A fifth ship would carry livestock, grain and trade goods. They would need to be well armed, too. His *Köbenhavn*'s armament consisted of eight cannon and the livestock ship could carry six more cannon. After they arrived, four could be unloaded for the defense of the colony. Along with forty arquebuses, powder, and shot, that should deter any but the most determined attackers. Trade goods to acquire the needed land from the natives should make for good relations with the new neighbors. They would also need at least one resupply of food with the second group of settlers, in case there were crop failures the first year. He'd have to make sure that group left early enough to avoid the tremendous storm the history books said would strike in the fall. Maybe he should mention it at the meeting. He hadn't heard any rumors about it yet. Something large enough to drown over fifteen thousand people surely would have generated some gossip!

The short walk to the *Köbenhavn* went quickly. Luke came out of his reverie as they arrived and he checked the rigging for any problems. A lifetime at sea had made that check second nature. His first officer, John Barrow, was efficient, as usual. All yards were squared off and the running and standing rigging showed no sign of excessive wear or stretching. The *København* was two hundred tons, painted black with a white strake, and was only two years old. It was the best ship he'd ever commanded. Sir Thomas had purchased her specifically for the expedition and refitted her with some new features based on the nautical writings Luke had found in Grantville. When Luke and Svend boarded, John Barrow met them at the entry port.

"Morning, Captain. I have your papers for the meeting in your cabin, just as you requested."

"Good! And by the way, you'll be going with us, John." John scowled at the news. His dislike of meetings was legendary, but Luke insisted. "You'll need to know our decisions and reasoning behind them, first hand, and I may need your expertise. You're the best man I know at loading cargo, and there are bound to be questions with all the equipment and supplies we have to take. Svend will be along to help carry the papers and books." Luke gestured to the low, gray clouds. "It looks like it might snow soon, so let's be off."

Just before they reached their destination, the prediction came true and a fine snow started to fall. John looked disgusted. "Hope the meeting goes quickly, Captain. These cobblestones will be slick if we get much snow."

"I'm afraid we're going to be a while today. Sir Thomas' note hinted that things were moving faster than we originally planned. I want you to speak up if you have any ideas or you catch anything that I miss."

John rapped on the door with the pommel of his knife. When the doorman answered, he announced, "Captain Luke Foxe and party to see Sir Thomas."

The doorman bowed and gestured for them to enter. "You are expected, sirs. The other gentlemen are here already."

44

They were greeted by a crackling fire in the brick fireplace of the study. Five men arose as they entered.

Sir Thomas made the introductions. "Captain Foxe, thank you for being so prompt. You know Saul and Reuben Abrabanel. And this is Adolphus Bamberg, the local factor for the House of Cavriani." The fifth guest was pointedly ignored.

"Gentlemen, Captain Luke Foxe, his first officer, John Barrow, and their clerk." Svend quietly placed the papers he was carrying on the table as Sir Thomas asked Luke, "What can you tell us about the ships you've found?"

Luke paused to pick up a list from the pile of papers. "Based on the number of passengers and amount of equipment that are needed for the first expedition, I calculate that we will need almost seven hundred tons of carrying capacity. The *Köbenhavn*, of course, and I've located four other ships that I feel meet our needs. Captain Thomas James, with his *Henriette Marie*, already has experience with Hudson's Bay. We've known each other for a number of years. He would be my recommendation as the second in command of this expedition. His ship and mine would carry most of the colonists. Captain Lars Johannson with his 90-ton *Kristina*, would carry the expedition's livestock and trade goods. Captain Jan de Puyter of the 150-ton *Wilhelm* and Captain Martin Rheinwald of the 120-ton *Hamburg* would carry some settlers, provisions, weapons, soldiers and equipment. This assumes that we are still looking at the planned numbers and leave in March. Captains Johannson and Rheinwald each have a charter to Luebeck to complete before they are ready to sail, but they'll be back in Copenhagen by mid-February."

Reuben and Saul whispered together for a moment, and looked toward Sir Thomas, who nodded agreement. Saul said, "This group is eminently satisfactory, Captain Foxe. We are on track with our plans for recruiting settlers and your recommendation for Captain James as your deputy coincides with our thoughts. March will fit our time frame." He gave the unnamed guest a quick glance, who gave a barely perceptible nod. "Now that we have decided on our ships, we need to discuss the details to make this expedition successful."

A loud rumble sounded from across the room. Svend started to blush. "I'm sorry, Captain. I was so busy this morning, I missed lunch."

Sir Thomas laughed. "A young man needs his meals. Why don't you see my cook? She usually has something to eat. The doorman will take you to the kitchen."

Svend beat an embarrassed retreat.

After the door closed Luke shook his head in amazement, "Thank you for being so understanding. I still remember what it was like as a young sailor, hungry all the time. He'll probably be happier there than listening to our boring discussions."

The group settled down to examine the details of the expedition. The Abrabanels were obviously concerned about the costs for provisions Luke had included in the plan. Saul opened a small ledger book and paged down with his finger. "I see where you want to provide provisions for all settlers for a full year. Surely, you'll have some deaths that will reduce that amount?"

Luke was appalled at Saul's callous remark, until he realized Saul was simply trying to force him to really look at his calculation for provisions. "We probably will have some, but we will also have some births. We will also have losses due to rats and accidents. I want to make sure we don't have any deaths from starvation. People fighting to just stay alive don't make the best miners and builders." Luke refused to budge and after repeatedly reminding them of the problems others had encountered with sparse provisions, they finally admitted Luke's provision list looked right.

The mention of deaths reminded Luke about the fall storm. "We'll have to make sure the second expedition sails on time. The research I did contained numerous hints that the western coast will be devastated by a huge storm in October. Nordstrand Island is just about wiped off the map and over fifteen thousand people will drown along the western coast."

Sir Thomas looked aghast. "What are you saying? Don't you mean the storm that struck in 1627?"

"No, this one will be worse than that. You mean you hadn't heard?" All three men shook their heads emphatically no. "Well, maybe you need to mention it to the King the next time you meet with him. I'm sure he would appreciate the warning. I know that if I hadn't been looking in all the books, I wouldn't have noticed it. I doubt anyone else has."

Sir Thomas looked pensive. "I'm certain he will. Not a breath of this has been whispered about in the court gossip. I'm sure this will be an unpleasant surprise, but appreciated none the less."

Always fast with a plan, Reuben turned to Sir Thomas. "While you're at it, see if he would be interested in encouraging the people that will be affected to emigrate. Moving to a new land would certainly be preferable to drowning. It would solve our problem of getting a large number of settlers and he might even pay us!" Sir Thomas made a note to ensure he remembered.

Reuben then questioned the amount and types of trade goods included in the inventory. He passed a list to Luke for items that might be added *and* eliminated. After studying the list, Luke agreed that the additions probably should have been included. He did comment, "I think the trade goods shoes may be too much. My experience is that the natives prefer their own style of footwear." The items to be eliminated were haggled over until both men felt equally uncomfortable with the result. A hard bargaining session on military supplies brought occasional comments from Sir Thomas and Factor Bamberg, but Luke noticed that the Abrabanels seemed to be Sir Thomas' experts. The source for the military supplies was one area that Bamberg seemed uncomfortable with, but he wouldn't elaborate as to why. After almost two hours, the discussion started to wind down. Then, a casual question concerning mineral rights started a heated debate between the Abrabanels, Bamberg, and Sir Thomas.

Luke nudged John, who was trying desperately to stay awake, "Why don't you see how Svend is doing? I think I can spare you for a while. Hopefully, we should be done here soon. I'll need him to help with the items we'll carry back to the ship."

"Thank you, sir!"

John quietly left the room. He spotted the doorman who had greeted them, cleaning and polishing some candlesticks, walked over and asked, "The young gentleman who came with us, can you show me to him?"

"Certainly, sir. He and Mistress Roe are in the kitchen with the cook."

The reply startled John. "Is she Sir Thomas' daughter?"

"Heavens, no! She's his ward. Her parents were his cousins. They died of the plague and Sir Thomas was her only living relative. She arrived on his doorstep during his last trip to England. I'm not sure he knows what to make of a young girl in his household. The cook is really who's raising her. Sir Thomas never had any children of his own. Since his wife died last year, she's the only close family he has left"

They squeezed through a narrow servant's hall that was still packed with some of the recently arrived furniture. The doorman ushered him into the kitchen. "Matilda will see you back when you're done. I have to return to my work."

A cherubic faced, matronly figure in an apron peered out of a cloud of flour. "Come to fetch the young master? He's been very well mannered. Mistress Roe will be disappointed that he's leaving. She doesn't get many visitors her age."

The cloud of flour she'd raised billowed along as she walked through it to fetch the youngsters. A moment later, they returned. The two youngsters were holding an animated conversation in whispers. Svend clutched a

48

small book tightly in his hands and nodded every time the small, dark-haired girl made some point.

"Agnes, this is Captain Foxe's first officer, John Barrow. Mr. Barrow, may I present Agnes Roe, a cousin of Sir Thomas," Svend said.

Agnes made a short curtsey and John bowed deeply. "My pleasure, ma'am. I come as a bearer of sad tidings. Svend's duties call. We will be leaving shortly and he must return to the library." Svend was downcast, but Agnes looked like a lost puppy. "Don't worry; I'm sure Svend will be back soon. The meeting's gone well and I expect the captain will send him by with messages from time to time."

They visibly perked up. Svend quickly promised, "I'll make sure to get your book back next week, even if the captain doesn't have an errand for me."

"Do you think he'll let me visit the ship? I would dearly like to tour your ship!"

John said, "Your ship? I didn't know Sir Thomas had sold her to you. The captain will be interested to hear this. Does this mean a raise for everyone?"

Svend blushed furiously. The hero worship in Agnes' gaze warned John to go easy on the boy. He recognized the signs of young love. He quickly replied, "I'm sure a tour can be arranged." With a flourish, he chivvied Svend out of the kitchen and back to the meeting.

When they arrived, John glanced through the crack in the door to see if the meeting was done. The mood in the room didn't seem promising. Sir Thomas stood by the fireplace, talking pointedly to Saul and Reuben. "My other investors have no problem with your proposal, Saul, but Captain Foxe is not familiar with it." The anonymous visitor stiffened noticeably. John started to clear his throat to announce their return but then stopped, having sensed the tension. He motioned Svend to stay where he was.

Sir Thomas continued. "Luke, As I understand, from time to time you may have settlers or others that need to be transported on short notice or have need of the goods we may be selling. The gentlemen here will be Adolphus' contact for those needs," Sir Thomas said. "What do you think, Luke?"

"Before I agree, may I ask who the other member of your party is?" Luke said.

Reuben deferred to Saul. "Let us just say he is from southern Germany and is traveling with us. If anyone asks you, he was never here. Rest assured, he supports our efforts and has significant influence in certain 'Swedish' circles. At this time, he is only here to bring news of our negotiations to the appropriate parties," Saul answered.

Once more, Luke was perplexed by the odd statements and then it hit. "You're from Grantville, aren't you?" The gentleman just smiled. "Forgive my interruption. The question was unnecessary." Many things fell into place. It seemed that Sir Thomas had established some contacts with Grantville outside of official channels. While the Danish and Swedish governments were technically at war and might not agree to the other party's support the proposed settlement, people with money and knowledge to help make a go of it were in support. In the long run, that might be even better. Full funding and full rations would go a long way toward a successful settlement, but support from both camps of the current belligerents might be even better. Future trading partners were an added plus. Luke thought for a moment, and then made his decision. "I agree to the proposal. As long as the passengers are not prominent Danish criminals, I should have no problems with transporting them. As for future trade, I hope we have a lot of what he wants!"

Sir Thomas noticed John and Svend waiting outside and motioned for them to enter. "I think that settles our last issue. We'll meet again, once the miners arrive."

The Grantville visitor added a last comment. "Don't take too long. Things could get very interesting come spring. The war could heat up quickly once the thaw sets in." No one seemed surprised by the comment.

50

* * *

Svend gathered up all the papers that Captain Foxe still retained, along with his book. He then had to find a place in the hall to keep them dry as he struggled into his coat and knit cap. A fine sifting of snow had found its way into the hall. When the door was opened, they were greeted by over six inches of fluffy, new fallen snow, with more still lightly falling. The neighborhood was quiet as a graveyard. Luckily, the snow packed down enough to keep the cobble stones from becoming dangerous underfoot. After a few minutes of walking, John broke the silence and spoke of his visit to the kitchen. When he mentioned that Agnes had loaned Svend a book, Luke inquired about the title.

"It's a copy of a book from Grantville that Sir Thomas bought for her, *Peter Pan.* It describes a magical land, pirates, and the adventures of a group of lost boys. I promised Agnes to return it next week."

"Make sure you keep that promise! You're likely to be going there on business frequently and you don't want to ruin your reputation. The young lady has trusted you with an important item. When I spoke with your mother the other day about your assistance, she spoke highly of your trustworthiness." He paused a moment, considering his next words, "We also spoke of your future. I need a good assistant who can be counted on. The skills your father taught you on navigation may come in very handy when we start exploring the new land. Would you be interested in the job? Think it over carefully because you would be gone for several years."

Svend's smile grew from ear to ear. "Mother and I already discussed this and I've thought and dreamed about it a lot. I don't need any extra time, the answer is yes!"

"Good, I'll sign you on as a member of the expedition, as Captain's Clerk, after breakfast tomorrow.

* * *

After a short, leisurely stroll along the docks the next morning, to help settle breakfast, Luke spoke with Mette for over an hour. He wanted her opinions on the various merchants he would be doing business with over the next few months; securing supplies he needed for the expedition. Her familiarity with most of the merchants in the harbor area was immensely valuable. Unlike Bamberg, she also had some pointed comments on the trustworthiness of some. Luke pointedly ignored Svend's squirming figure outside the kitchen door during the discussion, but finally broke down.

"Mette, I think your son has something to say. He's been very good for not interrupting, but I think I better let him have his say before he explodes from trying to hold it in."

With a look of mild concern on her face, Mette turned to Svend. "Is there something I need to know?"

"At the meeting yesterday, the departure date for the expedition was set. They plan to leave in March."

Luke was surprised by Mette's reaction to Svend's announcement. She turned toward him with a sad look, not the response that he had expected. For some reason, his heart seemed to flutter.

Oblivious to the byplay, Svend continued. "The captain has asked me to join the expedition as his clerk, with your approval. He says we will probably be gone for a couple of years."

Mette smiled. "Of course you have my permission. You've always been your father's son. I knew someday you would leave, I just hoped you wouldn't go so far away." She reached for Luke's hand. "I trust you to take good care of my oldest."

Luke realized Mette had left a lot unsaid. He felt twenty years younger. "Svend has a very bright future. We will need someone who can learn navigating overland and can keep a logbook. His father taught him well. I'll make sure that he stays out of trouble." He looked at Svend. "We have a lot to get done. Be ready to leave for the ship in ten minutes."

Luke's heart felt like a ship rising to the top of a rogue wave as he whispered to Mette as Svend was leaving. "We'll talk some more when we have some privacy and time." Her warm smile sent Luke off with a spring in his step.

Chapter 6

"Heave! Heave!" Each explosive pull inched the *Rotterdam* up the extended slipway of the dry dock. Dockworkers slathered on grease with huge straw brushes to ease the ship further into the berth. The temporary expansion of the dry dock's slipway to accommodate the *fregätten* had taken de Vries almost a month to complete, instead of his original estimate of two weeks.

Joris stood next to the dock master, watching his ship rise out of the water. The last hectic week, emptying the ship of all cannon and stores to lighten it to reduce its draft, had left his crew exhausted. Now, the critical point was fast approaching. He yelled at the crew on the ground, holding the lines to the mast tops. "Steady on those lines! Keep them taut!"

This was the critical point in the effort. If the lines weren't kept taut, the ship could topple in the dry dock. Everyone was struggling to use the last of the tide to pull the ship clear of the water. Their breaths steamed in the late fall afternoon. Two more turns of the capstan brought the ship as far up the slipway as it could go. Immediately, dockworkers swarmed around the dripping hull, setting braces to stabilize the ship. When the foreman yelled that it was secured, the ship's crews on the lines eased off and let out a cheer. Van den Broecke just let out a long sigh. He'd been holding his breath from the tension.

The dock master leaned over the side and pointed to the site where they had struggled throughout the journey to stem a leak. "See there, Captain? You were lucky to have made it here. It looks like you took a hit as you rose on a wave. The butt ends are sprung and the frame member is damaged. It's going to be at least a month before we can finish this properly."

Van den Broecke wasn't happy. "I've got to report to Tjaert. He'll want to know how long until we can sail again." He fixed the dock master with a hard stare. "You're sure it's going to be a month? A lot of lives could be in jeopardy if you run longer."

Huetjen bristled at the comment. "Captain, I know my business. With your crew to help, we'll be done by the new year. I commanded a ship once, too, before I lost my leg." He slapped his peg leg for emphasis. "I know what you're going through, watching it stuck on dry land. It's like losing a child. I'll hurry the work as fast as I can." He paused, pointing at the damaged planking. "You'll get it back when that's as good as new! I have family here and we need both your ships if we're to survive."

The captain chuckled. "Very well. I'll leave my child in your care, doctor. Get her well soon." He swung himself over the side and carefully slid down a rope. When he reached the ground, he proceeded to slowly walk around the ship, surveying the newly exposed damage before he set off in search of Tjaert to let him know that he would be sailing alone on his planned cruise after Christmas. Joris wasn't too concerned. In these waters, even one Dutch *fregätte* should be more than a match for anything she met. If she wasn't, a whole fleet probably wouldn't be enough.

* * *

In preparation for the council of war, Tjaert de Groot had spent the previous two weeks surveying the fortifications around New Amsterdam. He had even sailed the *Friesland* up the river as far as he could safely take her to "scout out the territory" as he told von Twiller. Tjaert then met with a few key members of the colony to learn more about the Dutch settlements further up-river. He wanted to lay the groundwork for his future plans.

During his discussions, Tjaert had learned that the debate over how to proceed had settled into three factions amongst the settlers. Some of the leaders weren't sure if there really was a threat and certainly didn't want to spend any more money paying workers to strengthen the fort's defenses. Von Twiller led this group. Others wanted to abandon New Amsterdam and return to the Netherlands immediately. The rest wanted to stay and fight, if they had to, to protect their lands. The council had been called to decide what the colony would do. When it came time for Captain de Groot's turn to speak, he surprised everyone.

"I agree with the Director General. I don't think we should spend anything on the fort *here*."

In the outcry that followed, only van Rensselaer noticed the slight emphasis on the word *here*. As the turmoil started to settle, he spoke up. "I think the captain has something to add."

"Thank you, *Mijnherr*. New Amsterdam is a wonderful city, but it is undefendable. Any force that is sent will have naval support *and* troops. The frontier forts at home work because the Spanish only attack from one direction. Here, an attacker can land troops on one side of the town, sail around the island and land troops at a second site, and then bombard the fort from a third. The *Friesland* and *the Rotterdam* cannot and will not be tied down to defend a city that cannot be saved." Tjaert tried to drive that point home as hard as he could. These tight fisted patroons would never *pay* enough to match the prize money his crews could make raiding the French and English. Raiding also hurt the enemy a lot more!

"But what choice do we have?" exclaimed a patroon in the back of the crowd. "I'll do whatever I must to defend my home, but I need to know what that is!"

"I'm glad you asked." De Groot's smile looked a lot like the one the mouse saw on the cat that had caught it. "Your house is near Orange?"

The patroon just nodded yes.

"While New Amsterdam is undefendable, the colony *is* defendable, but only upriver. If any fortifications are to be built, the effort must be made there. I've spoken with a number of traders and took *the Friesland* to scout the site in person. About twenty-five miles north, there is a spot along the river that's ideal for a fort. It's on high ground and could be defended from water attack with a log boom. *Our fregätten* are offensive weapons. We can do more good raiding the French and English shipping than sitting at anchor. We will work out of New Amsterdam and will fight if the enemy appears while we're in port, but the colony must be prepared to abandon the city if a large force appears."

Three merchants were immediately on their feet shouting for recognition. The Director General cut them off. "I understand your concern. We cannot possibly abandon the city now. It's the dead of winter. Captain, you must reconsider."

Tjaert just stared at him.

Van Rensselaer stood up. "If I might make a suggestion." Everyone turned to Kiliaen, because he had given no indication to that point where he stood. "Wouter is right. It is the dead of winter." He turned to face de Groot and gave a slight wink that went unnoticed by the group. "Captain de Groot, shipping off the Banks is slim this time of year. One ship should be more than enough to handle what's there. The other one can stay in port, finish refitting, and act as an additional defense for the colony. They can trade places by spring and we would be able to finish refitting both your ships completely, at our expense." Wouter winced when he realized what that statement meant to his purse. "Then, when the shipping season resumes, you both could cruise for prizes." He clasped his hands on the table. "In the meantime, construction of the fort you suggested could be started. Since it will benefit my manor upriver, I'd be willing to supply the land and pay for the work through the winter. We could revisit the issue in the spring. Who knows? We may even get good news and find our fears were unfounded. If the French never come, we keep our expenses down. I also think an embassy to our investors back home would be in order. After all, the charter does require them to help in our defense."

The city merchants nearly fell over themselves in support. Tjaert and Kiliaen looked at each other and nodded. Their plan had gone exactly as they had hoped. Tjaert would get his base for raiding and Kiliaen a base if the French ever came and possibly men, guns, and money to bolster defenses around his lands. It would also cover up his nephew's misappropriation of the fort's building funds.

Chapter 7

December 1633, Copenhagen

Luke sighed as he, John Barrow, and Factor Bamberg entered the shop of Gammel Bundgaard. Three fruitless weeks of excuses and apologies from Copenhagen's ships' chandlers and supply houses had finally convinced him that Mette's comments about who he would have to buy from were true. If he was going to get the cannon, gunpowder and small arms the expedition needed, his only choice would be to buy the needed supplies from Bundgaard. A cousin to the king's Minister of War, Bundgaard had the sole concession to sell military arms in Copenhagen. He used his monopoly to force people who wanted to buy armaments to also purchase their other supplies from him. Since word had gotten out that the expedition wanted to buy weapons, other potential suppliers were suddenly unable to meet Luke's requests or their prices were twice the rate they had been when Luke first started planning. Bundgaard had made a take it or leave it offer to supply all the expedition's needs. He hinted that the other suppliers knew what was good for them and Luke should too. His price was slightly higher than planned, but even Bamberg agreed, "He may be a scoundrel, but if we are going to sail on time, he's your only choice." With no other options and time getting short, it was time to negotiate the best deal they could get with Bundgaard.

"Greetings, Captain Foxe!" The owner met them at the door.

Bundgaard reminded Luke a little of a fictional character Svend had described, except without the hook. There were two unsavory looking toughs lounging near the fire who didn't bother to move when the owner greeted Luke.

Luke quickly got down to business. "We're here to finalize the order for the expedition. I brought Adolphus along because we need to add some additional mining tools to the list." Bamberg handed over a short list. "Can you supply these by the end of February?"

Bundgaard read the list. "I should have no trouble and your cost will be reasonable. Come into my office and we can work out the contract's details."

Luke thought Bundgaard's eyes reflected the stacks of coins he was expecting to count.

An hour later, after some serious haggling over terms and dates, Luke's party emerged. "Very well, half now and the remainder by the first of February. All supplies to be delivered by February fifteenth. My crews will load from your warehouse by the docks."

* * *

Once outside, Bamberg turned to Luke. "I hope we did the right thing. I don't have a very good feeling that we're going to get what we paid for."

"I know what you mean, Adolphus, but as you said before, what choice do we have?"

* * *

A short, stout Dutch captain and his bosun headed straight for the shop Luke's party had just left. When they entered, the two toughs immediately stepped over and blocked their way. "We're here to see that swindler, Bundgaard. Those provisions he sold us for our last voyage were mostly barrels filled with stone and sawdust. My men almost starved because of his thievery."

"Fister Bundgaard does not want to see you!" Both men blocked the doorway to the office Bundgaard had retreated into. The captain tried to force his way past, but one of the toughs tried to deck him with a round-house punch. The captain ducked, and then tripped over a chair, smashing it to splinters.

When the second tough moved in, the bosun pulled a belaying pin from inside his jacket and waded in to help his captain. Bundgaard emerged from his office with a cudgel and joined the fight.

Karl and his patrol were passing by and heard the commotion. About the time Karl reached the shop, the front door flew open and the fighters fell through the doorway in a mass of bodies, fists and weapons. The patrol judiciously applied their cudgels. In a few moments, the fighters lost all interest in each other.

"Who are you and how did this start?" Karl asked the captain.

Bundgaard interrupted before the captain could say a word. "These hooligans broke into my shop and attacked my men. I'm Gammel Bundgaard and I'm . . . "

Thunk! A quick rap with a cudgel by Gunnar silenced Bundgaard immediately.

"You were about to tell me before we were so rudely interrupted . . . " Karl said.

The captain picked himself up. He wiped the snow and dirt from his clothes and the blood from his lips. "I'm Piet van Hoorne, captain of the ship *Maastricht*. This swindler sold me provisions on my last stop here. Instead of salt meat and fruit, most of the casks and kegs were filled with stones and sawdust. My crew nearly starved. I came to get my money back!"

"That's a lie!" Bundgaard shouted. "You tried to attack and rob us. Sergeant, I demand that these men be locked up!" Like two bantam roosters, Bundgaard and van Horne tried to start fighting again.

Karl grabbed the fighters by their collars, "This is a job for the magistrate. You are both going to jail until we can straighten this out."

Sputtering and trying to get out of Karl's hold, Bundgaard threatened, "Don't you know who I am? I have friends in very high places. Your commander won't like this."

"I've been in trouble with the commander before. I've heard stories about you. You'll get your say before a magistrate," Karl said.

* * *

The next morning, Karl got a summons to see his commander as soon as he arrived for his shift. The commander rose from his desk, walked over, slammed the door shut and got right in Karl's face. "What the hell did you think you were doing arresting Gammel Bundgaard? His cousin is one of the King's ministers. You should have just hauled that fat Dutchman and his crewmen in and let it go at that. We're supposed to protect the people that pay us. Foreigners can rot in jail for all I care!"

Karl interrupted. "I've heard a lot of stories about Bundgaard, and they are all unsavory. He's a cheat and a thief. I decided to let the magistrate sort it out. Next time, maybe, I'll act differently."

"If there is a next time, you won't need to bother because you'll be out of a job. As of now, you and your patrol work the dock area at night, until I decide differently. Now, get out!"

Karl left, muttering under his breath, "Maybe I *should* look into becoming a farmer."

Chapter 8

The *Friesland* descended on the fishing fleets off the Grand banks like a hawk on a flock of chickens. The first sign for the fishing boat captains that something was amiss were the clouds of smoke on the horizon from burning boats. After the third ship was fired, the fishing boats started to scatter. The Friesland pursued and continued to capture boats, with a warning shot across their bows. Boarding parties were then sent to secure the boats until the *Friesland* returned. By late afternoon, four more boats had been captured and were hove to in a loose group awaiting their fate. In all, a very small Spanish trawler, an English dogger and a smaller fishing boat, and four smaller French fishing boats had been captured.

As the *Friesland* approached the impromptu fleet, Captain de Groot surveyed his captures with satisfaction. Pointing to the waiting ships, he ordered his First Lieutenant, "Pieter, see if they have any food supplies or spare sails we can use. Then transfer all the prisoners onto that larger dogger and prepare to burn the rest. I'd like to be there when you fire them."

"Aye, aye Captain!" De Beers replied. "I'll have the longboat crewed and away shortly. As soon as I retrieve one of the boarding parties' boats, I'll send it back for you."

De Groot arrived at the larger French fishing boat, the *Berthe,* just as de Beers was preparing to transfer the prisoners. An older man, evidently the captain by his manner, called out. "Why are you doing this to us? We're nothing but harmless fishermen. Our families will starve if you burn our boats." Tears were streaming down his face in frustration and pain.

"Go ask your King why. By now his treachery has probably destroyed my country. I haven't the means to strike back at his fleet, but I can still sting him in his colonies. And I'll keep stinging as long as I am able!" The Frenchman quailed at the vehemence in de Groot's answer. As he was descending into the waiting long-boat, de Groot grabbed a lit torch and descended into the open hold.

A few minutes later, Tjaert emerged with a bleak smile on his face. Wisps of smoke were already starting to rise from the open hatch. He hurried over to the waiting boat. "Push off smartly! The fish oil down below will feed the flames hotter than a furnace. You've all done a good job today. I just wish the Cardinal could feel the heat of these flames." As the boat reached the *Friesland*, flames engulfed the mainsail on the fishing boat.

Aboard the dogger, the prisoners also watched the flames. The French captain, Rene Chaumont, crossed himself and muttered a silent prayer. Tears streamed from his eyes as he watched his livelihood burn to the waterline. One of the Englishmen shouted out, "They're nothing but pirates! We must try and retake our ship."

Rene turned away as his ship started to settle beneath the waves. "You're crazy! If they were pirates, we would have been left aboard to die in the flames. May God forgive that Dutchman. His thirst for revenge burns as hot as my ship. If he's not careful it may consume him too. But if we try to take the ship, they would be within their rights to kill us. While we live, we may still find some way to return to our families. I just don't know how we'll be able to feed them with our ships gone. Has anyone heard what they intend to do with us?" The question was quickly translated among the crews, but no one had heard a thing. When Rene turned back, all that remained of the *Berthe* was some smoldering wreckage, bobbing on the waves.

Aboard the *Friesland,* Lieutenant de Beers was asking the Captain a similar question before he returned to the dogger. "What are your plans, Sir? Do we keep hunting? We've taken on enough supplies to stretch our voyage out for at least two more months."

De Groot paused, surveying the horizon that was now empty of sails. "I think it's time to kill two birds with one stone. We need to get rid of the prisoners." De Beers looked alarmed at the ominous statement. "No Pieter, I'm not going to do anything rash. What I have in mind is a visit to the English at Ferryland. We can dump the prisoners off on them and raid the settlement at the same time. Set course north by north nor' west. After we finish there, I'll decide what's next." He smiled, "Maybe we'll get lucky and catch a French trader heading for the Cabot Strait."

A week later, head winds still had the *Friesland* and the fishing boat almost a hundred leagues south of Ferryland. Aboard the fishing boat, the crowded conditions were raising tempers and complaints. The bosun, in the longboat, arrived with orders for the prize crew. Lieutenant de Beers assembled the prisoners, under guard, and made an offer. "Many of you have complained about the crowded conditions and wanted to know what is to become of you. I have an offer for you. Any man who will join our crew will be transferred to the *Friesland* and draw pay just like any other crewman. Those of you who choose to stay will be left at Ferryland once we make landfall there. I'll give you five minutes to talk amongst yourselves and then I expect your answers." He turned toward the stern to at least create an illusion of some privacy on the small deck. The prisoners broke into small groups, by their ships and nationalities. Only among the Spanish crew was there a heated discussion. When the five minutes were up, de Beers returned and asked the crews for their answers.

Captain Chaumont spoke for all the French. "We will stay together and face whatever fate awaits us at Ferryland. We hope to eventually return to our families. That's all I have to say." He deliberately turned his back on de Beers in anger.

The English captain shrugged his shoulders. "We're from Ferryland. We'll return home."

The Spanish captain stepped forward, "We four will also stay together." Suddenly his three crewmen pushed him aside.

"He does not speak for us! We want to join you."

The captain swung a wild haymaker that knocked the nearest sailor flat on his back. "You traitors! I say what we do!"

Before de Beers could intervene, one of the Spaniards pulled a short knife from his waistband and stabbed the captain below the ribcage. Eyes wide in surprise, the captain slid to the deck without a sound. The Dutch guards immediately seized the sailor and threw him to the deck beside his victim. De Beers was momentarily stunned by the violence and then quietly asked, "Didn't I tell you to search them for weapons? That could be me lying there."

Before the guards could answer, one of the other Spanish sailors spoke up. "He found it below in the hold with the fish. We're Maranos and the captain treated us terribly since we signed on. He'd threatened to turn us over to the Inquisition when we got back to Spain if we helped you." Pointing toward his compatriot he stated flatly, "He had no choice." The other sailor simply shook his head in agreement, too terrified to speak.

De Beers reached down and picked up the knife, after wiping it on the corpse. "Very well. Load them in the longboat and we'll let the captain sort this out." As an afterthought he added, "And load the body too. At least we can give him a decent burial." The guards quickly hurried the three sailors over the side before the rest of the prisoners could take advantage of the confusion.

The bosun pushed off as soon as the body was secured in the thwarts.

66

When they reached the *Friesland,* the bosun took all three sailors immediately before the captain and explained what had transpired. Captain de Groot fixed the three sailors with a stare that left them fidgeting. He finally pronounced sentence, "For what you've done before you come to this ship, you'll answer to God for those deeds. On my ship, you follow my rules and you'll earn your pay. This is a Dutch warship and we're fighting Spain, England and France. If you can't live with that, you're welcome to leave." He pointed over the side rail.

Francisco, the sailor who had knifed the captain, spoke up. "We will all gladly serve on your ship, Captain. We were no better than slaves where we were. Where do we make our mark?"

"The bosun will take care of that and show you where you'll hang your hammock." Tjaert signaled the bosun to show the men out. A hail from the deck for the watch to turn to heralded a favorable change in the wind. Tjaert had left instructions with the helmsman to call him only if necessary. When no messenger arrived, he took off his boots and lay down in his cot. The next few days would be busy.

* * *

The sun was just setting behind the hills as the *Friesland* dropped anchor just out of sight of the English settlement at Ferryland to its south. Captain de Groot assembled the crew on the main deck while he stood at the rail of the aftercastle to address them. "Men, we're here to burn the boats and land the prisoners. As soon as it's dark, the off watch will go ashore in two boats. Lieutenant Aamodt will lead you. Half of you will carry materials for firing the boats, the rest will carry cutlasses or clubs. I don't expect any trouble. Surprise should eliminate the need for guns. The lookout says there are only two ships there, so you can board both of them at the same time. When you're done, return to the dogger and land the prisoners south of the village. They can walk the last mile back. Lieutenant de Beers will be in charge of that part of this evenings fun. Dismissed!" He turned to the officer standing behind him. "Lieutenant Aamodt, see to your men and their supplies. I expect you to be ready inside the hour. Remember, keep the men quiet and keep the casualties to a minimum. We're here to burn the boats, not commit atrocities."

"Aye, aye Captain. I understand completely." Hinrich hurried down the ladder and started sorting out the crews for the two boats.

As the boats pushed off, Francisco whispered to his new messmate at the opposite oar, "Why does the Captain do this? Have these people done something to him?"

Without breaking stroke, his mate replied, "You weren't there when the French and English betrayed us. The Captain's got a good solid hate on for them, and so do the rest of us. These people may not have done anything then, but they're the only ones we can fight back at now. Maybe in time the Captain will end his private war, but only if he learns that Holland survives."

The lieutenant hissed, "Quiet! We don't need the English roused and waiting for us!"

* * *

Dawn found the *Friesland* and its consort heading back south. Captain de Groot paced the afterdeck, chatting with a weary, smoke stained Lieutenant. "Jan, you did a good job. Both ships destroyed, the prisoners landed and only one casualty."

Lieutenant Aamodt sighed, "There shouldn't have been any. That new man missed his grip as we boarded and drowned before we could find him in the dark."

Tjaert shook his head in sympathy. "God works in mysterious ways. Maybe it was his fate for his deed." He glanced up and checked the set of the sails. They were drawing nicely. "In any case, we're shed of the prisoners and the English can try to figure out how to feed them this winter. Now let's see what Frenchmen we can find in the Strait."

Chapter 9

"I never thought I'd be a duenna," John complained, while he walked behind Svend and Agnes through the snow. Today was Svend's big day to show Agnes around the ship. Agnes was so eager for the tour that she decided to accompany John and Svend on their errand beforehand. John pushed the wheelbarrow that would carry the wine Captain Foxe wanted for his own stores for the voyage down the cobblestone street. Luke had given Svend a list of what he was to purchase and a full coin purse to pay for it. It seemed that Bundgaard had passed the word that anyone who sold to Captain Foxe would be visited by his toughs. Sending John and Svend was Mette's idea, to avoid Bundgaard's monopoly and get a better price on the wine. John still felt uneasy about Bundgaard and hoped there wouldn't be any trouble for the youngsters. "We should only be here a short time. Then we can return to the ship for your tour."

Agnes smiled at Svend. The light snowflakes that had settled on her hair and eyelashes made Svend think of the fairies he had read about.

The wine shop owner was a rotund, red-faced gentleman who evidently sampled his own wares. Svend handed him the list and was surprised when the price quoted was half of what Bundgaard wanted. While the shop owner loaded the bottles, he kept up a constant stream of advice. "Remember young sir; let the bottles have a chance to settle before you have them served. Also, store them on their sides to keep the corks moist.

That will help preserve the wine's flavor." Svend paid for the purchase and then they left.

When they reached the ship, the snow was coming down hard enough to muffle all sound. Agnes' eyes lit up in delight. The rigging was covered in snow. "It looks like it's covered in lace!" Two crewmen spotted John and hurried down the gangplank to assist in bringing the wine on board.

"I must be old," John muttered, "pushing a wheelbarrow like this never was this hard before."

Svend laughed. "Mistress Roe, may I present the ship *Köbenhavn* and its crew, ready for your inspection."

Agnes dropped a curtsey. "Thank you, good sir. I am ready." She offered her arm to Svend.

John broke down laughing at their antics. The laughter spread to Svend and Agnes and all three boarded the *Köbenhavn*, unable to stop laughing.

The laughter brought Luke on deck to investigate. When he spotted John laughing, he called across the deck, "Mr. Barrow, I sent you to fetch the wine, not sample it!"

John looked like a fish out of water, until he realized the captain was just pulling his leg. He turned to Svend and winked. "I guess I'm in trouble. You'll just have to escort Mistress Roe by yourself."

Svend helped Agnes ascend the ladder to the aftercastle. "Here is where the captain runs the ship." Agnes walked to the railing and peered down. She stepped back quickly, "That's a long way down to the water."

"Not half as far down as the view from the masthead," Svend said.

"This is quite high enough for me. I'll never go that high up." She gestured back to the stern and asked, "What's the porch at the end of the boat for?"

"This is a ship, not a boat and that porch is the captain's walk. When Captain Foxe wants some privacy, he has his own deck area. If you'll follow me, I'll show you his cabin and where the officers and staff are berthed"

For the next hour, Svend guided Agnes on a tour of the ship. The cramped crews' quarters were warm, even though it was snowing on deck and were rank with the smell of unwashed bodies mixed with the smells from the bilge. They beat a hasty retreat from the smells and took a short cut through the half-filled hold to reach the ladder leading to the forecastle. When they were back on deck, Svend announced, "That's the tour for the ship. Do you have any questions?"

Agnes blushed but asked, "It's been a long morning. Can you direct me to the necessary room before we go?"

Svend felt like he had swallowed a fly. Captain Foxe and Mr. Barrow were nearby and overheard the exchange. "Didn't I tell you, John? Just the other day I said we should have Mette come by to get a woman's point of view! We'll have to make provision for any female passengers we embark! Mistress Roe, I must apologize but the only one we have is for the crew. It would not be appropriate for a lady. I imagine what Svend choked on was the thought of trying to explain the head to you. Master McDermott, escort Mistress Roe to the King's Arms Inn up the street. She can freshen up there and we all can have a nice meal before you escort her back to Sir Thomas' house."

* * *

During the meal, Captain Foxe regaled the youngsters with tales from his last voyage to the New World. Two hours later, while Svend walked Agnes to her uncle's house, she stopped to admire the ship again through the curtain of snow. "I truly envy you, Svend McDermott. So many adventures ahead. I wish I could go with you." She took Svend by his hands, reached up on tip toes and kissed his cheek. "Thank you for letting me see a little of your new world." She paused for a moment and then pulled him along as she headed off for her uncle's house. "I should be getting home soon. Cook will wonder what's become of me."

72

Even with the snow swirling around them, Svend could have sworn the sun was shining.

* * *

That evening, after all the supper patrons had been served and the main room had cleared, Luke asked Mette to join him. "Mette, I've come to value your advice. I need a woman's perspective on a problem that has come up. The expedition's planning has overlooked the women's needs and that could cause some serious problems. Could you take some time out from your busy schedule to help me identify what I've missed?"

"Of course, Captain. You've done so much already for me and my family; I would be delighted to help."

When she smiled, Luke screwed up his courage to ask the other question he had been afraid to ask. "Mette, I've also come to value my time spent here. I've never really had much of a family. My wife died during my last voyage to the New World and I have no close relatives. Svend has almost become a son to me."

"He's spoken highly of you, too. He's missed his father and you are such a good influence and so much like his father. The other children have enjoyed the tales you've told in the evenings. I have, too. You should consider publishing your journal. People would be interested in the New World. You've brought a joy to the house that hasn't been here for some time." She blushed a bit. "I've enjoyed your company, too, Captain."

"Please call me Luke. This is very hard for me. I know you lost your husband to the sea and I'm not a young man, but would you entertain an offer of courtship? I've nothing to offer but myself and my ship right now. But if this expedition is successful, we should be able to retire very comfortably."

Mette sat as though she were in a daze. Luke slowly rewrote Dante's Inferno in his mind, with himself as the main character, as he waited for Mette's reply. He had reached the third level of Purgatory when a smile lit up Mette's face. "I would be honored, Luke." In one galvanic leap, Luke's heart went from hell to heaven.

Mette continued, "I've had similar feelings, but was afraid to voice them. Let's wait to tell the children until your plans are more settled."

Luke took Mette's hand and drew her to him. It was quite some time before they remembered the expedition's needs.

* * *

The letter had arrived the day after Christmas, to announce that the miners Herr Cavriani had convinced to join the expedition were on their way to Copenhagen. Adolphus Bamberg had just enough warning to convert his warehouse into temporary quarters. When he finished, Sir Thomas and Reuben Abrabanel stopped in to check on the progress.

"Are these makeshift quarters going to be sufficient?" Reuben looked around skeptically. The canvas partitions gave little privacy. The two stoves, one at each end of the room, gave just enough heat to take the chill off.

"Once we get twenty or so people in here, it should be adequate. With all the refugees in town, they should be thankful that they have four solid walls and a roof. Captain Foxe says that he will quarter any overflow on board the *Köbenhavn*. Its temporary cabins are set up and can handle any families that arrive. We're just taking the single men here." Bamberg pointed to the door in the rear. "The sanitary facilities will be stretched, but the cold weather should help some. There was a new pit dug last summer."

Sir Thomas gave his approval. "You did a good job on such short notice, Adolphus. Two weeks seems like a short time for a group to travel in winter down the Elbe River. Have you heard how many miners are coming?"

"No, just that they left for Copenhagen about two weeks ago, and that I should expect a large group. Herr Cavriani was very sparse on the details. I'm not sure he was even there when they left. I'll send a note to you when they arrive."

* * *

Late the next evening, just after he had retired for the night, a loud pounding on the main warehouse door roused Bamberg. In a heavy dressing gown and cap, he hurried to the door. The local sergeant of the watch, Karl, along with another man, covered in snow, stepped in when he opened the door. "I have a group at the docks who say you're expecting them. They say they're miners from Bamberg and look down on their luck. I didn't want them wandering the streets at this time of night, and in this weather, without making sure they were who they said they were. This man is their leader, Ludwig Steinbrecher."

"You did well, Sergeant. They are expected. The families are to go to Captain Foxe's ship' the Köbenhavn. Do you know where she's docked?"

"Yes, sir."

"Have the families report there. The rest are to come here. Herr Steinbrecher, how many are there in your group?"

"I have eight families and eighteen single men. We also have two wagon loads of tools and household goods. I'll send those to the *Köbenhavn* in the morning. The wives are looking forward to dry, rat-free quarters."

"Rest assured, the quarters we have are dry, rat-free and heated. While you get everyone unloaded, I'll roust out my assistants. We will get the fires going here to warm up the living area."

Bamberg whispered to Karl, "See me in the morning; I'll have something extra for your help, Sergeant."

"Thank you, sir. My men will appreciate it."

Chapter 10

Over the next few days, the miners and their families settled into their new quarters. The trip from Bremen had been difficult due to the weather, but uneventful. All had experience working in the iron mines of the Upper Palatinate. Leopold Cavriani had found them and convinced them to join the expedition on a shares basis. Sir Thomas and the Abrabanels were extremely pleased with the skills Cavriani had listed for the recruits in the correspondence the miners brought with them.

Adolphus arranged for the Company's leaders to meet with the miners at the warehouse. Seating was crowded, but everyone had a place and the room soon grew warm. Sir Thomas called for silence. "The main goal of this initial expedition will be to start a colony in the south end of Hudson's Bay, with a layover station in Newfoundland. The colony in Hudson's Bay will initially serve as a fur trading post and provide a base for expeditions to locate and start mining operations for nickel and gold deposits. Herr Diedermann, your group of four families will be part of that effort. Your families will be housed at the fort, while your advance parties work at locating the deposits and start the initial site preparation. Yours will eventually be the largest operation but will take some time to develop.

"Herr Steinbrecher, your group will be able to start iron mining near the layover station in Newfoundland. There was a previous English expedition that located iron ore deposits on an island in the harbor we plan to use. Your group will develop that deposit. It has the potential to be the largest iron mine in the known world." He paused to let the information sink in. "Now that you've heard what's planned, are you still interested?"

The only sound in the room was from the logs popping in the fire. Diedermann and Steinbrecher turned to their groups to find out their thoughts. The discussion became quite animated for a time.

Steinbrecher's group finished first. "We agree, but have some questions and suggestions. You mentioned a previous expedition. Will there be any problem from that and did they leave anything there?"

Sir Thomas smiled. "My father was an investor with that group. All they did was identify the iron deposit. We've confirmed from another source that the size of the deposit is much larger than they originally thought. Nothing was done at the site itself."

"In that case, how many foresters do you have on the expedition? We will need some lumber for housing and a lot of timbers for the mine. Also, at least two pairs of oxen for hauling."

Sir Thomas and Saul looked to Reuben, who was shuffling through his papers.

"Aha!" Reuben brightened as he found what he was looking for. "We have seven families of foresters amongst the refugees with seventeen adult males. Will that be enough?"

"That should be adequate. You have yourselves a mine crew."

Diedermann's group was still vehemently discussing their options. At first, Sir Thomas appeared concerned with the level of apparent disagreement. As he concentrated on the exchange, he realized he could resolve the issue easily. "Herr Diedermann, if I might interrupt for a moment. We realize your group is mostly experienced with mining coal. Your concerns on whether those skills can be used in locating nickel and gold deposits are valid, since you don't know the source of our information. You will not be concerned with trying to find the deposits. We have maps and pictures from Grantville's library, and an engineer who is familiar with prospecting. Once the sites are located and marked, you will be responsible for opening the site. We will send for a second expedition to handle the refining and transportation of the metals." Sir Thomas sat down to wait for more questions.

From the back of the room, a voice rang out. "To the future of the Hudson's Bay Company mines!" Steins were raised in a toast and quickly downed. The crowd surged toward the tables to sign the work contracts.

The next day the sun was bright and the southerly breeze brought the temperatures up enough to start seriously melting the snowdrifts. Captain Foxe sent John Barrow to oversee the movement of the families' personal effects to the *Köbenhavn* and the tools to the *Wilhelm*.

John reported, "Everything's moved and stowed, Captain. The captain of the ship they arrived on kept them in squalid conditions. The scoundrel should be flogged for treating women and children like that! And speaking of scoundrels, have you heard when we can expect to start loading our supplies? Time is getting short."

"My latest contact from Bundgaard is that we can expect the tools, weapons, and equipment later this week. He said nothing about the food stores. I'm beginning to worry on that score. The siege at Luebeck has already driven food prices up and rumors are rampant about future problems. Thank God we bought when we did."

John walked down the forecastle, muttering, "I hope you're right, Captain, and the rumors I've heard are wrong. Otherwise that thieving bastard may ruin the whole expedition."

* * *

The last patron had left the inn and Anna was in the kitchen, washing the last of the pots. Luke and Mette sat in front of the fireplace in the dining area staring at the flames. Luke's shirt was open and Mette was playfully tickling his gray hairs.

"Mette, how can I concentrate if you keep distracting me?"

"You need some distractions. Your problem with Bundgaard is wearing you down. You need to relax. If you don't, you might not make it to the wedding." Mette joked about it, but her concern was evident. "You've been so worried with the food problem, we still haven't figured out how to tell the children we're getting married. If we don't tell them soon, we may have the first surprise wedding in history."

"I know!" Luke looked chagrined. "I just want to make sure that we do it the right way. Your late husband was a good father to them and I don't want that memory to be an obstacle. I've never had children and, quite frankly, it scares me more than a nor'easter. I'm afraid I'll disappoint them."

"Nonsense. You're wonderful with them and they love you! I'm sure if you just relax it will come to you." Mette kissed him and then went to check on Anna.

With the expedition's departure date rapidly approaching, Luke was overwhelmed with critical issues and just didn't seem to find a moment to solve the announcement problem. During the following week, small shipments of supplies continued to arrive, but no foodstuffs were included in the loads. Mette worked with him to review the supply lists. She discovered that he had overlooked many of the small, domestic items that the housewives would need. She pointed out that not only were these items needed, but they might also be good trading items with the natives. She asked Luke to come along with her went she went to buy them. It would give him a needed break and they could discuss the upcoming wedding without interruptions.

* * *

After the eighth stop, Luke wasn't sure how good an idea going shopping had been. He was in a daze and his feet hurt. Walking on cobblestone streets seemed worse than braving a heaving deck in a storm. As Mette dickered with a clerk for needles and pins, he started to daydream. Eventually his thoughts led to the one question still outstanding about the wedding, how to tell the children. As he stood there and pondered, the answer came. "Mette! I know how to tell the children!" Mette and the clerk looked at him as though he had lost his mind.

"Just what do the children have to do with pins?" As soon as she said it, Mette realized what Luke was talking about. "Men! Can't you ever concentrate on what's at hand?" Mette finished the dickering and paid for the sewing supplies. When she got Luke outside, she asked, "All right, what's the plan?" Luke explained as they continued walking home. By the time he had finished, Mette nodded agreement. "I just hope it works."

Luke reached over and took Mette in his arms, "I couldn't have done this without you. I can run a ship, but trying to handle children is something I have no skill with."

"You'll do fine, Luke. You just need a little more experience."

A child's shout caught their attention. "And speaking of experience, here's a chance for you to get some." The children came running up to greet them.

"Did you get us anything?" cried the smaller McDermott children.

"Not today, little ones. Now be good and go with the captain into the family room and maybe he will tell you a story. I'll have supper there soon."

Little Ilsa hugged Luke's leg. "Can you tell us the story of the bear? I missed it when you told it last time."

"All right, but first everyone get ready for dinner. If you do it quickly, I should have time. After supper, your mother may have another story to tell you.

The children scattered to get the table ready for dinner. When they were finished, they gathered in a circle around Luke and he recited the story of his ship's encounter with the polar bear. The children were entranced until the final scene, when, on cue, Svend let out a bear roar. All the children squealed and laughed. Shortly afterward, Anna came in with the dinner meal, followed by Mette with flagons for herself and Luke.

* * *

Ilsa and Sean clapped when Mette sat down in the "story" chair after dinner. The two little ones climbed in with her. The others settled down around Luke.

"And now, my story. It's very short and I'm not sure how it will end, but you can help finish it. There once was a widow with five children."

"Just like us, Momma?"

"Yes Ilsa, just like us." Mette continued, "She loved her children, but had been lonely for a long time. One day, a foreign prince stopped, seeking shelter. He was there on a quest to visit the king, but it took a long time to get in to see His Majesty. He was a good prince and treated the whole family well. Eventually, his great quest would lead him to seek an assistant to help with the journey." Svend looked from his mother to Luke, as he realized where the story was leading. He smiled, but Luke motioned for him to hold his thoughts. "The prince was lonely and he came to love the family. One day, he asked the widow to marry him. The lady sat her family down after supper that night and told them a story to see how they felt about having a new father. The end."

Luke rose and stepped over behind Mette. He took her hand in his and continued, "Children, your mother is the lady in the story. I've asked to pay court to her, but before we decided, we wanted to see how you felt first."

Luke was suddenly buried in a mob of happily crying children, hugging him. A smothered, "I think they approve," sounded from the bottom of the pile.

* * *

Luke and Mette planned for a small wedding but their friends decided otherwise. Time became a precious commodity. Two days before the wedding, Luke and Mette agreed that Mette would remain in Copenhagen until the resupply fleet sailed. That would give her time to sell the inn and for Luke to get a solid house built. They left unsaid the other reason for delay, the chance for famine the first winter. Luke was worried that the land near the planned site for the fort might not be productive enough. If none of the farmers chose to accompany the miners south or the crops failed, the first winter would be tough.

The day of the wedding arrived, bright and clear. Crews from the three ships, the stockholders, the settlers, and all of Mette's friends filled the nave of Vor Frue Kirk, the Lutheran cathedral, to overflowing. After a brief ceremony, everyone returned to the inn to celebrate; even the local watch stopped by to join the celebration. However, when John Barrow showed up later in the evening, Luke knew something was amiss. "John, I know you love a good party, but you told me you would be tied up all night loading the latest shipment of gunpowder. What's happened?" Luke had never seen John look so angry.

"We better go someplace quiet, sir. You're not going to like the news I just got." Luke motioned for John to follow him out the back door.

When they got outside, Luke said. "We should be able to talk here without being interrupted. Spit it out! What's happened?"

"That bastard Bundgaard has sold all our food! With the hoarding that's started from all the war rumors; on top of all the refugees already in town, Bundgaard says he won't be able to supply us with food until June. No extra cost, but we have to wait!"

Luke slammed his fist against the doorpost. "Damn! Mette said we shouldn't trust that scoundrel. I'll need to meet with our backers in the morning to decide what we can do. In the meantime, I want you to sniff around and see what really happened to our food. This could seriously jeopardize the entire expedition."

Trying to maintain calm expressions, they returned to the party. Luke walked over to Mette to join the circle of her friends. He did notice John leave the party with the sergeant of the watch.

Chapter 11

John stepped up nose to nose with the heavier of the two toughs at Bundgaard's office. "My captain is here to see Fister Bundgaard."

The guard glanced back at the door. "He's not available."

Bundgaard gave lie to the statement as he stuck his head out to call for a clerk. When he spotted Captain Foxe, he immediately put on a hang dog expression. "Captain Foxe, I assume you're here about your food stores. You have my apology. I've been forced to extend the delivery date. What with the war and such, prices and demand have gone up so much I would be foolish to deliver them now. I should have sufficient excess by June."

Luke was furious. He stepped forward but John caught him before he got to the guards. Luke shouted, "We have a contract and you've been paid! We have to have the food now!"

From behind the safety of his guards Bundgaard replied. "Captain, I would hate to have to call on the authorities. You will get your supplies, when I say so! Until then, don't come back here! Now get out!" The guards reached for their weapons.

John gently pulled Luke around and whispered in his ear." Not now, Captain. This plays right into his hand. We'll find a better way."

As they turned to leave, the guards laughed and jeered. John glared at them and muttered, "You haven't heard the last of this! We'll get even."

* * *

Bundgaard laughed. *Sailors never learn. They're all naive and so easy to gull!*

He entered his office and closed the door. A short, overweight, but well-dressed visitor stepped out from behind it. Giscard de Villereal had been waiting for Captain Foxe to leave. He had just finished negotiating with Bundgaard for supplies for the French fleet blockading Luebeck. They had also discussed France's concern with the Hudson's Bay Company. Luke's arrival had interrupted the discussion.

"I congratulate you, Monsieur! A secure source of food for the French fleet and this annoying enterprise foiled in one act. If they can't sail until summer, they will surely fail. I will deposit the funds in your account today, as agreed. The minister was right in recommending you to us."

After he checked to make sure that Captain Foxe was gone, Bundgaard escorted his visitor to the door. Villereal winced as if his shoulder hurt, but after rubbing it, continued out the door. Visions of future commissions brought a smile to Bundgaard's face. He watched his visitor disappear down the street.

* * *

Later that evening after transferring the promised funds and posting a report to Paris detailing his frustration of the expedition's plans, Villereal walked back to the house where he lived alone. As he walked, the pain in his shoulder returned. This time, it seemed to spread down his arm. Suddenly, his chest felt like someone was sitting on it. Gasping for breath, Villareal looked around for help. The street was dark; even the moonlight seemed to be failing. He landed face-first on the sidewalk.

The next morning, a partially clad body was found in the snow by the city watch. All items of worth and identification were gone, but there was no sign of violence.

When no one claimed the body in three days, it was buried in the potter's field outside the city.

Bundgaard didn't mind this at all. When Villereal failed to show to take delivery of the food, he put the word out that he had food for sale. Pure chance had delivered him an opportunity to sell those supplies three times.

* * *

"You were right Mette. Bundgaard is nothing but a thief! The whole expedition is in trouble," John said.

Mette looked to Luke, who just nodded.

Just then, a cabin boy from the *Wilhelm* entered the tavern and stepped over to Luke. "Captain de Puyter's compliments, sir. I was sent to tell you that the *Kristina* and the *Hamburg* have been sighted. They should be docking with the tide." He twisted his cap in his hands. "Is there any message I should take back?"

"Yes. Please inform Captain de Puyter to expect messages for himself and Captains Johannson and Rheinwald for a meeting here tomorrow evening. He's to deliver the messages to the other captains when they dock."

The arrival of the two ships helped Luke reach a decision. "Mette, I'll be up in our rooms. Would you send Svend up to help me prepare the messages?" Then he looked at John. "John, I've seen that look before. Usually about the time some sailor learns a hard lesson in seamanship. What are you planning?"

"With the captain's permission," John said, "I would like to bring an outsider to the meeting tomorrow."

"John, I've trusted my life and my ship to your judgment too many times to count. If you feel it's necessary, then by all means, bring your guest." When John didn't volunteer any more, Luke asked, "Do you want to at least give me a hint what it's about?"

"I need to talk to someone tonight about our problem. I think we may be able to use our problem to solve one of his. If it doesn't work out, then you can't be implicated."

* * *

Karl walked over and threw his cape over the back of the chair across from his friend. "I'm not surprised to see you, John. I hear our mutual 'friend' is up to his old tricks." John motioned to the barmaid for a beer for Karl and nodded. Karl sat down and took a long drink before continuing. "You're not the first ship he's played tricks on. You're just his biggest scam. His cousin, the minister, gets a cut from all his thefts. The minister has the local magistrate bought off so no one can touch them. The word is that he still has your food but plans to sell it to a new buyer for a higher price. It's all stored in his warehouse down by the docks. I wish I could help, but my commander has threatened my job if I interfere with Bundgaard again. If I had an alternative, I'd give up this job in a minute."

John smiled broadly. "Maybe I have an answer that can help us both. My captain is meeting with our backers tomorrow night and I'd like you to come with me." John set down his stein and fixed Karl with a stare. "Are you serious about taking a new job? We've been looking for a commander for our guard force. I'm confidant Captain Foxe would be interested in your skills."

Karl stared at the fire for a few minutes. This was exactly what his wife had already told him, *Try something new and turn the house over to Johann.* The chance to tweak his commander's nose was very appealing, too. "My wife has already said she was interested in going. I just wasn't interested in farming. What you've proposed changes everything. I will be there tomorrow night."

* * *

The following day was a flurry of activity. The captains of the *Kristina* and *Hamburg* reported that when they unloaded their cargoes for the forces besieging Luebeck, rumors were running rampant. The most prominent ones indicated that a naval relief force, commanded by Admiral Simpson, was expected once the weather moderated. The French were confident they would repel the force, but there were the fantastic claims about the strength of Simpson's new style ships. If they were to be believed, the combined fleet could be annihilated and Copenhagen would be next. The time to depart was getting short.

Word arrived on a French merchant ship bound from London that there were serious political problems in England. Fighting between the Trained Bands in London and the King's new mercenary companies had escalated. When Luke asked Sir Thomas about what it meant for him, Sir Thomas was very blasé. "Wentworth seems to simply be digging himself deeper and deeper into a cesspool. I'm not sure Charles knows how to make a rational decision on his own anymore. I've cut my ties there. I just need to make sure that they keep forgetting I'm here. If I get a summons, then I'll need to worry."

All the news wasn't bad. With the new plans to re-open settlements in Newfoundland, two fishing ship captains had contacted Sir Thomas to base a fishing port there. They would sell their catch to the colony and ship the excess back to Denmark. If the current food problems with Bundgaard could be solved, resupply should no longer be a problem.

* * *

Karl arrived early, and John escorted him to the back room where Luke planned to meet with the others. "Captain, this is the man I spoke to you about, Karl Andersen. He's a sergeant in the local city watch and a former captain of a mercenary company. He's interested in the guard force commander's position. I told him he had to talk to you about it. For what it's worth, my sources highly recommend him."

Luke motioned for Karl and John to sit down. "You've come at an opportune time, Mr. Andersen. We plan to leave soon, if some current supply problems can be solved. We were looking for a good man to handle our guard force. Initially, there will be fifteen men permanently assigned to keep the peace among the settlers and act as a cadre in case of attack. There are also four trained gunners to serve the cannons that will be landed. All able bodied men will be trained by the commander to serve as a militia. We have forty arquebuses for weapons. We don't expect any trouble with the local natives. Captain James had a local Cree tribal member return with him on his last voyage. He will act as an interpreter and the native has assured us his tribe will welcome us."

Karl was pleased with what he heard. This job wasn't much different from combining his current work with his previous duties in the mercenary company. And Luke appeared to be a big improvement over his current watch commander. "I'm interested," he said. "What's this I hear about land? My wife is adamant that we have our own land if we go."

Luke smiled at the question. It sounded just like something Mette would have said. "You'll have twice what a settler would receive, and regular pay." When they reached an agreement, Karl and Luke shook hands. "Pending approval of our backers this evening, welcome aboard, Commander Andersen." Luke turned to John, "I'm still a little mystified about your request last night, John. I know we were running short on time to find a good guard commander, but that didn't call for all the mysterious comments."

"Now that Karl is on board with us, we can go over that part. Tell him about the warehouse, Karl."

Karl checked to make sure they couldn't be overheard by any patrons in the tavern. He then laid out all the information for Luke about Bundgaard's operations.

He finished by saying, "Just as I told John, Bundgaard still has all of your food supplies stored in his dockside warehouse, but he is planning to sell them to someone else. Just how badly do you need those supplies?"

Luke could barely control his frustration. "If we don't get those supplies before April, the expedition will not sail and a lot of people will go broke! We have to have those supplies, now. That's what the meeting tonight's about. We need to find some way to solve this crisis."

John leaned forward. "Karl and I have a plan we think will get you those supplies. It may mean roughing up some of Bundgaard's men. I know personally, nothing would give me greater pleasure than to wipe those smiles off of his guards' faces. Our ships are already docked close to the warehouse. If we can wait until we have a moonless night and Karl is on patrol in that area, we should be able to, ah . . . liberate the supplies."

"That warehouse normally has only two night watchmen," Karl said. "I can make sure we don't patrol that area when the time comes. If anything should happen, I can come to check it out. I don't want my men involved. They'll still have to live and work here and my conscience could not allow them to be hurt because of my actions."

"We should have enough men," Luke said. "With the sailors and miners, we can move all the supplies quickly. But let's keep it quiet until the time is right. Just us and the men coming tonight will know. Too many with the details too soon could let the plan reach the wrong ears."

Mette's knock on the door announced the arrival of the rest of the attendees. "We'll settle this immediately." Luke introduced Karl as the new commander and got their approval. He then laid out the problem with the food stuffs and the proposed solution.

There was unanimous support for the plan.

Saul turned to Reuben, "Brother, I think we may want to plan a long business trip to somewhere else, shortly. It may be too hot here for us." He turned to Sir Thomas with a grin. "I guess that leaves it up to you to hold the bag."

"If the rumors I've heard about conditions in England are true, I may be joining Captain Foxe. If I'm not welcome in Copenhagen, I may be recalled to England to see what the Tower looks like from the inside. Wentworth was my friend at one time. I'm not sure anyone has a friend at Court now. I have enough enemies that my position is in peril. If Christian wants a scapegoat for this affair, I may be a convenient sacrifice."

Luke wasn't surprised by Sir Thomas' statement. "We can always use someone with your talents. We said to that man from Grantville that we would help those fleeing injustice."

Sir Thomas winced. "I just never imagined I might be the first!"

Luke tried to settle his fears. "If it comes up, I'm sure we can handle it. But first, we have to settle accounts with Bundgaard."

"Agreed!"

"The new moon is in ten days. Do we have all of our people and supplies ready?" Luke looked to the Abrabanels and Bamberg for the answer.

"Right now, we have one hundred and sixty seven settlers and soldiers. Karl and his wife add two more. We'll collect our head bonus when we move them on the ships. That timing could be tricky if Christian holds off payment. We probably should load them this week to make sure we get paid." Bamberg added, "Outside of food, the supplies are ready. Your suggestion to take on extra livestock and passengers when you stop for wood and water at the Orkneys will give you an extra month's food."

After the meeting broke up, Luke took Bamberg aside. "Adolphus, you aren't officially part of the company, so you should be all right. I have a favor to ask. It would be better if Mette and the children waited to come with our resupply ships. Can you watch over them and help her settle her affairs? She means so much to me, if anything untoward should happen, I could never forgive myself."

"You needn't worry, Captain. I've known Mette for a long time. I'll make sure she shows up safe and sound."

"Thank you!" Bamberg extended his hand to shake, but Luke grasped it with both hands, like a drowning man would grasp a rope. "A friend like you is hard to find."

Chapter 12

Eight days later, a warship arrived from England. Immediately after docking, two sets of visitors disembarked. The first headed directly to Rosenborg Castle to present the new ambassador's credentials. The palace was in turmoil. News had just arrived of a major naval action off Wismar. Assuming the English visitors were tied to that event, they were immediately escorted to the King.

The new ambassador was introduced and then handed his credentials to Christian. "Your Majesty, I have been instructed by King Charles to represent him at your Court. Due to distressing news the King has received concerning certain actions by Sir Thomas, I have been instructed to request Your Majesty's assistance in securing the former ambassador's return to England to answer for those actions. I pray that Your Majesty will look kindly on this request from your ally." He again bowed and awaited a response.

King Christian slowly turned purple with suppressed rage at the court fool that had escorted this problem straight to him at this time of crisis. *If they had only inquired as to the reason for the visit, I could have stalled for at least two or three weeks. Now I'll have to do something! Hopefully, Sir Thomas had his plans in order.*

"Baron Finch, I accept your credentials as the new ambassador to my court from England. You arrive at a time when I have many issues within my own kingdom to resolve. Word has just arrived that the League's naval forces near Luebeck may have suffered a reverse. I'm afraid that it will be some time before sufficient men are available to assist in locating Sir Thomas. As I understand, the last I heard he had been traveling out of the city. You may speak to Chancellor Scheel, when he is available, to request assistance in locating and detaining Sir Thomas. You are excused." Christian arose and left the room, ignoring the sputtered protests of the new ambassador. Once he was out of earshot of the room, he grabbed the majordomo by his collar. "Don't you *ever* bring someone into my presence without ascertaining what their business is! Now go find Scheel and make sure he's *unavailable to that man until* I tell him differently." He released the official with a shove and sent him on his way.

The second group was an officer and two armed men who asked at the dockside for directions and then marched off toward the house of Sir Thomas Roe. They had instructions that left no doubt that Sir Thomas was to be detained. Their only restriction was that they could not cause a major scene that would embarrass the ambassador. When they arrived at the house, the officer pounded on the door with the hilt of his sword. Michael, the doorman, cracked the door to see who it was.

The officer took a step back and announced, "I am here, by order of King Charles. Is Sir Thomas Roe in residence?"

Michael realized the worst had happened and stalled for time. "Sir Thomas is not here at the present. He's not expected back from his trip until late tomorrow night." Michael didn't bat an eyelash at the lie. Sir Thomas had actually just stepped out for his morning walk and would return within the hour.

"Very well, I shall return then. Please give him these documents when he returns." He handed over a sealed packet, turned and left abruptly. The two soldiers lingered behind, down the street from the house. They would insure that Sir Thomas didn't leave unescorted, once he returned

Agnes came out timidly from the library. "I heard what he said. Is Uncle in trouble?"

"I fear so, child. You know the pastry shop where he stops on his walk. Put on a cape and fetch him back quickly. He needs to see this right away. Make sure he comes in the back way, in case the two soldiers are still there." He held up the packet so that she could see the wax seal with the King's stamp on it.

Her eyes went wide, but she did as she was told. Five minutes later, Agnes reached the pastry shop where Uncle Thomas was chatting with the owner and eating one of his favorite kringles. Agnes paused to catch her breath and then entered the shop. "Uncle, Michael sent me to let you know that your expected visitor from England has arrived."

Sir Thomas successfully fought the urge to flinch. Agnes had thoughtfully phrased the message so that Inge, the gossipy pastry cook, wouldn't have anything to pass on to someone who might ask later. "I'll be right along, Agnes. Why don't you pick out a pastry? A brisk run deserves a reward."

"Thank you, Uncle." Once they left the shop, Agnes whispered. "Michael suggested that you might want to use the rear entrance. Two soldiers were left to watch the front door. He told the officer you weren't expected back until tomorrow night." She stopped and looked up at her uncle. "The soldiers scared me, Uncle. Are we going to be all right?"

"I hope so, Agnes, but we won't be staying in Denmark. What do you think about a long sea voyage?" The smile that lit up her face told Sir Thomas a lot.

As soon as they slipped in the back door, Michael handed Sir Thomas the packet. Matilda, the cook, stood by with clenched hands. Sir Thomas broke the seal and quickly read the summons. "What we've feared has happened. I've been summoned home to be questioned. England isn't safe for me now. I will not return, but instead will travel with the expedition. You are both welcome to accompany Agnes and me."

Matilda answered immediately. "If Agnes is going, then I go, too. She's like a daughter to me and I won't leave her. Someone needs to make sure you're both fed well."

Michael paused before answering. He hung his head, "I've met a lady, sir, and we were planning to get married. Her parents need her. I'm sorry, but I need to stay. I'll help to cover your departure if needed."

"Very well. I'll leave funds for you with Factor Bamberg to close up the house Michael and store what we can't take with us. You can have it shipped once we're settled in the New World. He'll also have a pension for you." Sir Thomas reached for the door. "I need to see Captain Foxe and let him know what's happened. Start packing. I'll be back late this evening with help to finish."

When Sir Thomas arrived at the *København*, he was met by John Barrow. "The captain is at the warehouse going over the plan with the miners, Sir Thomas. Can I help you?"

"It appears my niece and I will be joining your voyage. Do you have someone that can help load us tonight? We will need to do it discreetly. There may be watchers who want to interfere."

"Captain Foxe said this might happen. I'll have a wagon and five men at your back door after sunset. We've kept a cabin for you on the *Hamburg*." He paused, and then grinned. "I'll send two sailors to distract any watchers."

"Thank you, Mr. Barrow."

"Think nothing of it. It will be good practice for the bigger job tomorrow night.

* * *

"Now remember, no knives! The guards must *not* be killed. There should only be two of them. We'll surprise them and swamp them with numbers. We need to be able to come back here, so we take only what we paid for, nothing else!" Luke looked around to make sure there was no misunderstanding.

At a knock on the front door, everyone went quiet. Adolphus went to see who it was, then opened the door and motioned the visitor in. "It's one of your crewmen, Luke."

The man made his way through the crowd to the captain. "Mr. Barrow sent me to tell you, Captain, that Sir Thomas will be sailing with the expedition and that if you could spare them; he needs five strong men and a wagon to help load their belongings. He said there is some urgency and a need for men who can work quietly."

Luke turned to Steinbrecher. "We're done here. Would you choose five of your men you can depend on to work quietly and send them, with one of the wagons, to the ship?"

"Certainly, sir." He motioned to a group standing nearby. "Hermann, you and your brother, and you other three, come over here. The captain has a job for you. Hermann, you're in charge. Your brother will drive the wagon. Go with this sailor and follow whatever instructions Mr. Barrow gives you when you arrive at the ship."

* * *

Everything went smoothly at Sir Thomas' house. The soldiers had huddled at the mouth of an alley as soon as the sun went down and the temperature started to drop, to stay out of the wind. The two sailors simply walked up and knocked them senseless with belaying pins before they could even react. They rifled the soldier's pockets to make it look like a robbery.

The miners arrived with the wagon a short time later. Only the most essential books and furniture was loaded. Sir Thomas and Agnes were safely aboard the *Hamburg* before six bells. Svend helped with the unloading at the ship. He offered suggestions for what might be useful day to day and what could be stored in the hold. He was ecstatic that Agnes would be sailing with them.

It was a bittersweet night for Luke and Mette. When they married, they knew the parting would come quickly. They spent their time storing up memories for the months of separation that were coming.

* * *

The next day, just after supper, Svend donned a shabby set of clothes and an old boat cape and wandered down by Bundgaard's warehouse. He settled into a protected opening between two shops, a half block down from the warehouse; just like a street urchin trying to find a place to spend the night. His job was to watch the warehouse and warn the advance party if there were more than the usual two guards and play decoy for the raid.

Shortly after sunset, five sailors from the *Henriette Marie* came carousing down the darkened street past the warehouse. The two warehouse guards were stationed in front by the main doors, with a warming fire for heat and light. As they passed the fire, one sailor got boisterous. "We sail in the morning! I intend to spend this whole bonus tonight, drinking and wenching!" He shook a full money pouch and then a half empty bottle to emphasize the point. Fifty feet later, as they passed Svend, Svend signaled that no extra guards had been spotted. He waited a second and then darted out. He grabbed the sailor's pouch and ran back toward the guards. The victim yelled and then the five took off after Svend yelling, "Stop that thief!"

Svend appeared to trip on a cobblestone right in front of the warehouse guards and spilled the coins. The guards had only laughed when the sailor was robbed, but the sight of the coins spurred them to action. They pounced on Svend, just as the sailors caught up. They shoved Svend toward the sailors and scrambled for the few gold coins that glistened in the firelight. Two solid "thumps" and the warehouse was secured. The sailors picked Svend up, and congratulated him. "Nice piece of acting, sir. You nearly had us believing it." They picked up the rest of the coins, gave Svend a warmer cape to wear, and sent him off to bring in the rest of the raiding party.

While Svend was gone, they proceeded to truss up the two guards and gag them. They relieved the guards of their door keys and dragged them inside, so they were out of sight. Two sailors stayed out front to assume the guard's station in case someone wandered by. Ten minutes later, the rattle of four wagons could be heard approaching the warehouse. A silent group of men appeared at the rear of the building at just about the same time. Torches were lit and the loading of the supplies began.

* * *

At a tavern six blocks away a farewell celebration was in progress. All of the district watch that was on duty was there to bid Karl farewell. He had resigned from the watch and would sail in the morning.

"To Karl Andersen, the best sergeant in the whole watch!" Gunnar, the new watch sergeant raised the toast, "I just wish I could have seen the commander's face when you told him you resigned."

"Oh, he was happy. No more complaints from Fister Bundgaard. I'll be glad to never have to deal with that bastard again. He's your problem now, Gunnar!" Gunnar looked like he couldn't decide whether Bundgaard or the commander was the bastard. Karl laughed and downed the last of his drink. He thought, *Captain Foxe, I just hope you appreciate the hangover I'll have in the morning and that the seas aren't too rough when we sail. Two hours of drinking to go yet!*

* * *

At the warehouse, the supply loading went smoothly. John checked off the items as they were set in the wagons. When the last keg of flour was loaded, the two thugs were tossed in behind. John leaned over and whispered to them. "Cheer up. We have plans for you boys yet." The trip to the docks took only minutes. After the wagons were emptied for the third time that night and the supplies stored on board, John called for any empty barrels and crates on the *Köbenhavn* to be loaded into the wagons and covered with tarps. He then reported to Luke, "All secure, Captain. We're ready for the last phase. I'll head to the tavern. The wagons can start in five minutes." The sounds of the *Henriette Marie, the Wilhelm* and the *Hamburg* as they cast off in the darkness could be heard. "I hope your subterfuge with the ships works, sir."

"I do too, John. I hope the two fishing boats and the *Kristina* get back in time to rejoin us before we sail. In the confusion of sailing, people should only see the four ships they expect to see. If this masquerade works, we may throw suspicion elsewhere. If anyone tries to search us for missing supplies in the morning, our departing ships will be in the clear. We'll all rendezvous at Stromness Harbor in the Orkneys."

John headed down the gangplank to the dock. The two guards were now seated in the last wagon with three sailors as guards. Knives were out, but hidden. "You boys thought it was funny when Bundgaard threw us out." John had recognized the two from his visit to Bundgaard's office. "You're both in a lot of trouble for stealing Fister Bundgaard's supplies." The two started to protest, but a sharp prick with a knife silenced them. "We've left evidence and witnesses that you planned this theft. If you cooperate, you'll live and even profit for the experience. Otherwise . . . " John gestured with his knife, leaving the threat unsaid. "All you have to do is sit up here and drive a few blocks. When we reach a certain point, you will be met by some men with horses and money, who will escort you out of the city. And you'll be far away by sunup, if you know what's good for you." John's appearance from a lifetime of bar fights in foreign ports accentuated his threat. As he strode away, he called back over his shoulder, "I told you we'd get even."

Ten minutes later, John entered the tavern where Karl was partying. When he spotted John, Karl took his cue to start preparations to leave. When the group left the tavern and their eyes had adjusted to the dark, they had to wait for four canvas covered, loaded wagons to pass. Karl pointed to the last wagon, "Aren't those Bundgaard's toughs? I wonder what they're doing moving stuff this late at night?"

"Maybe someone needed a delivery before sailing early in the morning?" Jens suggested.

Karl watched the last wagon disappear around the corner. "But they aren't heading toward the docks. Gunnar, you may need to watch them. Moving goods this late at night ... maybe Bundgaard is up to something no good. Those two look like a couple of thieves"

"I'd chase them down now, Karl, but I don't think my legs would be up to it." Gunnar was only standing upright because of Jens' support. "I'll check around tomorrow, when we report for duty. Serve Bundgaard right if he got robbed, he's done it enough himself!"

John came out behind the group after they left. Karl started to stagger so John gave him a supportive shoulder to lean on. Karl said, "You know, Magda is going to kill me for getting this drunk." He staggered a little, but kept walking. John chuckled softly as they trekked back to the ship.

* * *

The next morning, an irate Bundgaard reported a major robbery to the watch commander, only to find out that the commander was already aware of the circumstances. An off-duty watch sergeant had seen two of the merchant's guards with a group of loaded wagons heading further into the city the previous night. The commander concluded that the guards stole the goods. The culprits were never found. Since he had already been paid twice for the goods, Bundgaard let the matter drop.

At the home of the former English ambassador, the officer tasked to escort Sir Thomas Roe to England arrived to an empty residence, with only some carters loading furniture for storage. No one knew where the ambassador had gone. The officer returned to his ship empty handed. When the ambassador protested to Chancellor Scheel that Sir Thomas had escaped, he was told icily, "If you've misplaced your man, that's your problem. We don't work for King Charles!"

Down at the harbor, four ships weighed anchor and set sail for the new world. Only a small group was at the docks to see them off. A mother and her children stood there until the ships were out of sight. She would see her new husband and son again soon.

Chapter 13

Early February 1634 Orkney Islands

"Land ho!"

Svend's navigation lesson with Captain Foxe came to an abrupt end. Landfall had been expected and the captain was needed on deck. Luke grabbed his boatcape and left to answer the hail. The wind was still fresh off the starboard aft quarter and the intermittent spray from the North Sea waves kept the aftercastle deck soaked. When Luke reached the deck, the first mate was standing next to the helmsman. "What bearing?" asked Luke.

John gestured to the left. "From the port beam to three points off the port bow. Scotland's off to port and South Ronaldsay Island's dead ahead in the cloud bank. Right when and where you predicted, Captain."

"That new chronometer is going to be a boon to navigators, John. Whatever Sir Thomas had to pay for it was well worth it."

Svend raced on deck and tried to sight the land. John walked over and rested a hand on Svend's shoulder, "You'll not see anything out there for a while, lad. You need to be in the foretop with a 'bring'em-near' to see beyond the curve of the horizon."

"An excellent suggestion, Mr. Barrow." Luke joined them at the railing. "Svend, go fetch my telescope, some drafting paper, and pencils. This is an excellent opportunity to continue your navigation lesson. Climb to the foretop, tie yourself off, and sketch each of the islands as we pass. It will help develop your eye for recognizing land features."

"Aye aye, sir."

Five minutes later, Svend began to ascend the shrouds to the foretop. The telescope hung on his belt by a strap, with a pack on his back for the paper and pencils. The swaying of the masts as the ship rose and fell on the swells made the trip up the shrouds interesting. He talked to himself to help concentrate on the climb up and to keep his mind off the deck below. His foot slipped on spray-slickened footrope and he spun around the shroud. "I'm glad I tied off the telescope. If I dropped it, Father would be fit to be tied." He looked up to the lubber's hole. "Just a few more feet and I'm there." After what seemed like an eternity, he reached the crosstree. He seated himself, carefully uncoiled the loose end of the rope he'd wound around his waist, and lashed himself to the mast. "At least now I can't fall." He heaved a sigh of relief. Looking down, he could see the ship's bow crashing through the waves. The slow pendulum motion of the masts as the ship rode through the waves suspended him out over the water at the end of each arc. He realized his stomach was queasy. Suddenly, the idea of sitting at the top of a tall mast swaying in the wind wasn't so pleasant. "I will not embarrass the captain by getting sick all over the deck," he said through gritted teeth. "What was it Father used to say about seasickness?" As he looked out at the land, he remembered: *Focus on the horizon.* He brought the telescope around and focused ahead. After a few tense minutes, his stomach slowly settled down. With the pad perched on his knees, a sketch of South Ronaldsay Island started to take shape.

* * *

The sunlight started to fade as the *København* entered Scapa Flow. The sound of the ship's bell startled Svend. He realized he'd been sketching for almost three hours. If he wanted supper, he'd have to finish the sketch from memory. It took a few minutes of stretching to work the kinks out of his legs. *I'll have to be careful going down. I don't want to drop anything, especially me.* He held out the last sketch and compared it to the island they were passing. "I think Father will be pleased." He stowed his gear and carefully untied himself. All the way down, he made sure he kept a firm grip on the shrouds.

John met him at the railing. "The captain was beginning to wonder if you were stuck up there. How did the drawings go?"

Svend handed over the pad. "After I got settled and used to the sway it was wonderful. The warm sun and the views made me forget everything else."

John flipped the pages slowly. The use of shading made the island views stand out from the page. "These are excellent. I'm impressed. Have you had training? The captain never mentioned anything to me."

"Nothing, I just tried to draw what I saw."

"You have a natural talent. These are better than most of the ones I've seen from veteran mariners. Run along to supper and show the captain." He handed the pad back to Svend.

The drawings highlighted a pleasant evening meal. Luke echoed John's praise. "These drawings show excellent skill. I want you to keep practicing when you have an opportunity. This will come in handy when we reach our new home." The conversation turned to the upcoming stopover at Stromness Harbor and Luke's concerns with taking on additional supplies and settlers. Svend just dreamt about a young lady on the *Hamburg*. When they finished, Luke reminded Svend, "You'll need to be up early in the morning if you want to see the harbor as we enter. We should reach Stromness around dawn."

"I'll be sure to be up before then," Svend replied as he left for his small cabin.

* * *

Svend awoke an hour before daybreak and wheedled a quick breakfast of hot porridge from the cook. When he went on deck, Captain Foxe was already there. He directed Svend aloft with a telescope. "See if the rest of the ships have arrived. Hopefully their passage was faster than ours."

Svend scampered up the shrouds to the foretop, and surveyed the harbor. Two fishing luggers were leaving the harbor, their patched sails damp from the dew. They appeared to be almost flying over the waves. Svend focused back on the anchorage. Eventually, he was able to pick out some masts against the shadows and clutter of the village. He called down to the deck, "There are two . . . no . . . three . . . ships anchored and one's definitely the *Hamburg*."

"Excellent. It appears everyone's made it safely so far." Luke turned and called to John, "Mr. Barrow, if you would please, steer for the *Hamburg* and anchor a hundred yards to seaward of her." He started to head for his cabin and a thought struck him. "Oh, and have the longboat ready. We'll need to get the extra men from the warehouse raid back to their wives as soon as possible."

Over the next hour, Svend tried to stay out of the sailors' way as the ships approached the harbor. The tide was full off Point of Ness. The wind off the port quarter required a number of tacks for the ships to reach the harbor entrance. As they approached the anchorage, Svend climbed onto the mainstays with the telescope and eagerly searched the people on the *Hamburg*'s deck for a familiar figure. Disappointment and worry started to set in until he spotted Sir Thomas coming on deck, with Agnes right behind him. Shortly afterward, Svend was forced to come down to make way for the sailors to furl the sails. By the time the ship's anchor was dropped, he had finally caught Agnes' attention and she had waved back.

"Master McDermott, do you feel up to a long session of note taking?" John Barrow had walked up unnoticed behind Svend, who was still watching the *Hamburg* intently. "The captain needs his clerk to take notes when he meets the other captains."

"I can be ready in two minutes, Mr. Barrow. Just let me get my paper, quill and ink." Svend carefully closed the telescope, handed it to John, and then disappeared down the hatch to his cabin.

John walked back to the captain, who stood watching the other ships prepare to send boats away. "He's got it bad, Captain, and I don't think he even realizes it."

"I know, John. Were we ever that young?"

"I don't know, but I think Mistress Roe will be good for him. I just hope nothing happens to them." The creak of tackle drew their attention. "The longboat's ready, Captain. Should I send it away with the men? It's going to be a long pull for the seamen to reach all three ships."

"Yes, but have them use the starboard side. Keep the port side free for the arriving boats."

"Aye aye, sir." John left to supervise the small boat handlers. The departing settlers were already bunched up, waiting on deck with their meager belongings in bundles.

* * *

The *Henriette Marie*, the *Hamburg*, and the *Wilhelm* had arrived in Stromness two days earlier. Their captains, along with Sir Thomas and Captain Andersen, arrived over the next hour and gathered in Luke's cabin. They traded stories on their departures from Copenhagen and their passage to the Orkneys. They all had a good laugh when Karl described his wife's reaction to his arriving home drunk. Only John's emphatic protests that it was in a good cause saved him from getting his ears boxed. The only incident of note was that Captain Rheinwald had discovered cracks in the *Hamburg*'s lower mizzen and bonaventure masts. Captain James politely inquired if they were serious. Rheinwald snapped back, "I'll be having my carpenters finish repairs soon." The looks of concern from the group caused Captain Rheinwald to get even more defensive.

"She's in just as good a shape as any ship here. As I said, Mr. Braun should have the boards fished on by the time this meeting's over." His emphatic nod cut off further comments.

Sir Thomas broke the awkward silence. "I've passed the word around the port that we're looking to take on extra livestock and have space for additional settlers. Three families have already spoken to me about joining. They're all sheep farmers and would bring their flocks. There was a dispute in the clan over an inheritance and they want to leave soon. They'll be ready before we finish wooding and watering and loading extra fodder. I've also added two pair of the island's horses. They're used to the colder conditions we'll be facing."

He reached down and took a document from a sealed pouch. "I have an announcement that I was directed to keep secret until we arrived. The Shetland and Orkney Islands have been returned to Denmark by England. We have been directed by King Christian to establish a Governor's Office that will be run by the Company. Our re-supply ships will bring out the new Governor. We will be using these islands on a regular basis for our trading with the new colony. I will need to find a site for a warehouse and residence for whoever comes with the next group. We will need to stay a few extra days until these needs are met. Captain Andersen, I'll need you to help me locate a suitable building to set up our offices and see to its protection." He sat down and surveyed the stunned faces of the captains. *Evidently the treaty had stayed a secret!*

Karl was not surprised by the announcement. Sir Thomas had spoken with him about this the previous night and he'd already spotted a site that looked promising. "I shouldn't think that will delay our departure."

Luke finally arose, "Excellent, Thomas! That's the best news I've heard in a long time. From past stops, I'm sure the islanders will relish the news. They've never been supporters of England. I can suggest two or three men that might make excellent factors here." Sir

108

Thomas gave a curt nod as Luke continued. "The only other point I think needs addressing concerns sailing instructions now that we're all back together. Specifically, what happens if any ships are separated during our next leg of the voyage?"

The captain of the fishing boat *Bridget* spoke up, "Lars and I already thought about this. Since we're going to be fishing anyways, we plan to save time and head directly to the fishing grounds and then to the settlement site. That way, you'll have fresh provisions soon after landing."

Luke paused to consider the idea. "That's an excellent suggestion." He glanced around, but no one spoke up, so he continued. "During a storm, if you are in distress, fire a signal gun. The nearest ship should try and render aid. Otherwise, if anyone just becomes separated, head directly to Bell Island."

Luke pointed to Svend. "Once a week Mister McDermott will visit all the ships to retrieve updates for the master log I'm keeping, and any routine issues you feel need to be brought to my attention. Status on food and water, and ship's conditions will be included in these reports." He refrained from glowering in Rheinwald's direction. "Again, if something urgent occurs, use your signal flags or fire a gun and we will come to your assistance. As Sir Thomas said, we'll sail once we finish replenishing our food and water and load the extra settlers and livestock." He looked around once more for questions but everyone seemed anxious to stretch their legs ashore. "That's all for now, gentlemen. If you can, let your crews stretch their legs on shore. This will be their last chance for quite some time."

As the group rose to leave, Luke drew two of the captains aside, "Thomas, Martin, would you stay a few minutes? I've some additional things I need to discuss with you." He motioned to the two cushioned seats. "I'll be right back." Luke saw the rest of the captains to their boats and then returned to his cabin.

As he reentered, Captain James asked, "Is there something wrong?"

"No, no. The two of you have some unique skills that may help our long term success. Thomas, the native that's with your crew, would he work with Svend to teach him the Cree language?"

"I'm sure of it. Svend showed Joseph around Copenhagen before we left and has already picked up a few Cree words. They seemed to get along well. They're not that far apart in age and Joseph is very quick."

"Good. Now Martin. One of the settlers on your ship was a mathematics teacher, has training as a surveyor, and has the necessary surveying tools. He started to train Svend shortly after he arrived in Copenhagen, but that was halted when the food problems arose. I'd like that training to resume."

" What I propose is that Svend alternate afternoons on your ships, working with his tutors. I know that will mean extra small boat work, but it will also give us an opportunity to communicate more frequently."

Martin chuckled. "I just hope he isn't too prone to seasickness. All those trips in an open boat could be trying."

"I'll give him Sundays off to recover! I'm sure he'll be glad to visit your ship so often. I think he's taken quite a liking to Sir Thomas' young ward."

"I wondered. She always seems to take a keen interest in where your ship is when she's on deck."

"Just make sure he applies himself to his studies when he's there. If he wants to talk to the young lady afterwords, it's all right, as long as Sir Thomas agrees."

* * *

The expedition remained at anchor three more days. The new territory's Government Office was set up in some empty rooms of a wool warehouse near the docks. Karl had two of his soldiers whitewash the walls inside to brighten the rooms. The owner was delighted to rent

110

the unused space. A small loft over the space would provide an office for the new 'Acting Governor', who was, coincidentally, the wool merchant. Luke and Sir Thomas had a good laugh when Karl related the man's reaction when the news of the reversion of ownership to Denmark was mentioned. He'd dropped to his knees thanking the Lord for deliverance from the English tax collectors. Sir Thomas just managed to get out between laughs, "I hope he realizes we'll be collecting taxes too! Though knowing English tax collectors too well, I don't doubt we will be an improvement."

The additions to the expedition were uneventful. The sheep were purchased and penned up outside of town. The additional families packed and loaded their belongings aboard the *Köbenhavn*. On the last day, Svend took the opportunity to go ashore with Agnes and Joseph. The afternoon was blustery. As they left the boat that had rowed them ashore and climbed the slime coated steps to the pier, one of the sailors called out, "Mr. Barrow said to remind you, sir, we sail this evening with the tide. He said we were to wait here and fetch you if you wandered too far."

Svend laughed. "I don't think we have any worries there, Kurt. The whole village is only two or three blocks long. We'll be back in plenty of time." The boat crew finished tying up and stretched out for a nap in the sun.

At the end of the pier, Svend stopped, "Now remember, Joseph, I want you to use only Cree while we're in town. I'll try to translate for Agnes."

"Âha."

Svend turned to Agnes. "That means, yes."

"Shall we get something to eat before we start?" Agnes asked.

Svend translated, "Â.hâw." Joseph nodded and pointed to the inn just off the pier.

Lunch was amusing for the young people as Svend stumbled over his translations. When they finished their meals, the innkeeper asked what was going on. Agnes explained. She pointed to Svend. "He is trying to learn the language of the natives where we are heading and Joseph is teaching him. He has to act as interpreter and translate anything we say, back and forth." She smiled. "He's still learning."

Svend immediately tried to stammer out to Joseph what Agnes said.

Joseph corrected two words and then added, "Ahay k"sposâkow. Tânitowahk wiyâs."

Svend turned to the innkeeper. "He says, 'Thank you for the excellent meal and wants to know what type of meat it was.'"

"Some of our local sheep."

As he tried to translate, Svend was stymied for a word for sheep. He tried a pantomime and then "baaed." He was saved when the sound of bells came through the open rear door of the kitchen. He quickly paid for their meals and called for Joseph and Agnes to follow him. The sheep that the settlers were bringing were being driven to the wharf. Svend pointed to them and said, "sheep." He then asked Joseph, "How do you say 'sheep' in Cree?"

Joseph looked at the wooly beasts, looked at Svend and said deadpan, "sheep."

Svend's jaw dropped. Joseph walked over to get a better look at the first sheep he had ever seen. Agnes was laughing so hard, she was nearly in tears. She gasped for breath and sat down, hard, on a nearby piling. Once she recovered her composure, Svend offered her a hand up. She stood up but slipped on a slime covered board and stumbled into Svend's arms. She murmured something and Svend smiled. Joseph asked for a translation. Svend replied in correct Cree, "None of your business!"

The three walked back up the path by which the sheep had entered the village. After a hundred yards, they were outside the village. Joseph looked around, "Not like Copenhagen, just a bunch of stones." They proceeded to walk around the hills at the outskirts of

Stromness and arrived back at the dock an hour later as the last of the sheep were being hoisted on board the *Kristina*. The noise from the flock was audible across the harbor.

"I'm glad I'm not on that ark." Agnes nodded toward the *Kristina*. "The noise and smell would be enough to make me want to row to Hudson's Bay."

"That's true, but they eat the best of anyone in the expedition." Svend looked wistfully at the ship, remembering the stew they'd had for lunch and the tough salted meat they'd eaten on the way to Stromness. Breaking out of his reverie, he motioned to the boat, "We'd better get back to our ships. The captain will want to sail soon, now that the sheep are loaded.

Chapter 14

February 1634

Frederiksborg Castle, Copenhagen

Prince Ulrik had never seen his father this angry, and sober to boot! The subjects of the royal rage stood mute before the King.

Word had reached the King that Dagmar Bundgaard had tried to use his family relationship with the Minister of War to feather his pockets at the expense of Sir Thomas' expedition. In addition, certain irregularities in the sales of supplies to the army for the dike repairs on Nordstrand Island had also been uncovered. All leading back to Bundgaard.

The War Minister, Asmund Poulsen remained mute as the King turned on him. "Asmund, if I had any hint that you were guilty of anything other than misplaced familial loyalty you would be standing in chains with your cousin! I can't afford to lose your knowledge of how the Ministry runs in the middle of this war and trying to stave off the disaster that will hit the coast in the fall. Neither can I risk any more supply fiascoes. You will turn over your supply duties with the army to Prince Frederik, the new research facility to Prince Ulrik, and the fleet to Captain Admiral Overgaard's adjutant. If I ever find that you are guilty of any other disloyal act, you will join your cousin in prison."

Ulrik's jaw dropped with the pronouncement. *What research facility was his father talking about?* Before he could ask, the King resumed his tirade.

"As to you, Fister Bundgaard, I don't know how someone as wealthy as you are could be so stupid.

Scamming foreign sailors with shoddy goods is one thing, but trying to scam an expedition sponsored by me defies comprehension. Even a bear knows well enough not to crap in his own cave. Selling damaged goods for the dike repairs puts the entire western coast of the country at risk. That could be construed as treason." Bundgaard blanched and sagged down further under the weight of his chains. The King motioned for the guards, who had tried to blend into the woodwork during the tirade, to remove Bundgaard. "Take this villain away to the dungeon. Hold him there until we can learn the true extent of his treachery. As for you Asmund, don't give me a reason to send you there too. Now get out of my sight before I change my mind."

The Minister bowed and almost scampered after the departing guards. Prince Ulrik decided to wait until his father was in a better mood to find out just what he had been handed so unexpectedly.

Early the next morning the answer came to him in the form of a knock on his door. Standing there when he opened it was a bear masquerading as a man. "Good morning your Highness. Your father asked me to visit you this morning and introduce you to your new job. My name is Baldur Nordgaard and I have been working for the King on his new research facility." His visitor noticed the nightgown he was wearing. "I see I wasn't expected. Shall I come back later for your tour?"

Ulrik paused before answering. The visitor seemed to be more at home in a thieves' den than doing research for a king. On the other hand, he did know about his father's comment. Besides the prisoners and the guards, no one else knew, so he probably was legitimate. "Give me a moment to dress and I'll be right with you. Come in and have a seat while I change into something more appropriate for *touring*." He stepped into the next room and changed quickly. While he dressed, he quizzed his visitor to make sure he was what he said he was. "So when did my father tell you to see me?"

"Last evening after his session with the Minister and his cousin."

Well, that confirmed the source of the message! "So what exactly is this 'research facility' I'm supposed to work with?"

"Your father sent for books from Grantville as soon as he heard about it. He spent a tremendous amount of money obtaining an 'encyclopedia'. When he saw the weapons in it, he hired me to try and duplicate them. I have a workshop set up on the castle grounds and have been working there around the clock since then. In the past few weeks, I've finally started making headway. I'm just not sure what the King intends to do with some of them. You'll have to see them in person. It's hard to explain something that no one else has ever seen before in this time."

Ulrik stepped back out clothed in some winter riding gear. "I don't normally keep work clothes around. The staff tends to dispose of them before they get to that state. Will these do for the tour?"

Baldur gave him a quick review. "They'll do just fine. If you'll follow me please?" As they walked down the hall, Baldur started to list the projects that the King had him working on. They ranged from the plausible all the way to bizarre. Ulrik still wondered if he was following a madman that had wandered into the castle.

Chapter 15

Late February 1634

Northwest of the Orkneys

Svend spotted someone on the *Hamburg*'s deck and stood up and waved back.

"Mr. McDermott, would you please sit down and quit rocking the boat? Captain Foxe would not take kindly to my reporting that you drowned while being rowed to the *Hamburg*," First Mate Barrow said.

"Sorry, sir. I wasn't thinking." Svend tried to look contrite but the object of his attention waved again and his attention was distracted.

"The sea's a harsh mistress and inattention can be fatal."

Svend waved again and John realized he was fighting a losing battle. "Very well, if you must wave, at least stay seated!" The two sailors that were rowing nearly missed a stroke as they laughed at Svend's reaction.

Five minutes later, they boarded the *Hamburg*. The trip had been brief and easy on the rowers. *The København* had launched them from ahead of the *Hamburg*'s course and they rowed towards the boarding ropes on the *Hamburg*'s side. They would repeat the maneuver when it was time to return.

Agnes met Svend at the entry port, along with their teacher, Jeremiah Redmond. Sir Thomas had arranged that she would join in the lessons, to further her mathematics education. Any concerns that Agnes might be a distraction had vanished after the first lesson. She was slightly ahead of Svend and a friendly rivalry had developed to see who could get the correct answer first.

As a result, they both showed excellent progress. Once they settled into the empty day cabin Captain Rheinwald had set aside for the lessons, Jeremiah started going over what he had planned.

"Today, we will cover calculating the area inside an irregular rectangle. Do you have the answers and drawings to the questions I posed last time?" They both dutifully handed over the calculations. Jeremiah quickly reviewed their homework. "Very good, Master McDermott; however, your answer on the second question is in error. It appears you forgot the offset distance. Otherwise, your other calculations are correct and your draughtmanship is excellent. Mistress Roe, your answers are correct. I see that you still need help sharpening your quills. The technique on your drawings still reflects your problem there." Jeremiah pulled out his knife and showed her the proper technique. He handed the knife to Agnes and had her practice. After three tries, he was satisfied she could do it properly and returned to the math lesson.

* * *

Shortly before the lessons ended a commotion could be heard on deck. Karl Andersen and his sergeant, Wilhelm Engle had arrived from the *Wilhelm* and started drilling potential militia recruits. The deck space was too limited to attempt any marching drills so Karl had chosen to train the farmers and miners in groups of five on the basics of the arquebus. A barrel had been attached to a line and tossed over the taffrail for a target. When the math lesson ended, the third and last group was preparing to fire their first shot. So far, no one had hit the barrel, and Karl was showing his frustration.

"Now, if you 'gentlemen' would be so kind as to load your weapons as the sergeant showed you, without shooting each other, we'll see if you can at least hit the ocean."

Two of the group snickered.

118

"You think that's funny? It won't be so funny if the natives attack and you forget how to shoot!"

"But, Captain, Joachim and I already know how to shoot, and we brought our own rifles along. They're a lot better then this crap we're using here!"

The statement stopped Karl dead in his tracks. It had never occurred to him that there might actually be some worthwhile recruits among the passengers. If these two really had rifles, his shortage of qualified scouts might be alleviated. "Go get them and we'll see!" As the two headed below, Engle roared at the other three. "The captain didn't tell you to stop! Keep loading!"

By the time Kurt and Joachim returned, the others had finally finished loading and stood at the taffrail, aiming at the barrel. Their wives and children stood to the side, watching. Karl chivvied Kurt and Joachim to get in line and load. As he saw what they carried, his eyes went wide. He had seldom seen weapons like these, but being the experienced officer he was, he hid his surprise with a roar. "Well, get loaded. I want to see if anyone can hit the barrel. So far, the barrel is winning this war."

The first attempt was by a farmer with an arquebus. He closed his eyes before he shot. The uproll of the ship sent his shot into the unknown.

Karl raised his eyes in supplication. "Not even the ocean!" When he looked back at the farmer, the fury was evident. "Keep your damn eyes open and aim!" He walked over to the next one in line, who was trying to stifle a laugh. "Think you can do any better? Let's see."

He was one of the miners from Amberg. He raised the arquebus, kept his eyes open and fired after the ship reached the top of the wave. The shot was in line with the barrel, but a little low. Karl was pleased. "Not bad, not bad at all. It's better to be low than high. A ricochet might still hit something. If you can do that again next practice, you'll rate out as militia. Give your name to the sergeant." The third in line never even got his weapon up before the gun discharged. He just missed a sailor scrubbing the deck. Karl grabbed the gun and kicked him back toward the group of women who were watching. He pointed with the butt of the empty gun at the last two. Kurt stepped up and took aim. The crack of the rifle was decidedly different from the previous shots. So was the result. The bullet left a two inch hole in the barrel. "That good enough, Captain?" Karl just stood there with his mouth open.

Joachim stepped up, raised his rifle, paused until the ship reached the next trough and then fired. He hit one of barrel's bands and the barrel exploded in a shower of staves. He rested the rifle butt on the deck. "My two brothers and I joined a mercenary company after the sawmill we worked at was ransacked."

"Well, you're back as scouts! Give the sergeant your names. It'll mean an extra bonus each month."

Karl walked over to Captain Rheinwald. "Pardon my intrusion Captain, but do you know where Master Mc-Dermott is? Captain Foxe asked me to give him a shooting lesson when I finished with the militia trainees."

"Here's your student now." Rheinwald motioned to Svend, whose head was just coming into view.

Joachim was showing his rifle to the sergeant as Svend and Agnes walked past. The simple lines caught Svend's eye and he paused to admire it. Karl walked over and spoke to Svend. "An interesting weapon, yes? Did Captain Foxe mention that he wanted me to give you a shooting lesson today?"

"Yes, just before I left. I was coming to see you."

Joachim tapped Svend on the shoulder, the rifle extended in his other hand. "Here, try this one. It was my younger brother's and it's a lot better then one of the old arquebuses." He reached for his powder horn "Let me show you how it's loaded."

Svend's delight with the offer was evident. "Thank you. I'll be careful with it."

After a twenty minute lesson in the care and loading of a rifle, Svend was ready to try his first shot. Joachim explained how to shoot. "Snug the rifle up to your shoulder. If you don't, you'll get a nasty bruise. Then sight down the barrel and line up your target with the sight on the end. Take a breath and hold it. Make sure you keep your eye on the target. Slowly exhale and then squeeze the trigger. Don't jerk it or you'll miss. Remember to allow for the roll of the ship and the movement of the target. Now try it!" A new barrel was pitched over the railing.

Svend went through the instructions in his head. Just as he pulled the trigger the ship pitched to the side a little and the shot missed by a foot.

"Not bad for a beginner. Now try reloading faster and let's shoot again." By the fifth shot, Svend had the reloading down to just over thirty seconds and had hit the barrel twice.

Karl stepped over. "Very good Mr. Hasselman. Your pupil learns quickly!" Svend also thanked Joachim and returned the rifle.

"You're a good shot, sir. I'd welcome you on a hunt with me anytime." Pulling out a cleaning kit, Joachim showed Svend how to clean the gun.

Karl watched thoughtfully. *I think I may have found my sergeant of scouts. I'll talk with him later.*

After the lesson, Svend managed to get Agnes to a quiet spot on the main deck where they could talk without being overheard. John was already hauling the boat in for the return trip and time was short. "I'll be back on Saturday to pick up the weekly reports. Do you think you'll have a chance to talk to your uncle before then?"

"I've already dropped some hints and he didn't seem surprised. I should have a chance after supper tonight."

"Then Saturday it is!" Glancing around to make sure no one was watching, Svend leaned over to give Agnes a quick kiss. She drew it out longer than he'd hoped for. A yell from John Barrow that the boat was ready hurried him off, with dreams of future happiness, but some trepidation about his upcoming meeting with Sir Thomas.

* * *

"I'm glad this is the last ship, Mr. McDermott. These waves are making for a long pull today." Svend was finishing his weekly rounds, picking up the ships' log entries. An oilskin packet had been needed today to keep the pages dry. As they reached the *Hamburg*, the boatman reminded him, "Watch the battens. They're awfully slippery in this weather. Wouldn't want you to get your clothes dirty." The old sailor gave him a knowing wink.

"I'll be careful, Mr. Dunn. I don't relish a swim in these waters." Timing his leap, Svend grabbed hold of the side ropes and carefully made his way up the side to the entry port. A seaman met him at the port and handed Svend the Captain's report. A second seaman dropped a rope over the side so the boat could be secured and towed until they reached a point ahead of the *Köbenhavn*. Svend excused himself to find Agnes and Sir Thomas. Time was short. He took off the boat-cape he had worn to protect himself from the sea spray. He was dressed in his best outfit. He had rehearsed all week what he planned to say. He reached Sir Thomas' cabin and knocked on the door. After a few seconds wait, Agnes opened it.

"Is Sir Thomas in?"

From the connecting cabin, Sir Thomas called out, "Come in, Mr. McDermott, we've been expecting you."

Agnes stepped aside and primly folded her hands behind her back. Svend took a deep breath and stepped in. Agnes stayed behind as he entered Sir Thomas' day cabin. Svend stood there, suddenly unsure how to start.

"Well, don't just stand there, come in! Agnes said you needed to see me today." Sir Thomas had a frown on his face and hands on his hips. A few of the planned phrases came back to Svend.

122

"Sir, I'm here to speak to you about Agnes. I . . . " He paused, unable to go on.

"I'm waiting, son." Sir Thomas' exasperated comment brought Svend back to his task.

"I'm here to speak to you about Agnes."

"You've said that already. Has she done something in class to offend you?"

"Oh, no, sir. It's not that at all."

"Well then, what is it? Your boat will need to be leaving soon." The look on Sir Thomas' face had gotten sterner. Suddenly, a giggle from the other room broke the tension. Sir Thomas broke into a broad grin. He couldn't keep the masquerade up any longer. "All right, son. Agnes has already told me why you're here. Let me have it in your own words."

Svend took a deep breath and said in a rush, "Sir, I would like your permission to court your ward, Agnes Roe."

"When Agnes warned me what you would be speaking about to me, I spoke to Captain Foxe about you. Your father had nothing but praise for your honesty, sense of honor, and future prospects. He said I would be a fool not to have you marry into the family. You have my permission, but nothing more than courting until we reach the new colony."

Svend's feet were frozen to the floor. "Thank you, sir."

Sir Thomas made a circling motion with his hand. "I think the young lady in question has something she'd like to say to you."

When Svend turned around, Agnes was standing directly behind him. She smiled at his confusion, shook her head, stood on her tip-toes and gave him a long, lingering kiss. After they finished, she looked to Sir Thomas, "Thank you, Uncle." A single tear was perched on her uncle's cheek.

* * *

Captain Foxe surveyed the gathered worshipers, concern evident on his face. Every Sunday since the expedition had sailed, an awning and lectern had been set up on the *Köbenhavn*'s maindeck for Pastor Bauman's Sunday sermon. If the previous five Sundays were any indication, the service still had another hour to go. The winds were freshening and the pastor was having trouble keeping his notes in place. Shortly after daybreak, the sun had disappeared behind the clouds and the overall atmosphere for the service was as gloomy as the weather. Luke checked the sails and then turned and whispered to his first mate, "John, the weather appears to be worsening. I think it's time to take in sail and start the other preparations we discussed."

"It'll mean interrupting the sermon," John's solemn tone was betrayed by his look of relief.

"So be it. I always did favor brevity in a sermon."

John rose and called out, "All hands prepare to take in sail!" The sailors in the crowd quickly headed to their stations.

Luke walked over to the lectern, "Sorry, Pastor, we'll have to end early this week. The weather's worsening and we'll need to clear the deck."

Three pages of the sermon escaped and were quickly blown over the side. "I understand, my son."

Luke called out, "Hoist the signal for the other ships to reduce sail. No sense in scattering more than we have to."

As the afternoon wore on, the winds continued to increase, along with the height of the waves. Just before sunset, Luke sent Svend to the foretop crosstrees to check on the other ships. After five minutes, he called down, "They're all still visible. The two fishing boats are just visible to the west, the *Kristina* and the *Henriette Marie* are just about a mile to the northwest, the *Wilhelm* is about two miles dead ahead, and the *Hamburg* is about a mile to the southwest."

"Can you see any problems?"

"I can see some activity on the *Hamburg*'s deck around the masts, but can't make out what's going on."

"Very well. Come down." As Svend descended, Luke mulled over the situation. Svend swung down from the chains and headed for the aftercastle to return the telescope. A large wave broke over the side and nearly knocked him off his feet. He came up sputtering. Luke decided it was time.

"John, rig safety ropes. It's going to get worse and I don't want someone swept overboard. I want just the foretopsail set and double reefed. Also, rig relief gear for the rudder and relieve the helmsman every hour. We don't need an accident from worn out gear or men."

"Aye aye, sir." John quickly set about his tasks.

A thoroughly soaked Svend handed the telescope to Luke. "Do you think that the other ships will be all right?"

"I hope so, son. We've done everything we can. I just hope the *Hamburg*'s masts hold up."

"I do too, sir." Svend was worried about a special person on board her. He certainly wasn't going to be able to see Agnes today like he had promised.

* * *

Throughout the night, the weather worsened. By morning, gale winds lashed the seas to twenty foot waves. The entire ship creaked as her hull flexed on the waves. The pumps were started to keep up with the leaks caused by seams gradually working open. Their monotonous clanking added to the din.

Breakfast consisted solely of dried biscuit. It was too rough to risk lighting a galley fire. After choking down a biscuit, Svend went on deck. He tied on a safety line, and went up in the afterchains to see if any of the other ships could be spotted. Only the *Hamburg* and the *Kristina* were visible. Two other dark shapes to the northeast might have been the *Henriette Marie* and the *Wilhelm*. When he reported to the captain, Luke didn't appear concerned about the missing fishing boats.

"They're built for this type of weather. They're probably well ahead and off to the northwest. We're about where they planned to separate from us anyways and they can run with the wind. They'll keep their distance so no one runs them down in the dark. We're more of a danger to them than the weather."

Svend reluctantly went below. The rough weather was affecting the passengers and the smells below deck were worsening. At least the cabin was slightly drier than being on deck.

When the evening watch ended an hour later, John came on deck to relieve Luke. "You need to get some rest, Captain. You'll be no use in an emergency if you're too tired to think quickly."

"You're right, John. I'll be in my cabin. The good Lord knows I need some rest. If the weather worsens, don't hesitate to call me!"

"You can count on me, sir!"

Chapter 16

The next morning, it was obvious the ship was struggling. The moan of the wind in the rigging set teeth on edge and the clank of the pumps continued. The smell below decks was revolting. No food had been prepared since the previous noon but many passengers still had the dry heaves. John reported to the captain on conditions below decks. From the companionway door, Svend was able to eavesdrop on them.

"The pumps are barely staying up with the water, sir. The hull's working so much from this action; the seams are leaking. We have to do something. We can't keep the wind and the waves on our quarter. The aftercastle's acting like a sail trying to turn the ship. If we should lose the rudder, we'll turn and broach before we can react."

"I agree. We need to change course. But, if we run with the wind, we could end up near Acadia. We need to hold our position. Summon the hands. We'll turn into the wind and set out a sea anchor. If we do it now, while we still have some men that aren't too worn out, it should succeed."

An older sail was brought up from the sail locker and modified to act as a sea anchor. Four extra men stood by the wheel to help the master. Another stood by with the captain's telescope. Svend just stayed out of the way and watched.

"As soon as the foretopsail's reefed, be ready to drop the sea anchor as soon as you're certain we're going to be able to come about."

"Aye aye, Captain." Fatigue was evident in John's face.

Luke turned to the group at the wheel. "All our lives are going to be in your hands. Once the sail's are reefed, she's going to want to try to turn from the wind pressure on the stern. You have to hold her! We'll go about as we reach the crest of a wave. Let the wind and the rudder work together. I'll give you a warning as the wave approaches. Understand?" The grim nods assured Luke they knew what to do.

As the ship reached the top of the next crest, Luke scanned to horizon to see if any rogue waves could be spotted. The rain and spray reduced visibility. Within the limited horizon from the storm, everything was normal. He called out, "Reef the foretopsail, Mr. Barrow, and prepare the sea anchor!"

John and the sailors in the foretop started to reef in the sail. Immediately, the master at the helm motioned for help. Luke was watching the waves approach from the stern, counting the time between crests. When one of the hands called out that the sail was furled, Luke stepped over to the wheel. "Mr. Cochrane, we're going to do it on the next wave. Let her sag a point off to port now. When I tell you, take her hard-a-port."

"Aye aye, Captain. Hard-a-port on your command."

The ship settled to the bottom of the trough and then the stern started to rise. As soon as he could see over the wave, Luke gave the signal for hard-a-port and the rudder was set hard over. The effect was immediate. The ship tilted to starboard and started turning. John cast loose the sea anchor just as the crest of the wave passed the bow. Two more men joined those at the wheel to hold it. Everyone held their breath, trying to turn the ship by prayer alone.

They had timed it perfectly. By the time the ship sank in the next trough, the sea anchor had taken hold and the result on the ship's motion was noticeable. With her head into the wind, the corkscrew action was gone and one man could handle the wheel.

A cannon shot sounded through the wind.

A quick scan of the horizon showed two ships still within view. The *Kristina* was about a mile astern, off the port quarter, and appeared to be readying for the same maneuver the *Köbenhavn* had just completed. The other ship was the *Hamburg* and she was definitely in trouble. She was missing her bonaventure mast completely and the mizzenmast appeared damaged. Rheinwald's only choice seemed to be to try and run with the wind. She quickly disappeared into the rain squalls.

Luke murmured, "May God have mercy on them," closed the telescope and returned to the tasks of steadying the *Köbenhavn* on its new heading. There was nothing he could do to help.

* * *

It took two more days for the storm to blow itself out. By noon the third day, the wind had veered to the south and brought a warm hint of spring. Four very bedraggled looking ships regrouped and hove to within hailing distance to begin repairs. After sunset, Luke retired to his cabin to eat his first hot meal in four days and consider the impact of the damage on the expedition. The *Kristina* had lost a mainmast spar that carried away a ten foot section of rail when it came down. Captain Johannson had been able to salvage the spar and was preparing to raise it back into place. The livestock had suffered minimal losses, thanks to an ingenious idea by one of the sheep farmers from Stromness. A little whiskey in the feed grain had kept the larger animals relaxed. The *Wilhelm* had suffered the only known casualties of the storm. Two sailors had been washed overboard and an older farmer had died of an apparent heart attack. Luke planned to be rowed over in the morning with Pastor Bauman to conduct a funeral and memorial service. The *Henriette Marie* had only minor damage. There was no sign of the *Hamburg* or the two fishing boats. Given the situation the last time he saw her, Luke was certain the *Hamburg* had gone down. The two fishing boats were probably already off the Grand Banks fishing.

An insistent voice finally broke through his musings. Svend repeated his question again. "How soon do you think we'll sight the *Hamburg*?"

Luke started to voice his thoughts, but paused when he realized why Svend was so concerned. There was a slight chance she was still safe so he softened the answer. "I don't know, son. Rheinwald's one of the best captains I know. Given the damage they had the last time I saw them, they're not likely to be able to rendezvous before we reach Bell Island. If the winds go foul or she meets another storm, we might not see her until after we reach Hudson's Bay."

Svend visibly brightened. "I know she's all right. I'd sense it if she was gone."

Luke started to ask how he could tell when a ship was all right when he realized who the "she" was. He put his arm around Svend's shoulder, "I know you're close to Agnes, but when the sea's harsh, how do you know she's safe?"

"I've known when people close to me were in trouble. I knew when Father died. I'm sure she's fine."

Luke's unspoken thought was, "*Keep your hopes, son. They're all we have now and they're thin at best.*"

* * *

The next morning, an unexpected cry roused the ship.

"Land ho, off the starboard bow!"

There was a rush of feet on deck as the passengers and crew hurried to catch sight of land. Svend went to Captain Foxe's cabin to make sure he'd been told. He passed John Barrow on the way. When he entered the cabin, Luke was slowly getting dressed.

"Sir, aren't you coming on deck?"

"There's no hurry, we're still nearly a week from land."

"But the sighting?"

130

"I believe we'll find out shortly that the land is nothing but an iceberg. I'm surprised we haven't seen them sooner."

Two minutes later, John knocked on the door and then entered, "As you suspected, Captain, just an iceberg. I'll have the boat ready for you after you finish eating."

Luke nodded and motioned Svend to have a seat at the table, "After you finish breakfast, make sure to dress warmly. I'd like you to accompany the pastor and me for the service. I'll have some words to say afterward and I'd like you to hear them."

After a quick meal, Svend ducked back to his cabin and picked up his cloak. When he emerged on deck, John already had the boat alongside. A quick glance around the horizon now showed a number of icebergs in sight, including a small one that was passing off the starboard side. In the early morning light, it appeared blue-white and sparkled like diamonds in the sunlight. A pair of bedraggled albatrosses were perched on it, resting. "I wish Agnes was here to see this. When I get back, maybe I'll draw a picture of it for her." He hurried across the deck and carefully climbed down the battens to the waiting boat.

The sea was smooth, with long swells. The rowers had the boat alongside the *Wilhelm* in less than five minutes.

Captain de Puyter greeted them as they boarded. "Pastor Bauman, thank you for agreeing to hold the service. The sailors also appreciate your offer to say a few words for their mates." As de Puyter shook the pastor's hand, Luke could see his own exhaustion from the past few days reflected in Jan's eyes.

Captain James was the last to arrive. When he joined the group by the starboard rail, Captain de Puyter hove to, summoned the remainder of his crew on watch and the service commenced. The canvas wrapped body of Johannes Brueck was already resting on a board at the side port. His wife and grown son stood by as Pastor

Bauman read the commitment service. When he finished, Captain de Puyter signaled for the seamen that had been standing by. The board was tipped and the body slid quietly into the sea. After a few private words of comfort to the new widow, Pastor Bauman continued with the memorial service for the sailors.

Svend stood quietly with Luke; the Captain's hand on his shoulder, waiting for the service to end. When Pastor Bauman started to speak on those lost aboard the fishing boats and the *Hamburg*, Svend took a deep breath and was ready to speak out. Luke's grip tightened in warning. He cautioned in a whisper, "Not now, son. Many of the sailors and settlers had friends on the *Hamburg*. It will calm them for the moment and means nothing if he's wrong."

Svend gave a sullen look, but held his tongue. After the service, Luke stepped forward to add some remarks. "We've come through trials in the past few days on our journey that would have taxed the Israelites. But the journey is nearly done for many of you. Within the week, we will make landfall on Bell Island. When we land, those of you who will be staying will immediately start to build their new homes. When that's finished, you'll be called upon to establish the rules and laws you will live under. Our charter allows a great deal of latitude in how you govern yourselves. Before we reach Newfoundland, each ship will appoint three delegates for a committee to draft laws. I plan to explore the coast with the *København*and don't expect to remain more than four weeks before pushing on to Hudson's Bay with the rest of the expedition. Hopefully, our missing ships will rendezvous with us before we leave. I have a copy of the founding documents from the Virginia and Plymouth colonies and also some suggestions on your convention. We're going to be in a New World and that calls for new ideas. Choose your delegates well.

"Captains, if you would see that your ships' companies receive the same directions and these copies, I would be obliged."

The passengers gathered around those who could read to learn what the documents said. Luke steered Svend through the crowd toward the boat. He spoke just loud enough for Svend to hear. "This should give them something to take their minds off the tragedies of the past week."

As they rowed back to the *København*, Luke contemplated the mood of the settlers. By and large, they appeared to have stoically accepted the recent setbacks. The probable loss of the *Hamburg* would cause problems in the future for the entire expedition, but he'd solve those as they arose. Suddenly, a scream from the deck of the *Wilhelm* broke the silence. Two passengers were pointing ahead of the boat. The rowers lost their stroke as they turned to see what the passengers were pointing at. A dark shape rose out of the water within yards of the boat. A spray of water drenched all aboard. The younger of the sailors screamed, "A monster!" and scrambled for the stern.

Luke grabbed him by the collar and threw him back on his seat. "Belay that! That's no monster. It's a whale." The other sailor stood in a defensive pose with his oar raised. Luke waved him back to his seat. "It won't hurt us if we don't anger it. Put the oar down. You wouldn't do more than tickle it with something that small."

Svend was fascinated. A moment later, two more whales broached the surface. The smallest of the three, a baby by its size, was curious and swam within an arm's length of the boat. The look in its eye convinced Svend it was friendly and meant no harm. Without thinking, Svend reached out and stroked its smooth skin.

"Be careful, son," Luke said.

The baby stayed nearby for the rest of the trip back to the *København*. When Svend boarded, it disappeared below the waves. John was standing by the rail, staring at the two larger whales as they cavorted on the surface, almost as if they were dancing.

"Did you see that, Mr. Barrow? The little one let me touch it. It looked like it wanted to talk." Svend was nearly breathless from the excitement.

"Aye, it did look friendly, but next time you might not be as lucky. We're going into the unknown and you need to think before you act." John gave him his best glare but realized it was a lost cause.

The whales remained in the vicinity until the afternoon. Svend completed a series of drawings and showed them to Luke. The picture of the baby near the boat seemed to be almost alive. "Svend, you have a real talent. It's a shame you won't have a teacher to work with you further."

"That's all right. I like to do it, but I really am looking forward to the exploring. If the drawings help that, I'll keep it up."

* * *

By the time the sun set, all repairs were completed. The ships shook out their sails and the course was set to the north-northwest. Luke surveyed the remaining ships. Everything appeared to be in order. He had the log cast. They were making five knots.

"Well, John, if this wind holds, we should sight Bell Island in three to four days."

"I hope you don't jinx us, sir. I'll settle for a safe arrival."

Over the next two hours, the winds became erratic, and then died down. For three days, the winds barely gave the ships steerage way. Finally, they resumed a steady southeasterly breeze. The next two days passed uneventfully. Svend spent his free time sketching the increasing varieties of birds that portended landfall. The most interesting was a strange, large billed bird; Captain Foxe called it a 'puffin.' The next morning, the sky to the southwest was red. Svend noticed John and Luke pointing and commenting. The only part of the conversation he caught was, "storm to the south, but it should miss." The sky turned cloudy as they day wore on and the seas were choppy. There was no chance to take a noon sight aboard the *København*. An hour before sundown, Luke passed within hail of the *Henriette Marie*.

Taking a speaking trumpet, Luke hailed Captain James. "We're very close by my reckoning. For safety, we'll reduce sail to topsails only tonight. We should sight land in the morning." The passengers on deck took a moment to realize what had been said. A cheer started and soon all the ships heard the news. Sails were quickly taken in and the four ships gathered together to await the dawn as they steered north-northwest.

Svend rose early and dressed by the light of the false dawn. After checking with John for permission, he ascended the foremast with his papers, pencils and a telescope. The western horizon was still dark but shortly after the sun rose, a reflection from what could only be distant hills brought a call of "Land ho!" from the lookout at the mainmast. The passengers and crew boiled on deck hoping to catch their first glimpse of the New World and not another iceberg.

Soon after the lookout confirmed that they had sighted land, a delegation of passengers approached the aftercastle to inquire when they would be landing. They were somewhat crestfallen when Luke informed they wouldn't make their anchorage until the next evening or the following day. A light breeze from the south helped to make for a smooth passage. Around noon, under cloudy skies, a second headland appeared to the west. Svend kept busy sketching the views as they headed north. As the sun was setting, a final headland appeared. He only had time to do a brief sketch before the darkness forced him down to make way for the sailors furling sails for the night.

The next morning, the sun broke through the clouds. At noon, Captain Foxe was able to get a solid position fix and the ships turned to the southwest. As the ships tacked back and forth to make their way in the variable wind, the day seemed to drag on interminably. At dusk, the ships hove to near the north end of Bell Island. The northern facing shores were covered in huge piles of ice. Luke repeated the previous evening's maneuver and hailed Captain James. "It looks like the ice is out. We should have clear sailing from here. We'll heave to and wait until morning to explore the coast for the best anchorage. I want a full day and sunlight when we land."

Captain James agreed. "The days are still short. If we run into hostile inhabitants, we'll need all the daylight we can get. I'll pass the word to the other ships."

The weather held clear that night, but no lights were visible from the distant shore. The land seemed deserted. At the first hint of light, sails were shaken out and the ships headed south. Just before noon, the cry of "sail ho!" interrupted the exploration.

Luke called to the lookout, "How many?"

"Only one, Captain!"

"Can you make out who it is?"

"It's the *Bluefin*. I recognize the cut of her sails. They appear to have a number of fires going on shore. I can see their smoke!"

"Mr. Barrow, set a course toward her. We'll anchor just offshore from her."

As they glided up to the anchorage, Luke studied the activity on shore. "It appears they've been here a few days. They're building drying racks for fish and huts for the crew. I hope they have news for us." He continued to survey the shore. The size of the clearing hinted at earlier visitors. Snow was still visible in the shadows and the ground was churned up mud around the huts.

At an hour past noon on April 5th, Captain Foxe landed at Newfoundland. Captain Nielsen met him as he set foot on the rocky shore. "Welcome, Captain Foxe. It's been quiet since we landed. We found some broken tools and three graves, but the natives haven't shown themselves"

136

Anxious for other news, Luke asked, "What happened after we parted? Do you have any word on *the Bridget* or the *Hamburg*?"

"Nothing on the *Hamburg*. We sailed with the *Bridget* to the Banks as agreed. Shortly before we arrived there, we met an Englishman loaded with cod and bound for England. He passed word that a Dutch frigate was raiding English and French ships on the Banks. Captain Anders and I agreed, I would head here and prepare the site for whatever he caught." He motioned over his shoulder past the huts. "Before I forget, we've already found plenty of fresh water."

"You did well, Lars. We will start landing supplies and the settlers immediately. I just want to explore the coast and see if anyone else has settled here."

Chapter 17

Jacque le Brey huddled near the warming fire in the guard house, trying to get some feeling back in his hands. While the fire's heat was mostly illusory in the early morning cold, the fort's walls at least kept the wind at bay. Why he had ever left France for Acadia was now a frozen memory. Why he had guard duty on such a frigid morning was still very fresh in his memory. He'd finally managed to overcome Claudette's objections. He hadn't been the first one to plow that field and he doubted her father knew. They were finishing dressing when her father, Sergeant Bascom, returned early from the tavern. Luckily, he thought that Jacque was just starting to seduce Claudette. Bascom swore that he would serve guard duty until hell froze over! This was his third week on night guard duty and no end was in sight. If the sergeant really knew what had happened, he'd probably be dead.

He glanced toward the ramp leading to the firestep and realized he needed to make some rounds before the Sergeant made his sun rise inspection. Why the sergeant was so strict on procedure, he'd never understand. Nothing ever happened here. The light snow that had fallen during the night left a virgin blanket that the sergeant was sure to notice if there were no tracks showing that he'd at least made some effort to make his rounds. He grabbed his halberd and wearily trudged up the ramp.

When he reached the top, he stopped and scanned the harbor. The ice was starting to break up and the first supply ship of the year was expected. The blowing snow obscured the view, but a brief lull revealed a ship anchored some distance off shore. He rubbed his eyes to make sure he wasn't dreaming. He continued to stare, until he realized that this was his chance to get off his punishment detail. If he alerted the town the ship had arrived, surely the Sergeant would relent! Before he could take two steps, a loud roar sounded from offshore. *Too late! The ship had beaten him to the announcement!* He continued down the ramp. At least he could tell them it was a large ship. Maybe that would be worth something. When he reached the bottom of the ramp, he stepped on a patch of ice and went sprawling. Then a huge explosion lifted him into the air and flung him against the wall. The guard house was completely destroyed. "Those idiots! They forgot to unload the shot in the barrel." He shook his head trying to clear the cobwebs. "I have to get to the Captain and tell him what's happened. As he struggled to stand up, he heard another roar. "I think we heard you the first time!" he growled. He started toward the gate. The world suddenly was a mass of flying splinters and dirt. Everything went dark.

* * *

Jacque le Brey was the first of many casualties that day. Sergeant Bascom was just leaving home for the morning inspection when the first shot rang out. He started to run toward the fort, but stopped short when the first shots struck. From where he was standing, he could see the ship in the harbor. His first thought was that the English had returned and were attacking New France again. As the ship unfurled its flag, he was dumbstruck when he recognized the Dutch flag. *They're our allies! Why are they firing on us?* But then he remembered the passing comment made by the last ship's captain before winter. He had heard rumors that France might be fighting again soon. Who or where he hadn't heard. This answered part of that question. He ran to the fort's gate and started to ring the alarm bell. "To arms! To arms! We're under attack from the sea!" Within a few minutes, the first men reached the rough parade ground between the fort and the village, many still struggling to don their coats and hold on to their pikes. A second broadside struck the fort's bastion, unseating two of the small four pounders mounted there to discourage pirates. As the Captain arrived, a third broadside struck, leveling a ten foot section of the seaward wall and wounding two men who had gone toward the fort for shelter.

"Sergeant, what the hell is happening?" Captain Bouchard's hat had been blown off by the blast and he was looking around trying to spot it in the snow. He found it alongside a wheelbarrow in a snow bank and jammed it back on his head. "Who is firing on us? The English?"

"No sir. It's a Dutchman. It appears to be only one ship, but it looks like a frigate." Bascom pointed toward the harbor. "It's anchored just off shore. I don't know why that idiot le Brey didn't sound a warning. If he's still alive, I'll make him wish he were dead!"

The settlement's leader, Sir Isaac de Razilly, arrived, dressed in his buff coat, with his nightshirt hanging out of his trousers. A servant was trying to catch up to him, clutching a loaded wheelock pistol and a scabbard. Men were crowded around, trying to ask questions. De Razilly pushed them roughly away and demanded attention from the sergeant. "Never mind him right now! Have they landed anyone?"

Bouchard deftly pulled de Razilly aside. "Sir Isaac, I don't know. As soon as I can sort out this mob, I'll send parties down to the beach in each direction to check." He turned and yelled at the men that had arrived, "Line up and shut up! I'll tell you something as soon as I find out." Looking at the damage the ship's fire had already done to the fort, Bouchard didn't have much hope for the near future. The straggling mob of settlers would have a hard time stopping a bunch of old women with brooms, much less a determined attack.

In the woods, Lieutenant de Beers watched the assembling militia with interest. The *Friesland* had anchored a mile up the coast and sent a large raiding party ashore. The *Rotterdam* had timed its broadside perfectly. De Beers muttered under his breath, "So, what's going to go wrong now?" He surveyed the crowd of sailors trying to imitate marines. "Form a line just inside the trees here and prepare to fire a volley!' He drew a line in the snow so that no one would step past the trees and spoil their surprise. Amazingly, all twenty men with guns managed to get into line without one gun discharging. Another twenty with boarding pikes bunched up in a group behind them. Pointing toward the forming line of militia he announced, "Ready, fire!"

The Captain's fears were confirmed by a ragged volley from the woods that stretched down the hill to the shore. A cloud of powder smoke showed that at least some men had landed from the ship and intended to attack the disorganized mob near the fort. Three settlers were down, thrashing on the snow covered ground. One look at the red pools staining the snow and the rest took to their heels, leaving the Captain, Sergeant, and de Razilly alone on the parade ground.

Sir Isaac started screaming at the militia to return to ranks, but Bouchard laid a hand on his shoulder to calm him. "They won't stop running until they reach their homes. I suppose I might as well see what terms they're offering."

De Razilly turned purple and turned his rage on Bouchard. "You will fight to the last man! I will not see New France surrendered to the enemy again. The King personally gave me command here! You will follow my orders or I will have you hanged for treason!"

Bouchard spun around and clipped de Razilly with the basket of his sword. He fell backwards into a snow drift before Bascom could catch him. Bouchard stared for a moment, pondering his shrinking options. A line of sailors with muskets and boarding pikes were approaching slowly through the knee deep snow. "Sergeant, see that Sir Isaac is taken somewhere warm until he calms down." He unbuckled his sword and held the hilt out for the onrushing Dutchmen to see.

* * *

The settlers stood around in sullen silence as the landing party emptied their homes of valuables onto three makeshift sleds. Lieutenant de Beers stood off to the side with the militia captain who had surrendered the fort. "For the last time Captain, I do not care what happens to your settlement. The fort will be burned. If you have so mistreated your Indian neighbors that they choose to attack you, that's your problem. Your King chose to stab Holland treacherously in the back, without warning. Count your blessings that we aren't burning your houses too! If you choose to stay here and not return to France, we will return and the next visit won't be as pleasant. We do not make war on women and children, unless they choose to remain in danger." Smoke from the fires lit along the fort's remaining walls sections started to blow back across the village. De Razilly was nearly frothing at the mouth in rage and was barely being held back by three settlers.

Bouchard looked back and then asked de Beers, "Can you at least do us one favor and take him with you for ransom? It would make my job of convincing the settlers to leave at lot easier."

De Beers was taken aback by the unusual request. After watching de Razilly a moment he laughed, "Done. No man should have to endure that much spite. I think a sea voyage would do him a world of good! It's the least we can do for the inconvenience we've caused. Now, how soon do you expect before your supply ship comes? I need to insure we leave you enough provisions."

Without thinking Bouchard answered, "We thought you might be them. That's why we weren't prepared when you fired." De Beers' smile made him realize his error. He'd just doomed the ship to be taken by these marauders!

"I think we may leave a few more weeks than that. It may be a longer period before you see another ship." De Beers walked back to the guards. "Take that one along." He said, pointing at de Razilly. "He should be good for some ransom. Then finish loading the sleds and we'll push off. I don't like the look of those clouds. I want to be back at sea as soon as possible. Their supply ship will be the real prize!"

* * *

The storm arrived much quicker than expected. Luckily, the *Friesland* and *Rotterdam* were able to anchor in a sheltered cove and rode out the storm in relative safety. They split up in order to cover more sea, in case the supply ship had been blown off course. On the third day, a brig was sighted just before the midday meal. The lookout shouted down, "She's a galleon Captain, and sitting low in the water. She's heading straight for us."

De Groot waved his hat in acknowledgment and then turned to de Beers. "We'll let her come to us. Break out that old French flag and run it up. We'll greet our fellow countryman just as he expects!"

Two hours later, a sputtering Frenchman was brought before de Groot. 'Monsieur, what is the meaning of this? You flew a French flag!"

"But you are mistaken *Mynheer*. As you can see, we hoisted our Dutch flag before firing." Tjaert pointed aloft to the small Dutch flag now flying from the aft rigging. "You are my prize. We will ransom you and your crew once we return to port." He turned and left the

Frenchman to contemplate his fate. "Pieter, see to your prize crew and secure the prisoners onboard in our hold. No sense giving them an opportunity to seize their ship back from a small prize crew. Then we'll find the *Rotterdam*and plot our next move. The weather looks like it might be worsening again!' Later that evening, the lookout spotted the *Rotterdam,* towing a prize of her own. Before they could rendezvous, a new storm broke.

Chapter 18

The anchorage for the new village of Christianburg bustled with activity. The sound of axes chopping trees echoed across the water. The crew of the fishing boat, *Bridget,* was busy transferring cod to the drying racks a quarter mile from the main landing. Small boats from the larger ships were shuttling settlers and their belongings ashore to waiting tents. The *Kristina* was the centerpiece of the activity, just offshore, offloading sheep. Three seamen stood laughing at her entry port. As they joked, another sheep rose from the hold on the end of a rope and belly band. The protesting animal was quickly set down by the port and the band removed by one of the seamen. Before the sheep could realize what was happening, the other two sailors grabbed it by its wool and shoved it through the port. It hit the water with an indignant "baaah!" The sight of land and new grass just fifty yards away drew it like a magnet and it swam quickly to shore. When its feet hit bottom,it let out another 'baaah' and started to run. Every other step it tried to shake its wool dry. A small rainbow followed it ashore.

Captain Luke Foxe stood nearby watching as Taggert MacDonald supervised the growing flock's unloading from shore. When the flock began to crowd the landing, Luke pointed toward the gap in the bluff where the stream flowed down the hillside. "Mr. MacDonald, as soon as you're finished, move your flock inland. We'll need this area to unload the equipment next."

The beach was ideal for unloading. Boats could anchor close-in, while the hills started right behind the

protected the beach from winds. The seamen
een helping the sheep over the side waved to
ey were done. Luke raised his speaking trumpet
the *København*. "Mr. Barrow, you may start un-
g the sawmill." Luke had decided the sawmill was
the most urgent need. The foresters were already clearing a larger area on the nearby hills and logs were available for sawing. Sawn lumber would speed the housing
construction and let him clear his ships of the settlers
that would be staying. He was already three days behind
his planned departure for the exploration expedition
around the island. Luke turned, once he was certain
John had heard him, and headed for the hill where Captain Andersen was overseeing construction of the fort's
palisades.

Back on the *København*, John Barrow ordered the
sailors to lower the cargo sling into the hold after
checking it quickly. The sling showed signs of wear, but
appeared adequate for the day's needs. He decided to
continue. Time and tide were their enemies today. He
yelled down to the men in the hold, "Lash that crate securely. That's worth more than all your scrawny car-
casses. I don't want it coming loose when we hoist."
John was more concerned about the barge waiting below than the sling. The crude barge that had been built
with green lumber to unload cargo leaked like a sieve. It
looked like a gentle tap would sink it. They would have
to be extra careful lowering the crates. The first crate
was quickly tied off and the sailors on deck heaved on
the line to raise the load. As it cleared the hatch, they
swung the spar with its block and line and positioned
the load over the barge. As they started to lower away,
John spotted a strand of rope part on a sharp crate
edge. Then the remainder started to unravel. He
shouted at the bosun guiding the line. "Lower away *now*,
or we'll lose it!" The bosun tried to obey but the crate
still dropped with a crash onto the barge. The sound of
wood breaking was very clear. John grabbed four sailors
and they dropped down to the barge. He tossed them

oars and roared, "Row like your lives depend on it! I'll not lose this cargo!"

With water rising in the barge, they made slow progress toward the shore. Just before the water reached the low side rail, the barge grounded. John heaved a sigh and jumped into the waist deep water, yelling for the idlers on the beach to help unload the crated sawmill. The sawmill crate was cleared quickly and then the barge was hoisted up and carried beyond the high water mark. A bottom board had been sprung with the crate's impact. John yelled to the ship for the carpenter to fetch his tools. He had planned to finish unloading the rest of the cargo before the tide changed but now he would have to wait until the repairs were done.

Luke had heard the commotion and started to turn back to the beach, but stopped when he realized John was handling the problem. He had to delegate or he would be swamped. As he turned back and continued his trudge up the hill, he remembered why he preferred the deck of a ship. It was flat and level. Climbing hills was agony on his calves. "I'm getting too old for this foolishness." He paused and sat down on a rock to massage his legs. Captain Andersen came down to greet him. Luke took the proffered hand to stand up. Back on his feet, he pointed up the hill. The stockade was going up quickly. "It looks like you've made excellent progress. Do you have enough men?"

"The extra sailors have been a big help. It freed up some of my men for the scouting work you 'suggested.' The Indian boy, Joseph, went along as well. They returned this morning. They explored the entire island and found only one abandoned village. It appeared to have been wiped out by illness quite some time ago. They found graves, but no evidence of violence. Otherwise, all they found were some older campsites. Right now, we're the only ones here. We should have the palisades finished by the day after tomorrow. The well is fresh and has a plentiful water supply. Captain Nielsen chose the site well. If someone should attack, we'll have a strong place of safety to retreat to." He motioned toward a work party digging a trench outside the wall and piling the spoil inside the seaside bastion. "I'm still going to mount the two cannon where we discussed. With the added height, we can cover the settlement from both land and sea attacks. The guns aren't large, but they don't need to be with a plunging shot like they'll have. Natives aren't my only concern. If that Dutch ship we heard about shows up, we'll be able to give it something to think about!"

The site looked good, even to Luke's unmilitary eye. He was pleased with the choice for military leader. He pointed toward the boats, "Unless something happens to delay the unloading, I plan to finish landing the settlers tomorrow. They can continue to live in tents while the cabins are built. The good weather seems to be holding. I'll leave with the *København* Saturday and explore the coast. If all goes well, I'll return in four weeks. That will leave an extra week before the rest of us head to Hudson's Bay. You'll be in charge until then. I don't want to run any longer or we may have problems trying to get established at the Hudson's bay site. Captain James will be responsible for the rest of the ships' unloading." Luke gave a wry smile. "I expect the bulk of his time, though, will be spent leading the convention for the new laws." Thomas had put up a vehement protest when he found out he would have to replace the missing Sir Thomas Roe as the leader of the convention. He detested politics but had grudgingly agreed he was the best one remaining to do the job.

Karl looked like he wanted to say something, but was hesitant. Luke decided to ask, "Is something on your mind? When I've seen that look from you before, you've usually had a good idea that meant work."

"Captain Foxe, I'm not sure yet. If the *Hamburg* is truly lost, I may need to relook where my remaining soldiers need to go. I'll have a better idea by the time you get back from your trip." He gestured to the walls going up nearby. "If this works out as well, and as quickly as it seems, I may not need as many military people to stay here. That would still keep my forces for Hudson's Bay up to strength. I'm just not sure how feeding a garrison there will work considering all the settlers we lost."

Luke had missed that point in his planning. The repairs and landing hadn't left much time to consider the impact of losing the *Hamburg*. Svend's optimism had also helped delay the realization that the *Hamburg* wasn't going to show up. Now he'd have to reexamine the equipment and supply lists and decide who would still go to Hudson's Bay and what they could do when they arrived. "Captain Andersen, you've raised a very good point. I think we may have to reconsider what we can accomplish this season at Hudson's Bay and how we'll do it." Karl seemed satisfied. Luke made a short tour of the site to encourage the workers and then went back down the hill on his aching legs.

* * *

Saturday morning dawned bright and clear. Neat rows of tents were sheltered close to the new palisade. Off in the woods, a work party was already busy setting up the sawmill. They would be ready to start cutting planks later that day. A nearby stream had been dammed up and a millrace built to supply power. It was quieter this morning, now that the sheep had been taken to the next valley, where new grass was abundant. The work animals grazed in a corral close to the fort. They were too precious to leave unguarded. At the fort, Captain Foxe was going over last minute instructions with his ship captains and Captain Andersen.

"I don't plan to be gone more than four weeks. If we're gone six, send one of the fishing boats to search for us. I don't fancy walking back." Everyone laughed. Luke's aching legs had become a topic of humor. "By the way, Karl, thank you for the use of the scout. He'll be valuable for escorting our landing parties. The miners know their business, but they would be lost without guides. And Thomas, while I'm gone have them continue with clearing the land for planting and cutting the timber for planks. The sooner we can get the settlers and supplies in solid buildings, the healthier and happier they'll be."

"And the sooner we can return home!" Captain Johansson voiced the sentiment of all the captains. An idle ship made no profit. The consensus had been to offload all of the livestock at Christianburg. The few animals that were going to Hudson's Bay could be reloaded when the time came for the ships that would push on. They would stay healthier that way. Without the *Hamburg*, the settlement at Hudson's Bay this season would be just a small trading fort and base for the surveys during the first year.

Luke continued, looking at Captain James. "And make sure the convention gets us a set of laws the people support. You've got a copy of the framework Sir Thomas planned to support. With his loss, I'm counting on you to make sure they get something done. That has to be finished before I can leave for Hudson's Bay." It was the first time Luke had publicly acknowledged the loss of the *Hamburg.* That Svend wasn't there to hear the remark probably had some bearing on the timing.

An hour later, the *Köbenhavn* raised anchor and set sail on a nor-nor'east course. Svend was at the rail with drawing pad and pencils out trying to capture the beehive activity of the new settlement. He'd been kept so busy by Luke that he hadn't had time to think about the lost ship. Luke walked over to admire the effort. "Very nice work, son. You've captured the essence of the bustle onshore."

"Thank you. I've really wanted this to turn out well. Since Agnes isn't here to see the start, I wanted something to show her what she missed when we get back."

"I hope you're right, Svend, but we have to face up to unpleasant facts. If they aren't here when we return, they won't be coming."

"I'm sure they'll be here."

150

Luke just stared ahead to the open bay. Youthful optimism was hard to kill. If Svend could keep it in this new land, that spirit could overcome all challenges. Otherwise, the challenges would consume his soul.

Luke planned to retrace part of their voyage, sailing clockwise around the main island. He'd marked likely landing points on his map where minerals were indicated. The first evening, they remained under topsails on a course to round Cape Bonavista. The next morning they approached the first likely site. The exploration party was standing by the entry port as soon as the ship hove to. Besides the gear they needed for prospecting, each member of the party was armed. Captain Foxe had been adamant on that point. They were venturing into unknown territory where humans or animals could be hostile and deadly. The two scouts, Heinrich Reinhardt and Joseph, the Cree Indian, checked everyone's gear a second time to make sure it was secure and comfortable. Heinrich was in overall command.

He gathered them all for one last review of instructions. "Once we get ashore I don't want anyone wandering off alone. Two men together, all the time. That way, if something happens, the survivor can save the gear." That brought some nervous laughs. "Pick out your partner now." He pointed to Svend. "You're with me. The captain said to show you all I can so you can record it for his journal and can learn how to lead a group like this. He said you may get a chance when we get to our final stop."

Svend was taken aback for a second. This was the first time he'd been told what plans Luke had for him once they reached Hudson's Bay. "Don't worry, I'll stay close. I've heard the Captain's story about the bears around here."

Heinrich laughed, "Those are further north! But there are other dangers that are just as likely here. I wouldn't want to face him if I lose anyone, especially you." The group piled into the two boats and headed for shore.

The landing was uneventful. The beach was level and the boats were pulled up above the tide line. Heinrich told the two sailors with the group, "Stay with the boats, but stay alert. We may need to push off with little warning. If you spot any natives, push off out of range of their weapons but stay near. We may have to abandon our gear and swim for it if troubles develop." The two men nodded energetically. Heinrich turned to Svend, "Which direction does the Captain's map say from here?"

Svend pointed toward a hill just inland, to the south.

Heinrich had a private conversation with Joseph, who then headed off in the direction Svend had indicated. Heinrich turned back to the prospectors, "We'll follow along in a few minutes. Get your gear and be ready. Joseph will scout ahead and blaze the trail. Watch for two axe notches on the trees, about shoulder height." Svend carefully folded the map and returned it to his pack. After shouldering the light pack, he opened his drawing pad and started to sketch the forest opening Joseph had disappeared through. Before he had even finished roughing in the scene, Heinrich passed the word quietly to start out. Svend closed the pad and joined Heinrich at the head of the small party.

An hour later Svend was beginning to have second thoughts about exploring. The short stop at Christianburg had not toughened his legs from the long sea voyage and his shins were sore. As if reading his thoughts, Heinrich called a rest halt. Svend gratefully sat down on a nearby, fallen log. Before he could stretch out, Heinrich came over and asked, "How far does the map say to the site?" Svend opened the pack and pulled out the map. After studying it and checking for landmarks, it appeared that the stream should be just over the next ridge. Before he could answer, there was a rustling from the undergrowth ahead. Heinrich started to raise his musket, but a quiet hail revealed it was only Joseph returning.

152

As he stepped into view, he pointed back over his shoulder. "I think I've found the site. It's just up ahead." Heinrich looked to Svend, who nodded agreement.

"Very well. Let's get there and we can take a longer rest." Shouldering their tools and weapons with groans for their aching legs, the group set off. Fifteen minutes later, they broke through a patch of brambles and found the stream. Heinrich called a halt and started directing the setup of a temporary camp. Svend stood to the side and watched as Heinrich started a fire for cooking a noon meal so that no smoke showed. The three miners chose their spots to excavate and then guards were set out to give warning of any intruders. Everything was done quietly and with a minimum of fuss. Hopefully, he could do as well if he was called upon to do this in the future.

After a warm meal of boiled salted beef and cabbage, work started on the excavation. Svend stood by and sketched the three men as they worked their locations. Gunther was working the rocky hillside, trying to determine what was in a very small vein in the rock formation. He was the only one of the three with any schooling on mining and minerals. Luke had told Svend to stay close to him and learn what he could. The other two, Karl and Franz, were alternately panning along the stream and digging and sluicing their spoil to see what was near the surface. After about an hour, Gunther had gathered a large enough sample to take back to the ship for testing. Karl and Franz packed up their gear. Franz showed Svend a miniscule speck of yellow. "Your map was right. There is gold here. If I worked for a month, I might find enough to pay for one good meal at the *Schwein und Stein* back home." He spit on the ground in disgust. "I thought we would find gold by the bucketfuls. That's why I came." Karl nodded in agreement.

Svend vigorously defended the map. "I'd think you would be happy. The map said there was gold here and there was. It didn't say how much, but maybe the next stop it will be plentiful. That's why we have to search."

Karl chimed in, "This seam looks to be just the end of an outcropping. He's right. We may have better luck if we can locate a main seam. I've worked twenty years hunting for metals and this is the first time I've at least had a lead on where to look." He seemed satisfied with his day's effort.

Heinrich had Joseph recall the guards and they all headed back to the boat. During the whole time, not one alarm had been raised. By the time they reached the *Köbenhavn*, the sun was just touching the top of the hill. Gunther reported to the captain on what was found and Luke then gave orders to set sail for the next site.

154

Chapter 19

Bundgaard stood by his cell door, listening to the cannon fire. Ever since he had been thrown into prison for dealing with the French, he had been trying to escape. Hopefully, his cousin was working on getting him out. Without his signature, none of his funds could be claimed by anyone else. Once he got out, there was one expense he would definitely pay. His old acquaintance, Oskar the Silent, would be given a job. If it was the last thing he ever did, that bitch at the inn, who had turned him in to the Swedes, would die. Then her brats could starve on the streets.

It sounded outside like the American *wonder ships* had finally arrived and were shelling the palace. Bundgaard smirked, "I hope they drop a round right on Christian." The next broadside sounded, then everything went black. Sometime later, he woke to see daylight streaming in around a huge pile of rubble. Pushing aside the timber that had knocked him out, he said, "Well, it looks like the King will have to forego the pleasure of hanging me for awhile." Crawling through the opening, he saw the way out was clear. Still hobbling from a twisted knee, Bundgaard hurried as quickly as he could to freedom.

Mette Foxe watched the evening crowd as they arrived for dinner. Two ships had arrived that afternoon and both captains had chosen to dine at her inn. They were in deep discussions with an American that she knew worked for Francisco Nasi. Since she had helped Nasi identify a French spy ring in the harbor area, the inn had seen a rise in foreign visitors. Francisco had even hinted once or twice that he might be interested in the inn as a cover for his work. When the time came to join Luke she would have to see if he was still interested.

A commotion at the door caught her attention. A disreputable looking vagrant had pushed past a departing patron, knocking him into the door frame. As the intruder swept aside his cloak and reached for something, the American kicked back from the table and drew a gun. As the thug reached back to throw the knife he'd had concealed in his belt, the American fired. Mette heard a thud and turned to her left. The knife was buried in the post next to her. She turned back in time to see the assailant sink to his knees and then fall on his face.

The American turned to face her. "Sorry about that, ma'am. Mr. Nasi has had a number of us watching over you. Gammel Bundgaard managed to escape last month and we had heard he might try something." He nudged the corpse with his foot. "Looks like he tried, but was too much of a coward to do it himself. The town guard has been looking for Oskar here for some time on another matter. When I recognized him, I didn't have time to warn you. We thought all Bundgaard would try was some intimidation. That was his modus operandi in the past. It looks like he really doesn't like you."

Mette didn't know exactly what modus operandi meant, but the context was clear. She was in trouble. Maybe it was time to talk to Mr. Nasi further about selling her inn and joining Luke in the New World earlier than planned.

Chapter 20

Off Bois Island, Newfoundland, May, 1634

Captain Foxe sat in his cabin in a funk, staring at the mineral map of Newfoundland without seeing it. His thoughts were far away, wondering how Mette was doing. This was pleasant, but not solving the problem! He really needed to concentrate on what his next move should be. Five sites had already been explored and so far, no rare metals had been found that were worth mining.

Gunther was ecstatic about some unusual metals that had shown up in the samples, but as far as Luke could tell, they were of little commercial value. So far, all that the *valuable* information he'd found in Grantville had done was cost him time. If it weren't for the iron deposits at Christianburg, the expedition would have little to show for itself at this point. He stared at the map. It showed coal deposits on the west side of the island, but they were some distance inland. The iron deposits would be much more valuable if they could locate a ready source of coal to smelt the ore into finished ingots. His eyes wandered across the map. Too bad he couldn't get to Cape Breton. The coal deposits there were substantial and closer to the coast for hauling. But without a contact, the possible trouble with French officials was more than he cared to risk.

Their next stop in the morning would be the English settlement, Ferryland, on the east coast of the island. Rumor had it that the Lord Baltimore had abandoned the settlers after building a good port and defenses. Maybe they might have some knowledge of the interior of the island and the Boethuck natives that no one had seen yet. Or maybe they had news on the Dutch ship that was raiding in the area. In either case, worrying about "maybes" wasn't going to make tomorrow come any faster. It was getting late. He reached up, extinguished the flame of the lantern, and headed for his cot. His dreams that night weren't of coal.

Ferryland, Harbor, Newfoundland, May, 1634

A fog had risen during the night, but the morning sun was rapidly burning it off. Captain Foxe waited by the wheel, trying to sight the settlement he knew lay just to the west. The long boat was already swung out to send a party ashore. He handed his telescope to Svend and motioned aloft. "Go see if the shore is visible. I think we may just be in an isolated fog bank."

Svend hurried aloft. As he faded from sight in the fog, he paused and called down. "You were right, Captain; the fog bank ends less than a cable west of us. It's clear from there to the shore. We're about two miles from the dock."

Luke passed the order to the first mate, "Take her in Mr. Barrow, just like we discussed. We'll anchor offshore and send the boat in. Oh, and have a signal gun ready. The map I have shows they're spread out a bit and may not have a watch set."

"Aye, aye sir!"

The sun and the westerly heading soon had the *Köbenhavn* clear of the fog. Svend kept the deck posted from aloft on the situation ashore. "The dock seems to be intact, but two boats pulled up on the beach appeared to have burned. It looks like someone has tried to start repairing the least damaged of the pair. I can't make out any activity in the few houses in view." The *Köbenhavn* continued to sail toward the dock. It was barely making way. The cutwater off the bow was not much more than a child would raise in a puddle after a rainstorm. "Still nothing moving."

"Fire the signal gun, Mr. Barrow. Maybe these farmers are still asleep!" Luke's expression suddenly changed, "Or maybe something has happened."

The discharge of the gun on the forecastle banged out and then reechoed from the nearest hillside. "Do you see anything yet, Svend?"

"There's some movement behind the wall back from the beach. I'm not sure . . . "

The rest of Svend's answer was drowned out in an answering blast from behind the wall. Two clouds of smoke rose from the concealed cannons there. Seconds later, there was the sound of ripping linen and two holes appeared in the mainsail.

"Come about, Mr. Barrow, and get us out of range. These folks don't seem to want visitors." As the ship came about, it seemed to slow down and then stayed heeled over a degree or two. The tide was at ebb and the *København* had slid up on a small sand bar. As the crew tried to sort out what had happened, another volley sounded from shore. This time, one ball hit the fore-top yard and it split in two. The pieces flopped but their supporting chains held them aloft.

Luke gave a quick glance to where the guns were hidden. His cannon could not bear on the battery. "Mr. Barrow, get two more boats lowered. We'll shift the forecastle guns back and try to tow her off." As the crews lowered the boats, another volley slammed home. Both shots hit the hull but bounced.

"They're only using a pair of four pounders Captain." The bosun who had called out had served in the Danish navy before joining the *København.*

Luke snapped, "I don't care what they're using. If we stay here much longer, even a rat could nibble us down." He turned to Svend, who had nearly run down the ratlines when the first shots had been fired. "Raise a white flag. Maybe we can parley and find out why they're so belligerent."

Svend raced below and returned with a bed sheet from his cot. Another two shots rang out, but this time they were clean misses. The sheet was tied on to a line and quickly raised. After ten minutes without another volley, Luke relaxed a little.

"John, you're in charge. I'm going ashore to find out what this is all about. Keep trying to get us free from the bar. And keep sounding the well, in case we sprung something. Svend, grab your notebook. I want you along as my aide." Luke stepped to the ladder and headed down to the maindeck and the entry port. Svend ran back to his cabin and packed the paper, ink, and quill into a pack. He reached the boat just as a seaman passed a small white flag to one of the rowers. Svend took it after he settled in. Hopefully the people on shore would honor the flag.

As the boat approached the dock, an armed party of about fifteen men came out to meet them. Even at a distance, angry shouts in English and French could be heard. The seaman in the front of the longboat tied the line to a piling and Luke stepped up to the dock. He was met by an old, weathered man, who probably had been the captain of one of the burned boats. "Who are you and where are you from?" he demanded before Luke could say a word. The question had been accentuated with a wheelock pistol in his hand.

"I'm Captain Luke Foxe, of the Danish ship *København*. We're here on an exploring mission." Any comments on settlements and other ships could wait until the situation was less tense.

"Then why did you shoot at us? Are you in league with that damned Dutchman?" All the guns were pointed at Luke and his sailors. The rage was evident on all the faces in the crowd. Unless something was done quickly to defuse the situation, a single tense finger on a trigger could cause a massacre.

Luke laughed. "That was our signal gun! From the water, it was evident something had happened here. Since no one showed themselves, we fired to attract your attention. We heard from a passing ship that a Dutchman was raiding these waters. If there were desperate survivors, we wanted to let them know succor was at hand. Now put down that pistol before you shoot a fellow Englishman."

160

"But I thought you said you were Danish?" Uncertainty was starting to replace the rage.

"We're chartered to a Danish company that's partly owned by Sir Thomas Roe." Luke noticed that everyone in the crowd looked gaunt, so he added, "We're provisioned for a two year voyage. If you need supplies we'd be glad to share. How many are you?" The instant smiles told Luke he had hit the right note.

"We've forty-three English settlers and twelve French sailors that were marooned here by the Dutchman, with no supplies. We tried to rebuild one of the boats they burned but we didn't have anything for a cordage or sails. It's been over a year since our last supply ship arrived from England. Our food is almost gone."

Luke called to Svend, "Return to the ship and ask Mr. Barrow to hoist out a barrel of flour and some cabbages as soon as he has the ship off the bar." Even as he said it, he heard a cheer from the ship and could see that the *København* had refloated with the returning tide. "Come back to me as soon as you've delivered the message." Luke was now surrounded by well wishers pounding him on the back, grateful that the specter of starvation had been lifted.

Later that evening at a modest feast laid out in celebration of their rescue, Luke sat down with Captain Willem Holmes, the leader of the group in the morning and Captain Rene Chaumont, the leader of the French sailors. As Luke poured them all mugs of wine he asked, "So, what's the story on this Dutchman? All we heard was from a passing ship that a Dutch ship was raiding off the Banks."

Rene raised his mug and pointed at the crews in the room, "We were all fishing off the Banks, minding our own business. Next thing we know the Dutch comes sailing into view and fires a shot across our bow. He sends a boat over and tells us we're his prisoner. We ask why and he says that France stabbed Holland in the back and that we're at war. They gave us five minutes to gather our personal belongings and then they whisked us into the boat and set fire to my *Berthe*! Two more times that day they do this. The entire fishing fleet from Baie de Mordienne he sinks! Even if we get back, our village is ruined!" He slammed the mug down to emphasize the loss. "He tells me he wants to hurt the English too, since they helped the French. Since there were few Englishmen working the Banks at that time, he decides to kill two birds with one stone and sails here, to Forillon and sets us off without supplies and burns the English boats."

Willem nodded agreement and added; "It was already a rough winter for us, with no supplies from England. We knew nothing about any war. We were just trying to hold on." Tears started to roll down his check. "We've already lost six this season from sickness and the start of scurvy. One was my youngest daughter."

Luke's mind was racing. These people were facing the same problems he had worked so hard for his expedition to avoid. He couldn't undo the harm they had suffered, but he might be able to give them a better future. The problems facing the village presented an opportunity for all of them.

He recalled the charts from the previous evening. Baie de Mordienne would become Port Mordien in another future. The Port Mordien that would also become the site of the first coal mine in Cape Breton. He just had to present the solution the right way. "From what we heard before we left Copenhagen, it sounds like Lord Baltimore may have decided to cut his losses here and go elsewhere. Our major backer was Sir Thomas Roe, an English diplomat to King Christian's court. He has friends in England that know Lord Baltimore and they had told him that Newfoundland was being abandoned. That's why we're here. We're setting up a mining settlement near Bell Island. From there, we plan on expanding into the Hudson's Bay area. This harbor would make an idea second site for the fishing boats we plan on supplying the settlements."

162

Willem interrupted, "I don't know what the others here will say, but good riddance to the Calverts if they want to treat us that way. We don't owe them nothing! We'll talk it over, but I think you have your port."

Rene sat there with a long face. "But what about us Bretons? What do we do?"

"Patience, my friend. First I have a question for you." Luke tried not to let his eagerness show. "As I understand, you are under the French, *non*?"

"*Oui*, the *Compagnie* holds a charter for our territory."

"But do they have any administrator living there?" This was the key.

"*Non*. They only show up about once a year to collect taxes and sell us shoddy trade goods. They keep us in servitude by forcing us to sell our fish cheap, back in French markets, and control the prices we pay for goods. If there was some way to change that, we would. With no fishing boats now, they'll let us starve and start over with new victims."

"We'll make sure you get home. When we get there I'll need to contact your leaders. There may be a way for you to break your chains to the *Compagnie* and we'll all be rich men. Just how badly do you want to stay a fisherman?" Rene and Willem both smiled broadly and leaned forward to listen to Luke's proposals.

Chapter 21

Mid May, 1634, off the coast of Newfoundland

Captain Luke Foxe again sat at the desk in his cabin, staring at the maps and data graphs spread out in apparent, random confusion on the desk and pinned on the bulkhead. A closer examination revealed a method to the madness. This time he may have found an answer.

The maps contained handwritten notes and symbols on mineral deposits throughout the country that would have someday become known as Canada. He'd gathered up the maps for the Newfoundland and Cape Breton regions and added a chart that was titled "Characteristics of the Ingredients for Steel and Iron." He stood up and held the chart so the candle lamp overhead gave enough light to read it easily. His eyes weren't getting any younger. For a long time, he went back and forth between the charts and maps trying to reach a decision. The Grantville researchers he'd paid to scour the library, offices and private papers for any hints of minerals in Canada had hand written a wealth of information on the maps. What they hadn't done was tell him where he should search. He finally set the papers down and closed his eyes in exhaustion.

"Do I dare try it? The gamble has so many risks." When he opened his eyes, a paper on the corner of the desk caught his attention. It had been part of the package he acquired in Grantville. It was a short copy from an encyclopedia on the "Life and Death of Captain Luke Foxe." He'd forgotten that he'd made a copy of it. Supposedly, he would die in the very near future. He smiled at the implied contradiction. "Well, for a dying man, I seem to be doing quite well. I've beaten the odds so far."

Many things had happened since he originally read that article. He was now the de facto Hudson's Bay Company's leader and had to make the decisions since Sir Thomas Roe appeared to have been lost at sea with the *Hamburg.* He thought back to his conversations with the Abrabanels on how to conduct the exploration operations once they got to the New World. Reuben had said something that had brought a chuckle at the time but now seemed very apropos. "How did that saying go?" Luke concentrated on the memory, "Ah yes, playing with the house's money!" The iron ore discoveries around Christianburg already promised to pay for their efforts. Anything else, from this point, was found money. If a way to easily convert that ore to pig iron or steel could be developed, the profits would more than double. They could ship refined metals back to Europe, instead of ore. For roughly the same weight, they could triple the value of each load. The only catch was that the French nominally controlled the coal deposits around Cape Breton, even if they didn't know they were there. The sailors he had rescued at Ferryland and was returning to Baie de Mordienne would provide an opportunity if he could just find the right way to use their influence. They had already agreed that they wanted to improve their lot, but the specifics were what needed to be resolved.

They should sight the Cape Breton coast in the next two days and he needed to come up with a workable plan. Too bad Reuben hadn't come on the voyage. He always had a crazy plan to solve a problem, just like that offer of his to give land to the settlers. Sir Thomas had almost had an attack of apoplexy, until Reuben explained that giving away some of the land just made the company's land more valuable. Luke leaned back and closed his eyes. Something was there in that thought, if he could just recognize it. Suddenly, he snapped his fingers. "I've got it!" He picked up a pistol he had been using to hold down a stack of maps and used it to hammer on the nearest cabin partition. He called out to his stepson, "Svend, are you finished studying?"

A muffled reply came back, "Yes, sir!"

"Can you come here, please? I need you to do something for me."

"Right away." A moment later Svend entered. He paused to take in the mass of papers spread around the cabin. "I hope you don't need this straightened in the next five minutes. Mother always said I never was very good at straightening up."

Luke looked perplexed before he realized what Svend was talking about. "The mess can wait. I'll take care of it later. Would you please go and find Mr. Barrow and ask him if he would come, at his earliest convenience, to my cabin. The three of us have some planning to do."

Svend nodded and hurried off to find the first mate. Two minutes later, the pair knocked and then entered. John was tucking his shirt tails into his trousers. "You sent for me, Captain? I was just getting ready to turn in. In case you forgot, I've got the late watch tonight"

"I'm sorry to interrupt your rest, John, but it seems I have some work for you and Svend to do before we sight Cape Breton. Pull up those chairs while I finish clearing a space on the desk. Then let me explain what I want to do. Hold your questions until I'm done explaining."

Fifteen minutes later Luke finished and then waited for the questions. John rubbed his forehead and chuckled. "Captain, you and I have done some pretty crazy things in our day. That time we killed the polar bear with a pike and a pistol when it tried to climb aboard ship from that iceberg ranks right up there, but this one takes the prize. Do you figure we can just sail into this fishing village, ask them to move, and the French won't care if we start mining the coal? If you can pull that off, the rest of the plan sounds reasonable. But unless you have some warships hidden somewhere, I don't see how it can be done in the long term. What you're talking about is an act of war!"

Svend saw the slight smile trying to hide on his step-father's face. "Mr. Barrow, I think there's something that he still hasn't told us yet."

"You're right, son. My plan revolves around something Reuben Abrabanel said to Sir Thomas. Land is only worth something if it's developed. We need some French partners to act as our agents to secure the land for us and provide local workers. We'll cut them in for a piece of the profits without their having to risk one *sou*. If my suspicions are correct, things are probably still in some turmoil from the Kirke brothers' invasion and the *Compagnie des Cent-Associes* may not have much, if any, presence this far from the mainland. If we can keep a low profile, we may be able to operate a long time before someone in France gets wind of our adventure. By then, who knows? Maybe the French company will have gone broke, the king will have died, or we will have our own fleet of warships!" The last line got a laugh from all three.

"John, here's what I need you to do. I've already spoken to Rene about my idea, in general terms. I need to know what the others are thinking. During the evening meal, mingle with the French and find out what the situation is around Cape Breton. Be subtle! Their friendship is important and I don't want them to feel we're just using them. Anything at all about how the *Compagnie* is treating them, how they handle trade, what the situation is on land ownership, is important. Even something as simple as where their leaders are and what defenses are used against smuggling could help our cause. If you need to enlist some help, make sure the men understand what's at stake and can keep their own counsel. Do you think that's possible?"

"I'll sit down with Chaumont and see what he has to say over a bottle. He's pretty smart and seems to know what's going on there. He can fill me in on who we need to influence in the other crews. If I run into a blank wall, then I'll see about asking for some help."

"Good. I'll trust your judgment, John."

Luke turned to Svend. "Your job will start after we arrive. I want you drawing and surveying as much as possible. Start with pictures of the village and the people to ease any fears. When we get to the mining site, I also want views and maps of the surrounding countryside and views of the seaward approaches. Captain Andersen isn't with us, but we will want his advice on whether the sites are defensible and we'll need pictures to help him plan those defenses. We'll also need you to map out the land for future building and mining work. I'll have Reinhardt accompany you to watch out for any trouble."

"I can take care of myself! I don't need a wet nurse!" Svend looked to be on the verge of rebelling.

"He'll not be there to be a wet nurse. It will be to discourage busybodies. The fewer questions asked, the better for everyone. This won't be your typical village we'll be visiting. This is a fishing village. These are hard men, with few women along. A young man like you could easily get into trouble without even knowing why." The concern on Luke's face defused Svend's response.

"All right, since you put it that way." Svend still didn't seem pleased with the prospect.

John rose from his chair and stretched. "If it's all right with you, Captain, I'll get ready for my part. I'll find Rene and invite him to share our mess tonight." Luke nodded and John left, steering Svend out in front of him.

* * *

Luke woke the next morning, tired and nervous. John had not gotten back to him before his watch and he was apprehensive that something had gone wrong. After a cold shave and a quick meal, he dressed and was getting ready for his watch when John knocked on the cabin door and entered.

"You look like something the ship's cat caught and threw away, Captain! Did you have a bad night?" John acted positively cheerful. "I got the bosun to handle the rest of my watch, so I could fill you in on what I learned." He sat down and stretched his legs, not saying a word. His exhaustion from a long night was evident. He started to nod off.

After a minute, Luke gave up in exasperation and demanded, "Well, what did you find out? I can't read your mind!"

John shook his head in chagrin for nodding off. "You won't believe it, but Rene was wondering why you hadn't asked him these questions when you first discussed possibilities with him at Ferryland! The local situation is just how you explained it to Svend last evening. It's simply an overgrown fishing camp, with crude huts. There are a few families, but mostly single men. He thinks there may be one or two boats left, if the Dutchman didn't get them too. In any case, their situation is tenuous at best. The *Compagnie*'s control doesn't extend beyond the territory immediately around their capital, La Have, on Isle Royale. They used to show up about once a year to collect a 'tax' on whoever was there. Since the Kirkes' freebooting expedition, things have been jumbled. The revenue cutter was sunk and not replaced, as far as he knows. France just got the lands back from England and no one seems to care what happens in the farther reaches. The locals would welcome anyone who could give them trade and security. Rene promised that he would give you his full support, no matter what you planned."

"You didn't tell him of our plans, did you?" Luke asked with alarm.

"Rest easy. I said nothing. He's worried for what will happen to his people without their fishing boats to support them. He's like a drowning man, grasping at whatever branch is available. I think he suspects what you're planning and fully supports it. It looks like your plans may be possible after all."

"Excellent. Go and get some rest, you've earned it! I'll relieve the bosun early. When I finish my watch, I'll meet with you and Rene and we'll lay out a plan for our arrival."

Chapter 22

"Land ho! Dead ahead" The lookout called down from the maintop.

Captain Foxe took a quick sighting with his telescope, then closed it with a satisfied click. He stood at the port rail of the aftercastle, with John Barrow and Rene Chaumont. Rene shook his head in amazement, "Just as you predicted, Captain. Those new instruments are amazing. I had some doubts about your stories, but this feat of navigation supports your claims." He looked to the sky and then asked, "We still have good weather and some daylight left. Do you still plan on laying over here 'til dawn?"

"These are new waters to me and I'd rather arrive at Mordienne in daylight. Besides, this will give us all a chance to see what the area looks like. The anchorage looks superb. Tell me, Rene, why didn't you use this as your port, rather than Baie de Mordienne?"

Rene stood with his left leg on a coil of line on the deck, watching the approaching shore. "We thought about it, but Mordienne already had some abandoned huts there when we put in and we didn't know who or what might be here. Besides, this is more closed. Anyone could arrive here and we'd be trapped. At Mordienne, it's more open and we can escape to sea easier. I just hope the Dutch didn't come calling while we were gone. Nothing we had could have stopped them." His concern was written all over his face. "One day won't matter and you're right. Seeing what's here will help me convince the rest of your plan."

"You won't be disappointed, Rene. We have a good military commander at Christianburg who will help build adequate defenses here to protect the settlers and the mines. I plan to send for him right away." John Barrow frowned at the statement. Luke hadn't mentioned this to him. Before he could ask, Luke continued, "John, would you ask Svend to gather up his drawing supplies and start making the sketches we discussed?"

"Very well, Captain." John descended the ladder to locate Svend down below. He could take the boat ashore that was just being lowered.

Later that evening, after the ship was safely anchored, John sought out the captain. Luke was in his cabin with Svend, going over the drawings that Svend had finished that day. John rapped on the door frame and then entered. "Do you have a moment, Captain? I need to ask you something." Svend started to rise but John waved him back to his seat. "It's not a secret. I just was wondering, Captain, what you meant when you told Rene we would be sending a message back to Christianburg? Are you planning on cutting the exploration short?"

Luke paused for a second, trying to recall the conversation. "No, nothing of the sort! Just a new idea, based on something you said the other night and Rene's reactions today. If they have a fishing vessel still intact, I will try to convince them to send it to Christianburg with some letters. Hopefully, some of the ships will still be there and can take them on to Copenhagen. The vessel could return with some of the miners and we can start work here immediately."

Svend quickly asked, "But what about our voyage to Hudson's Bay? Is that off?"

Luke shook his head, "No, we will still leave for there after we finish this exploration trip. I had already decided to limit our efforts there this season to establishing a site." *The loss of the Hamburg is going to limit our efforts this year more than I want to say.* "If reinforcements arrive from home before the winter ice blocks the way, we will remain there for the winter. Otherwise, we will return to Christianburg and return again in the spring. The opportunities here are too good to pass up.

If we can get a firm toehold here before anyone else realizes what we're doing, we may accomplish much more than we first envisioned. We would have bases on both sides of the Cabot Strait. If the French get too obnoxious, we could even try repeating what the Kirke brothers did, but we would have a much better chance of holding on." The fervor in his voice showed that much more thought had gone into the plan than either Svend or John had been aware of.

Svend still had some concerns. "What about the directors? Are they aware of these changes?" He left unsaid his thoughts on the fate of the *Hamburg*.

"No, that's why I must send the letters. If they don't approve, all we'll have lost is a season. If they can raise the funds to send more miners and equipment, a whole continent may open up for us. The risk is great, but the possible rewards are tremendous."

John answered dubiously, "I hope you're right, Captain. A lot of lives will be depending on you."

"I hope so too, John. If I'm wrong, I'll still do my best. We'll sail in the morning, once the rest of the shore party returns"

* * *

The next morning, Rene Chaumont was like a bridegroom on his wedding day. When John started to tease him, Rene was quick to reply, "It's been almost half a year since we left. They certainly believe we've perished. I pray they're still there and in good health. If that Dutch bastard attacked the village, I don't know what we'll do." He pointed to the rocky point they were approaching. "We're almost there! The *baie* is just around that headland."

Svend had spent the morning in the crows nest, drawing the coastline as they passed. He called down to the deck. "There's a small ship ahead. It looks like a fishing boat. It's tacking into the bay off our starboard side."

Rene stepped over to Captain Foxe and begged the use of his telescope. Luke handed the glass over and pointed to the maintop. "Of course, man, take it and find out if she's one of your people's." Rene made his way up the shrouds as fast as his aged body would allow. When he reached the crosstree, he paused. He couldn't wait to go higher. He got a firm grip with one hand, opened the telescope, and tried to sight the ship. After a moment, he started waving the glass and almost lost his hold. "It's the *Coquette*! I'd recognize that patched topsail anywhere! They're still alive!" He slid back down the stay, ignoring the burns on his hands. Luke met him as he jumped down from the railing.

Rene embraced and kissed him, "Captain, thank you for bringing us home!"

Embarrassed, Luke accepted the telescope back. "I'm glad they're there. I pray everyone is still safe." He looked up to see how the sails were drawing. "We should be there in two hours." He glanced at Rene's hands. They were scorched, but the calluses had kept them from serious injury. "Go take care of those burns and get your people ready. I'm sure they'll want to go ashore as soon as we arrive."

Rene looked at his hands, wondering what Luke meant. They were just starting to sting. "Just like a landlubber! You'd think someone my age would know better." He headed below, shaking his head at his stupidity, to get some grease from the cook.

* * *

The Baie de Mordienne was just as Rene had described. Once past the headland, the bay opened up, with low, wooded hills behind it. In the winter, it would be a dangerous anchorage. Any easterly winds could bring ice and a ship would be trapped. There were about two dozen rough huts and cabins on the hills behind the beach. One boat was onshore, being cleaned of weed and caulked. Nets were spread along the beach

174

and fish was being dried on racks. The arrival of the *Coquette* had everyone down to the beach. The *Köbenhavn* was still hull down to the villagers and the *Coquette* had no way to signal, if the sailors had even sighted the *Köbenhavn*. As the *Köbenhavn* entered the bay, someone dockside spotted her. The *Coquette* was too far inshore with the prevailing breeze to escape an enemy, so she tied up at the ramshackle dock and awaited the visitor. The villagers scattered over the hill in case there was trouble. Luke had a French flag raised to signal that they were friendly. He then anchored a cable length from the dock and prepared to lower his boats to return the fishermen to their friends and families.

As the boats were being lowered, Luke surveyed the small group of sailors on the dock. Everyone held some type of weapon, whether it was a belaying pin or a fish gaff. He walked over to Rene. "I feel like I just went through this scene a week ago. I'm glad you're going first!"

Rene laughed. "See the gal with the spear? That's my sister-in-law, Anna. Looks like she's still mad at me for convincing my brother to come here! Maybe you should do the honors again, Captain." He bowed and waved Luke to the waiting boat.

"Very well. But this is the first time I ever saw a Frenchman scared of a woman." That brought a roar of laughter from the waiting survivors.

"Touché, Captain!" Rene clapped him on his shoulder. "Let's face the foe together!" The two captains descended the battens to the boat. The rest of the survivors, with their meager belonging, and the boats' crews clambered down and prepared to row ashore.

As they approached the dock, the man next to Anna shaded his eyes and then called out, "Is that you, Rene?"

Rene stood up and roared back, "Jacques, your eyesight really must be failing if you can't recognize your own brother!"

Others on the dock started to point and shout. Weapons were dropped in place and the crowd rushed to the arriving boats. The bedlam and obvious shouts of joy brought the rest of the village back to see what had happened. Luke, and the boat crews, were a small island of tranquility on the dock, until the villagers realized they were responsible for the return of their friends and family members. Gallic passion then swept them up in a tide of embraces and kisses. Luke soon found himself in the bear hug of an older, gray haired matron. With Rene hovering behind her, he realized that it must be Rene's wife. Just then, a larger wave hit the dock and it gave a small shudder. Rene shouted out over the noise, "Everyone ashore. We can tell our tale better there and we won't risk getting drowned!"

As they walked toward the village, Rene leaned over to Luke to make himself heard. "I wonder what else suffered while we were gone? That dock wasn't rebuilt this spring like it should have been."

"Maybe you won't need to worry about it if things go as we hope." Luke gave a vague nod toward the north.

"You're right, my friend. We can build a new one there."

* * *

Supplies and spirits were brought from the *København* and the celebration lasted well into the night. When the singing quieted, Rene walked over to the bonfire and called for everyone's attention. "I know I speak for everyone here when I say we owe a debt of thanks to our rescuers. Captain Foxe, thank you!" Luke stood, made a small bow and sat back down. Rene continued. "We've been rescued from the devil, but we still face the deep blue sea. With only two boats, we cannot support a village this size, we can't all return to France, and we have nothing with which to build any new boats." The fishermen around the fire nodded in agreement. "So what do we do? Stay here and slowly starve or do something about it?" There was a scattering of 'Non!' from the men. "The *Compagnie* has done nothing to help us." He pointed to Jacques. "From what you've said, they can't even help themselves. The Dutch leveled La Have after they captured us. This village is now the largest French settlement on Isle Royale. Our new friends here have already settled a large group in Newfoundland and have reached an arrangement with the English at Ferryland to support them in the future, too."

Rene paused to take a swig from a wineskin. After he wiped his mouth with his sleeve, he continued, pointing at Luke. "They have financial backers that see a bright future for this country. They need settlers that want to make a good future for their families. Strange and wonderful things are happening back home. They say people from the future were brought to the German lands with knowledge beyond our wildest dreams. I've seen a small part of this in the new navigation tools Captain Foxe used to sail here. He has maps of this island far better than any available. He asked me to speak to you about a proposal he has made. Just north of here is another bay that is protected and can be secured. It also has large coal deposits his company is interested in. He has proposed that we move our village to that site. They will help build new homes for us to live in and new boats to replace those we lost. What they ask in return is that we supply food for the miners they will bring to dig the coal and the militia that will defend the new port. Anyone who wants to quit fishing and work the mine will be welcome too." Rene turned to Luke and gestured for him to add anything else.

"What Captain Chaumont has said is true. I represent the Hudson's Bay Company and we are looking at mining the nearby coal. We want to be partners with those people already settled here."

Jacques interrupted. "What about the *Compagnie des Cent-Associes*? We're French and you're Danes. What will they do when they learn about you? They may not be here now, but they will return, just like locusts."

Luke answered, "Well actually, I'm English, and most of our investors are English, Germans, and Swedes. As for the *Compagnie*, as Rene said, they seem to be pretty scarce around here. Even some freebooters like the Kirke brothers could kick them out and the Dutch just did it again. I don't see them giving two clipped *sous* for this area. They just bought the English colonies further south and they should be tied up there for many years to come. You will be just like the English at Ferryland. Abandoned, because new and better opportunities came along for their investors."

"What says you won't abandon us, too?"

"Over forty million *livres* in steel and precious metals says we won't."

The villagers were dumbstruck. Finally a voice was faintly heard. "Forty million?"

Luke knew he had struck just the right note. "Yes, forty. We have information that indicates where the deposits are located and the tools to mine them. What we need are people smart enough to see a future with us." He waited for the buzz of conversation to die down before he continued, "I know this is unexpected and I don't need an answer now. Talk it over tonight and we can meet again in the morning. My crew and I thank you for your hospitality and bid you good night."

Luke gathered up the crew that had come to the party and returned to the ship. The conversations around the fire could be heard well into the night.

Chapter 23

Late the next morning, after his hangover had dissipated, Luke went ashore with just Svend and Mr. Barrow. They met Rene as he emptied the night slops. He too looked much the worse for the night's festivities. Luke commented, "You look how I feel this morning. Two old men like us should know better."

"Yes, Captain, but how else do we keep the young ones in their places?" Rene winced, but smiled.

"It went well after we left? We could hear some, even out at the ship."

"They all eventually came around. Old Berthe wanted to know if he would have to build a new hut himself. I told him no, that your crew would do it. Was I wrong in saying so?"

"No, Rene. As I said when we spoke before, the cabins will be built before they move. Will they send the boat with the letters as I asked?"

"Yes, they saw the wisdom there. And the benefits too! The pay you offered did the trick."

Luke took Svend aside. "I want you to get an accurate count of how many cabins we will need to build at the new site. Make sure you allow extra space for families. Let them know why you're asking and make note of any special requests. Get me a count of people and a rough idea of the cargo we will need to move. Can you handle that?"

"Yes, sir. One census coming up." Svend went off with Rene to start the counts.

"John, I want you to get with the captain of the *Coquette* and make sure of the arrangements. Give him copies of my charts to reach Christianburg and find out how soon he can leave." Luke returned to the ship to complete his letters to the Abrabanels and Mette.

* * *

Two days later, both ships prepared to sail. The few people remaining in the village turned out to wish everyone Godspeed. They would use the time available to finish careening and repairing the other fishing boat. The *Coquette* raised anchor first and cleared the headland on a long reach. The *København* took longer, since they needed to finish loading supplies that would be moved to the new settlement. Rene helped John stow the gear. An hour later John reported back to the captain that everything was secure. "Very well, Mr. Barrow. Weigh anchor and let's be on our way. We've a fair wind and should be there before nightfall."

"Aye, aye, Captain." As he walked forward, he called out, "Man the capstan and prepare to make sail!" As the anchor broke free of the bottom, the *København* paid off at her head and followed in the path of the *Coquette.* When she cleared the headland, she turned to the west northwest and headed for Spanish Bay. Late that afternoon she dropped anchor just west of the river that flowed into the bay. Luke surveyed the shore through his telescope. "It still looks peaceful, but we'll stay on board tonight." He closed the glass and handed it to Svend. "Please find Mr. Reinhardt and bring him to my cabin. The three of us need to discuss how we will proceed from here." Svend slid down the handrail to the main deck and then ran below to find Heinrich. Luke remarked to John, "I just hope he has that much energy in two weeks. He's got a lot of hiking and survey work coming up."

* * *

The next two weeks were a blur of activity. Throughout the first week, the need to reach Hudson's Bay in good weather remained as a concern for Luke. To the crew and the new partners, Luke was very upbeat, but Svend heard the mutterings through the thin cabin walls at night. All he could do was try to finish his tasks quickly. Svend accompanied Reinhardt and the three miners during their survey for the coal deposits. They rowed across the bay, to the town site, Sydney Mines, shown on the uptime map. After an hour of hiking, they discovered a large area of surface coal that gave every indication that was just the tip of a larger, underground deposit. They spent the rest of the day helping Svend lay out the area for the mine and set stakes for future excavation work. They finished two days earlier than planned.

When Svend returned with the maps and drawings, a meeting with the French was held at the site. It was decided that the mine would have cabins nearby for the miners, but the fishing village would be across the bay. As Svend said, "The mine will need a large area for the works and for the docks. No need to have everyone living on top of the tailings. With all this space to use, let's make it a healthier site to start with."

Luke looked surprised. He hadn't expected such forethought in someone so young. "That's an excellent idea. Show us how you plan to lay out these sites." Svend unrolled his drawings and Luke, Svend and the village leaders studied the plans. It took a while to explain what the drawings meant, but once they understood and could relate them to the land, they gave a hearty endorsement. The next morning, clearing began for the new mine and settlement.

Shortly after the first foundations were laid out, a delegation from the village workers came to Captain Foxe. Their spokesman asked, "Captain, I know this may be presumptuous, but we would like to ask a favor."

Luke was surprised by the request but said quickly, "We're all working together. What can I do to help you?"

"Can we include a church in the construction plans? We know we have no priest now, but maybe in the future someone will come." The spokesman stood twisting his cap in nervous anxiety.

Luke relaxed, since he had already anticipated this moment when he sent the letters off. "I apologize for not saying something sooner. A church will go up just as soon as the houses are done. As for a priest, I requested that one be found to accompany the next group of miners. While there may not be a state church, there will be churches for those who want them. I can see this place growing fast enough that that would have been a grave oversight. Rest assured, you will have a priest before the year is out." Luke had to struggle to keep from being hoisted on the shoulders of the group. He was too old for that type of celebration. Seeing the signs of the cross and prayers among the group left him with a feeling that the decision for religious freedom may have been the best decision for the new lands.

While the clearing was progressing, Svend and Heinrich set out with their party to survey the surrounding countryside. Captain Andersen would need detailed maps of the area to decide the best defenses for the terrain. Joseph worked as the scout, and the three miners continued to search for additional mining sites. The fourth day out, they paused near a large pond for the evening meal. Heinrich directed the set up. He tossed some empty water skins to Svend.

"Would you go back and get some water from the spring we just passed? Karl can collect some firewood while Joseph keeps watch." He pointed at the two remaining miners. "Gunther, you and Franz break out the cooking pot and start preparing a stew. I'll follow in a minute, Svend, to help carry the water skins back."

As Svend left to get the water, with his gun and the water skins, Heinrich reminded him to watch out for trouble. Svend told him one mother was enough, thank you. Heinrich then pulled out a flint and steel to start a fire. Karl already had a small pile of kindling ready and in a few strikes, the fire was lit. Heinrich picked up his rifle and followed after Svend. He heard Karl mutter that some fresh meat would be nice for a change. He caught up quickly to Svend. After a short hike they reached the spring and filled the skins. As they walked back, he said, "I think we may stay here a day and do some hunting. Our supplies could use some fresh meat to stretch them out and there were quite a few signs of game around that spring."

"I don't know if we can afford the time, but I'd like to go with you, if you don't mind. I've never gone hunting before and father said I should learn from you."

"I don't see why not. I've heard you're a good shot and you seem to be able to handle yourself in the woods. We can leave Joseph to guard the camp." With that settled, they continued on quietly toward the camp. When they arrived, Franz was tending the fire. Heinrich asked quietly as he set the water skin down, "Where's Karl?"

"He went down to the pond to see if he could catch some fish. He said he was tired of the dried meat." Franz poked at the fire, and then added a larger branch.

Heinrich raised his eyes skyward in supplication for deliverance from fools. A commotion in the brush in the direction of the pond caught their attention. They all turned toward the sound. When it came again, Heinrich and Svend grabbed their rifles and raced off toward the pond. Heinrich was furious, "I told him to stay close. We don't know what's around here."

As they approached the pond, they could see Karl struggling to pull a fish ashore. There were already two large ones lying at his feet. He let out a whoop when the fish he was fighting broke the surface in a leap. It was at least a foot long. At the same time, a roar sounded from the brush about thirty feet away. All three men turned to see a large black bear rear up. Heinrich called out, "Karl, set the pole down and back away slowly." The bear dropped to all fours and stared in Karl's direction. Karl just stood there, too petrified to move. The fish flopped on the ground in front of him. Heinrich broke from cover, yelling and waving his gun, trying to spook the bear. Instead the bear started to amble toward Karl. The scent of fish had his full attention.

Heinrich dropped to one knee, brought the rifle up, and fired in one smooth motion. All he got was a misfire. Waving the rifle had somehow dislodged the priming. Without thinking, Svend raised his rifle and took aim. Time stood still as his training kicked in. Aim, lead, hold the breath, and gently squeeze the trigger. The bear was just about to Karl when he fired. The impact of the bullet sent the bear sprawling. It also broke Karl's trance and he started to run. The bear rolled over and started to chase Karl, but its pace was labored.

In the meantime, Heinrich had reprimed his rifle and took careful aim. This time the rifle discharged and the bear dropped dead in his tracks. A head shot had taken him down. Svend came running up, reloading as he ran. Heinrich motioned for him to slow down. "It's over. You don't need to trip and shoot one of us." Svend stopped and grounded the butt of his rifle. He still finished reloading, just in case. Heinrich walked over and clapped him on his back. "Your shot was excellent, but a lung shot would have taken a couple of minutes to kill him. Luckily, I was able to reprime in time and get a close head shot. Bears that size are notoriously difficult to kill."

Karl staggered back as they checked the bear to make sure it was dead. "You saved me! Thank you."

Heinrich fixed him with a furious stare, "No thanks to you, you fool. This is why I told you to stay together. It's spring and they are hungrier than usual. To him, you were just his next big meal. Only luck, and Svend's shot, kept you alive. Grab those fish and take them back to camp. I hope you enjoy them, because they almost cost you your life." He turned back to the bear and started to show Svend how to skin it.

They spent the day butchering the bear and preparing the meat and skin for transport back to the landing site. When they arrived, the story spread quickly. By the evening, even Heinrich and Svend didn't recognize the tale. Everyone enjoyed the fresh meat that night.

* * *

After two weeks, Luke decided that they had done all they could with the building supplies they had and announced that they would sail as soon as the *Coquette* returned. If he waited any longer, he might not be able to sail for Hudson's Bay this season. "We'll take a day of rest and then start loading fresh water and wood. The *Coquette* should be here by then." As they finished loading the last of the water casks, two sails were sighted to the northeast.

The *Coquette* returned with the *Wilhelm.* As soon as they anchored, boats were lowered and their captains came ashore to confer with Luke. He greeted them as they landed. "Jan, it's good to see you. How are things in Christianburg?"

"It's going well. Your timing on the letters was excellent. Both fishing boats were loaded with fish and just about to sail when the *Coquette* arrived. Captain James had copies made of your letters and sent them on both ships. In case something happened to one of them, the other should still get delivered."

"Just like Thomas, always planning for possible problems. How is the convention doing? I know he wasn't happy to be stuck with running it."

"It was finishing when I left. As you surmised, it was raucous, but Thomas handled it well. From what he told me, just before I sailed, the results were exactly what you two had worked out beforehand." Jan gave Luke a cynical stare.

Luke feigned surprise. "I'm shocked, shocked I say! Why would I do such a thing? It was all decided by the people." He managed, just, to not smile when he said it.

De Puyter shook his head in disbelief. "In any case, it's done. I brought the tools and extra lumber we had cut to help start up here. Four of the miners came along to get things started. What are your plans now? Thomas assumed you probably would finish your voyage, but won't be worried if you miss your deadline. He said to tell you, just make sure you're there by late July, or things might get dicey for Hudson's Bay this year. That is, if you still plan to go this year."

"Yes, yes. We're still going. I'm ready to sail now. If you and Captain Gilbert would join me for a celebratory drink, I'll fill you both in on where we are here and what needs completing." Luke pointed toward a roughly finished cabin. They all walked over, admiring the work that had already been done.

The next morning, the *Köbenhavn* raised anchor and set off on the remainder of her exploration voyage.

Chapter 24

Mid June, 1634, West coast of Newfoundland

The trip along the west coast of Newfoundland was quick and uneventful. The *København* made landfall twice, once to check for mineral deposits and once to replenish food and water. Gunther reported that the terrain was favorable, but nothing significant was found by the prospectors. Luke's frustration was mounting. The trip was running much longer than he had planned. Coal and iron were valuable, but they didn't have the appeal that gold and silver fostered. If he was going to get the miners they needed to realize the enormous profit potential of the coal and iron, he had to have the lure of gold, or at least silver to lure them to the undeveloped land.

The days were long and much warmer than when they had left Christianburg. The good weather just served to highlight that summer was moving on. If they didn't return soon to Christianburg, the entire expedition would run into serious problems if they still tried to sail for Hudson's Bay this year. A decision was needed, but Luke still held out hope that at least a start could be made in Hudson's Bay this season. He once more had his cabin covered in maps and paper. The west coast had been his original goal for coal deposits, but the events in Cape Breton had relegated the smaller Newfoundland deposits to a remote contingency. Their location, and questionable size, turned his final hopes to the possibility of rare metals along the north coast.

The charts seemed to indicate the north shore was where the best possibility for a substantial strike could be made. He had to find some indication of gold and silver, or his backers, and the miners, could be fickle and desert him. The long term profits from the iron and coal should prove to be enormous, but he needed something now. Time was becoming a factor. He had to concentrate on one area or he would miss sailing for Hudson's Bay completely this year. The problem was, which one? Nothing seemed to jump out and say 'Dig here!' He asked Svend to join him as he reviewed the maps one last time.

Luke handed Svend a map covered in hand written comments. "Here's what I have for information. These markings indicate where the up-timers mentioned traces of the metals we're seeking. The researchers that helped me tried to include everything they found. The problem is that many of the references didn't say exactly where and how much was found. The writing has gotten smeared and I can't read all of it. It seems the whole north coast has traces, but nothing is positively identified." Frustration was written all over his face and in the set of his shoulders. "I'd hoped a fresh set of eyes might help."

Svend leaned over and studied the maps. "What's this sign mean, by Baie Verte? I can't make out what the legend says this symbol is for."

Luke picked up the map and stared at the spot. "I can't tell either. I'm afraid my eyes are getting old," he said. "Can you make out anything better by the light?"

Svend took the map and held it up to the hanging light. He could see something, but it was faint. On a hunch, he turned the map over and checked the back. In the light shining through the paper, he could read the legend in reverse. "It says new strike. They found something there. Some type of mining must have been done!"

"Then that's our destination." Luke called up through his cabin light, "Mr. Barrow! Check your charts and set a course for Baie Verte!"

Five days later, the *Köbenhavn* dropped anchor off a rocky cove. The high expectations that Luke felt had been conveyed to the crew and everyone was anxious to get the surveyors ashore to start their work. Luke gave them some words of caution before they departed. "I know this area holds a great deal of promise, but don't forget to exercise care." He looked straight at Karl. "Last time you got careless and almost died because of it. I don't want to have to read a funeral service before we get back to Christianburg. Do your jobs right and find what we've been searching for. Good luck. Carry on, Mr. Reinhardt!"

"You heard the captain! Into the boats and let's shove off. Sooner started, sooner finished." The six members of the survey party went over the side and down the battens to the boats. Their gear was lowered to them and they shoved off for shore.

* * *

The map showed an area that should be about a day's march inland. Gunther stared at the topographical map, trying to relate the elevation lines to the forested area they had stopped in. They should be just about there. The problem was, *all* the area was forested. One rocky slope looked just like the next when you couldn't get a clear view of any distant landmarks. By dead reckoning,with the compass and hiking times, they should be near the stream on the map. He folded up the map and placed it carefully back in the waterproof pouch. "We'll head north for another half hour. If we haven't hit the stream by then, I'll need someone to climb a tree and try to get some bearings on the hills we should be near." Everyone looked at Karl, who was the skinniest of the party.

"Alright, I can take a hint! I'll do it if I have too." He shouldered his pack and headed north, hoping they hit the stream soon. The party crested a rise that had left everyone scrambling for hand holds on the scrub trees, to try and pull themselves up the rocky ground. When they reached the ridge line, the sound of rushing water was could be distinctly heard below.

Karl looked relieved that he wouldn't have to climb a tree. Joseph walked up behind him and said deadpan, "Looks like you get to save your climbing skills until you run into your next bear." Karl turned beet red as the rest of the party broke out laughing.

Down the slope, two streams joined just before a small waterfall. Gunther pulled the map out in a hurry. He thought he recognized the terrain from the map. After a moment comparing the map to the scenery he announced, "This looks to be about a half mile downstream from where the uptime mine was located. We'll start panning here to see what the stream might have washed down from there." They all shrugged off their packs. "Let's set up camp first and start after we have a good meal."

After a meal of venison stew, tools were passed out for the survey work. Gunther handed Karl and Franz pans and pointed toward the waterfall. "I want the two of you to work around the base of the falls. Hopefully, you should have some luck with the pans. Joseph and I will head upstream and see if we can locate the main vein.

* * *

Ten days passed without any sign from the survey party. Tempers aboard ship were starting to fray. That night a lookout thought he saw signs of a fire on a hill to the west. Later the next morning, Gunther and Joseph finally arrived back at the beach and were rowed out to the ship. Gunther boarded with a grim look on his face. Luke hurried over to the railing. If only two had returned, something serious must have happened. He had been increasingly worried about time, since this had taken so long. Now it looked like he might have a service to read. As he reached Gunther, Luke saw him break into a broad grin. "We found it, Captain! Your researchers were right about the area. There's a stream with paying metal in it and it eventually led us back to the main deposit. It's a combination of copper and gold. It's not going to be easy to mine, but it should pay handsomely, with the right gear. The others stayed at the site. They wanted to make sure the vein we found didn't peter out just below the surface." He reached into his pack and pulled out a large leather bag. When he finished untying the knots, he spread it open to reveal a handful of gold and copper encrusted rocks. "There's a whole wonderful, beautiful vein where these came from!"

When the word spread through the crew, they raised a huzzah and started celebrating.

Gunther took Luke aside to fill him in more on the extent of the find. "We didn't see any sign of any other people the whole trip. Game was plentiful and didn't act afraid at the sight of us. I felt it was safe to leave the rest of the party at the site. Joseph came back with me as a guide. He'll head back now to guide the rest back to the ship. Now that we know the route, it shouldn't be more than four days until they're back. Franz and Karl are doing some additional surveying and digging to see if there're more indications in the area." He held up the bag. "This should make our voyage."

Luke looked toward the shore. "It's already been made, Gunther. This just means the workers we need will come. They won't all find gold, but they can all find work." He took Gunther to his cabin for a toast to their find.

* * *

A week later found the *Köbenhavn* standing off the new loading dock at Christianburg, preparing to tie up from her journey. A boat from the *Henrietta Marie* had just brought Captain James ashore and was tying up. Captain James and Captain Andersen stood on the dock as a welcoming party. The *Kristina* was anchored downwind from the dock. She and the *Henrietta Marie* were the only ships in the harbor. Svend's heart sank at the implication. Suddenly, from the fort, a salute rang out and a new flag was raised. Forest green with a maroon colored beaver outlined in gold. Luke had his gunner return the salute with a four-pounder on the main deck.

Captain James called out after the last echo, "Were you successful?"

A grinning Luke leaned over the rail. "In all respects Thomas. Summon the settlers, we'll tell the story to them all at once!"

An hour later, all the settlers who could steal away from their duties met in the new community hall. The air was full of resin scent from the unfinished boards. Luke recounted their adventures on Cape Breton and then gave the news on the gold discovery on the north coast. Captain James then read the results from the convention and proudly pointed out the new flag. Luke got back up and motioned for silence. "When we left three months ago I prayed that God would grant us success in starting a new life. Our original intentions were to start a small outpost here and then sail on to Hudson's Bay with the majority of our settlers. With the loss of the *Hamburg* and these new discoveries, we need to revise our plans and expand our efforts here. I still plan to lead a group to Hudson's Bay this season, but it will be smaller and will simply start a new settlement for others to join next year. Over the next few days, I will meet with Captain Andersen and your new leaders to determine who will need to stay and who will go. I still plan to sail this month." Luke sat down. Someone at the back of the hall stood up, "Three cheers for the Captain! Huzzah, huzzah, huzzah!" By this time, the cooks were ready with the feast and everyone settled down to some serious eating. As the meal was winding down, a dejected Svend approached Captain James. "Has there been no word on the *Hamburg*?"

"I'm sorry, son, but it looks like she's gone."

Svend hung his head and walked slowly away. With the ongoing festivities, no one heard him mutter, "I still don't think she's gone." From across the room, Joseph saw the exchange and walked outside to join Svend in case he needed a friend. They sat by the harbor in silence until the sun set.

Chapter 25

The morning after the celebration of the *Köbenhavn'*-s successful return saw many of the younger participants trying to shake off their hangovers. Luke took the opportunity for fewer interruptions to tour the new settlement with Captain James, Captain Andersen, and Ludwig Steinbrecher and see what had already been accomplished in the short time he'd been gone. He wisely started at the fort, while his legs were still fresh.

Karl was justifiably proud with what his men had accomplished. From atop the main bastion he pointed out the new features. "When you left, we were just finishing the palisade. We now have all four cannons mounted to cover the entire waterfront. Any attackers would have to face plunging shot to even get close to the settlement." Luke considered the view from an approaching sailor's view and nodded agreement. Karl turned toward the fort's interior and pointed toward an earthen mound with a door. "The ammunition is all safely stored in that bunker and the nearby well has a plentiful supply of sweet water. The main blockhouse can shelter everyone in the settlement and we have enough men to man all four walls, if needed. When we finished this two weeks ago, I sent the militia to help the miners starting to excavate the main mine shaft. The ground there is ideal for digging and they are already down to the first signs of ore!"

This was the first news that Luke had that progress had been that swift. "I don't recall seeing any hoist gear. How are they getting down into the shaft?"

Ludwig Steinbrecher pointed toward the east. "See that fill there?" Looking closely, Luke could just make out that there was an evenness that was man made, along the hillside, extending toward the harbor. "That's the spoil that's already been excavated. We're going in at a gradual angle. It takes more framing, but we'll be able to haul ore out with carts, instead of hoists and buckets. In the long run, it will be more efficient and we can run tracks right down to the harbor to load directly onto the ships. If you can follow the line of the fill, it will intersect down at the harbor where those men are driving in the pilings." When they had arrived, Luke had wondered why pilings were being set so far from the landing.

He was impressed by the progress. "How soon will you be able to start really mining the ore?"

Ludwig paused, "We should see the first significant amounts later next month. The real question is; what do *you* plan to do with it, once it's above ground?" All three men faced Luke, waiting for the answer to the question they had all been contemplating since the previous evening's announcements.

Luke borrowed Karl's sword and started sketching a map on the bare ground. Pointing with the tip of the sword he explained, "Here's Christianburg and here's the coal mines in Cape Breton. Both have good harbors for loading, but they're too small for more heavy industries." He stabbed the sword into a spot on the southeast coast of Newfoundland. "This is where I plan to ship the coal and iron ore to be turned into usable iron. The harbor is protected and the surrounding countryside is suitable for heavy operations. We'll bring the coal in and convert it to coke there. Likewise, the iron ore and limestone will be shipped in and it will all be converted to pig iron. Eventually, we'll start making steel there and just ship the finished product back to Denmark.'

Luke leaned on the sword for support. His feet were feeling the effects of too much time on land. "When the resupply ships arrive later this summer, that's where the new workers will go." *And now for the hard part. He had to approach this very carefully.* "Thomas, you'll need to stay here and lead that work, now that Sir Thomas is gone. Your mate will have to sail the *Henrietta Marie* to Hudson's Bay." Captain James started to protest, but Luke cut him off before he could get on a roll. "Thomas, I know you're a sailor, but you're the best leader here for the job. We're simply too stretched to waste your talents simply sailing your ship to a known destination. This job has to succeed if we're to have a future here."

Thomas glared at Luke, "Very well, but I'm still not happy about it. What do I do in the meantime for an engineer? I assume Karl's going with you?"

The flattery worked, as Luke knew it would. "That's right. He'll need to get the fort built where we land, before winter. I'll send him back as soon as we're ready there to start breaking ground for your site. Svend has made maps and plans for the site and Karl can work with him before we leave to add his thoughts. It should give you enough to keep busy for the rest of this season. We all have to do more than was anticipated. On the voyage out, I plan to leave Diedermann and a few others near where we found the gold to start operations there. I pray they don't encounter any problems beyond mining. I can't leave any militia with them. They won't be needed at Hudson's Bay until next season and they can get those deposits working now. We've lost too much time to try and press on there this year. I'm worried we might all have to return here in the fall if we don't get resupplied or we can't acquire adequate food stocks there. The growing season is short enough, and an early frost could be deadly." Given his normally positive attitude, Luke's admission that not everything was going well left all of them uneasy. Captain James relaxed as he realized he might get to play the hero if events turned out badly.

Breaking the spell, Luke pointed downhill. "Thomas, I see you've done wonders with the settlement. Show me what's there! I don't see the tents that were there when I left."

The trek down the hill was much faster than the journey up. As they reached the first cabins, Luke asked casually, "Thomas, before I forget. What happened with the widow that lost her husband in the storm?"

Captain James pointed to a nearby cabin. "She's now a newly remarried wife! Two weeks after we landed, one of the miners, Hans Kleindorf, asked her to marry him. She and her son are farming a small garden plot while Hans works in the new mine. With her wedding and two christenings, we're keeping Pastor Bauman busy and out of mischief!" Thomas' smile left Luke wondering what else had gone on in his absence. The group continued through the small settlement, admiring the work that had been accomplished in the short time.

Two days later, under a cloudless sky, the *Köbenhavn*, *Henrietta Marie*, and *Kristina* set sail for Hudson's Bay. Up in the crosstrees, Svend sat sketching their departure. On the opposite page was a sketch of Agnes as he last saw her. He was smiling as he finished the sketch. He remained aloft, sketching the coastlines as they passed. On the aftercastle, Luke watched his stepson with a heavy heart. For someone so young, Svend had suffered a great deal, but he didn't know how to ease his pain. John walked over and cleared his throat to interrupt Luke's thoughts. He nodded toward the figure aloft. "I hope he's alright. He can't seem to accept what's happened."

"I know, and I don't know what to do. I never had any children of my own and I just can't seem to break through that false optimism he's holding onto."

"Give him time Captain. He's a smart lad and should come around on his own. We'll just need to keep him busy so he can't brood."

"I hope you're right John." Luke hung his head in frustration and turned to watch the horizon.

The first few days were uneventful. Diedermann, and his five miners were dropped off to start developing the gold field. They were anxious to see the vein that was supposedly going to make them rich. All thoughts for their safety, in the event there were unfriendly natives around, were forgotten. As they rowed off, Luke called out to them one last warning to exercise caution. When the boats returned, the ships then set sail north for the passage to Hudson's Bay. The weather held fair but as they neared the Hudson Strait, ice floes started increasing in size and quantity. The temperature hovered barely above freezing at night, but the days were bright and the sun barely set at night. Whales were now a common sight and speculation about their edibility was rampant. Luke asked Joseph to his cabin to discuss the broader question of food at their destination. "I'm concerned about food for the coming winter. When we locate your tribe, we'll want to be able to start raising food for our needs. Is there enough tillable land in the region for us to be able to plant our own crops?"

Joseph looked perplexed. "I'm not sure what you're asking Captain. We only grow a little of what we need to get us through the winter. We hunt and fish and gather what we need. We don't have fields like I saw in Denmark. We certainly don't have extra food."

Luke shook his head. "You misunderstand. Maybe I didn't say it right. What I need to know is whether the ground will be able to be turned and planted by the time we get there. And, is there an area nearby that we could use without crowding your crops?"

Joseph mulled the question over before answering. "The ground should be soft enough to dig when we get there, as long as you don't go down too far. You can still find some frost, even in summer, in the shaded areas. There is land south of our village that should be open enough for the small gardens I saw in your city. If you want better land, you'll need to travel south for some distance to get good land for growing."

Luke sighed, "That's what I was afraid of. We may need to send out whaling and fishing parties to supplement our food stocks. That will take up valuable time and energy."

Luke seemed to focus on some distant point that Joseph couldn't see. "At least we'll be able to start a settlement this year. Unless the resupply ships arrive before September, I'll have to send some of the workers back to Christianburg for the winter." Realizing he was wandering he nodded to Joseph. "Thank you Joseph, you may go."

Looking out the stern windows, Luke stared at the ice flows curling back into the *Köbenhavn's* wake. It reminded him of a task he'd been considering. He'd need to make contact with some of the Inuit to establish a shelter along the route, in case any ships were stranded by ice. They would also be a good trading source for whale meat and oil and furs.

Chapter 26

July 1634, off Danby Island, Hudson's Bay

"Ahoy the deck! Smoke off the port quarter!"

Captain Foxe hurried on deck. "Can you make out what it is?" Hopefully, it was an Inuit hunting party. The lookouts had specific instructions to hail the deck if any possible sightings occurred.

The lookout was an experienced sailor from a previous Arctic expedition. He surveyed the activity at the base of the smoke column. "It appears to be a hunting party. There's something in the water by the beach that looks like a whale carcass. They may be butchering it. I can't be positive, but it looks like three or four boats pulled up on the shore. One of them appears to have some sort of mast, almost like a Thames River wherry! I can't make out how many are in the party."

Without waiting for orders, John Barrow started preparations to lower the longboat. The Captain had been so anxious to make contact with the Inuit, John knew he would be personally going to meet the hunters. It still took almost an hour to reach a safe anchorage. Even though it was summer, there were ice floes that slowed the ships' passage. Even before the *Köbenhavn's* anchor touched bottom, the longboat had pushed off for shore. The other ships simply stood off with their sails furled. Luke had the guide, Heinrich, Svend, Joseph, and four sailors accompany him to the meeting. All carried some type of weapons. Heinrich, Svend and Joseph were armed with muskets, Luke had a pistol and sword and the sailors had boarding pikes. Luke wasn't expecting trouble, but he'd always insisted that any landing party going into unknown territory had to be ready for any type of trouble.

As they were being rowed ashore, Luke was still instructing Joseph how he wanted to approach the hunting party. "Are you sure you can handle their language? I want to make sure they know immediately that we come in peace."

Deadpan, Joseph replied, "I think I remember how to say that. Then again, most of the Inuit I know dealt with meeting their girls. For all I know, you may have an extra wife when this is all done." Luke looked aghast, until Joseph and Svend broke out laughing.

Between gasps for air Svend managed to reassure Luke, "Relax Father. Everything will go fine! You've been grilling Joseph ever since we sighted the hunters. He knows what you want him to say. If there's any doubt, the gifts you're bringing should help bridge any misunderstandings."

Luke ruefully admitted his misgivings. "You're right. It's just so important we make this contact." The rowers started to ship their oars. "Well, we're here!"

As the longboat beached on the shore, a group of five Inuit gathered a short distance away between the landing site and the whale carcass. They presented an interesting sight. All wore animal skin clothing that was liberally drenched in blood and spotted with patches of blubber. The apparent leader was somewhat taller and more weathered than the other hunters. He was unusual, in that he had a full beard. One of the younger men had a flaming red head of hair. The other three were typical shorter, dark haired Inuit. Four others hung back and continued their work on the carcass, carving off long strips of blubber.

Joseph stepped out of the boat with his hands empty and raised. "*Uvagup qaijuq saimmavuq.*" He paused and waited for a response. The leader simply stared at the landing party. Joseph turned back and said to Luke over his shoulder, "I think I said it correctly. What should I do now?"

The leader stepped forward. "You said it correctly. It's just that your Cree accent is atrocious!"

The landing party was dumbfounded. The leader had answered in English with a slight London accent! Luke was the first to recover. "Who are you sir, and how do you come by your English?"

The leader answered, "I might ask you the same! I've been waiting here over twenty years for rescue. My name is Jack Hudson. My father was Henry Hudson."

Luke studied the leader intently, trying to ascertain if he spoke the truth. "I've heard descriptions of your father, and you do bear a resemblance. I've also read everything from the trial of the mutineers." He turned to the red haired youngster. "Was your father the ship's carpenter? I heard he was a red head."

In halting English the red head, Adam, answered, "I'm told he was. I never knew him. He died of the lung fever shortly before I was born."

Jack Hudson interrupted, "You said mutineers? So the *Discovery* did make it back. Did they hang them all?"

Luke took a deep breath, "None of the mutineers were hanged. Greene and Juet didn't even survive the return trip. In all, only eight returned."

Hudson seemed to shrink with that news. "Those bastards deserved to die, especially Greene and Juet. They set us adrift and then taunted us, just keeping the ship out of reach. We rowed after them for almost a day, hoping they would relent and take us back aboard. Many of us were deathly sick. Four of our group died within a fortnight of the cold and deprivations. Two more were killed by a white bear, trying to save a seal we'd killed for food. For me, the worst was watching my father die. I think he died simply of a broken heart. After we buried the two the bear killed on the island, the rest of us tried reached the mainland. We were starving and threw ourselves on the mercy of the locals. When we proved we could be of assistance, they reluctantly took us in." Jack stared out across the open water.

"I've waited twenty years for rescue and vengeance, and now you tell me those that did this went free? Thank God I made a life here for myself. I've helped my clan grow, with the knowledge I had of ships and metal." He pointed to the wherry. "That used up all the nails salvaged from our boat and what little we could trade for. It's let us range much further to sea, hunting whales and returning with more from the catches. We've almost doubled in size since I became their leader." He looked back to the workers who continued to strip the carcass, almost finished with the work of packing the meat aboard the wherry. "I'm forgetting my manners. Will you have a meal with us and tell me more of what transpired with the *Discovery?* I can't promise an elegant fare, but it's the best we have."

Luke quickly accepted. "I'd be honored." He pointed to the goods wrapped up in the stern of the longboat. In the confusion of the stunning discovery, he simply used his prepared speech. "Let me present you with these goods as a token of our appreciation of your hospitality. They may help to make life easier for your people."

Jack nodded. "With many thanks." He turned to the distant group of butchers and yelled, "Yutu! Kirima! We have guests. Start preparing food and drink."

It took a few minutes to unload the presents. Svend stared at the hurried meal preparations and the ingredients going into the pot. He started to get queasy. Joseph leaned over and whispered in his ear, "Now we can get some real home cooking. Not some of that tough sheep we had in the Orkneys!" Svend turned a light shade of green.

Luke looked surprisingly pleased. "That sounds delicious. I've looked forward to that all during my voyage. I'm sure the rest of the party will be just as *pleased."* His look quelled any possible objections.

The bosun saw the look on Svend's face and decided to poke some fun at him too. He'd been with Luke on the previous voyage to the Bay. "That sounds excellent

Captain. Lot's better than the rat we had to eat on our last trip!"

Luke looked back to the ships offshore to hide his smile. "I'm afraid you'll just have to wait for your share, bosun. I need you and your crew to return to the *København* and inform Mr. Barrow we will be remaining here until morning. He's to have the other ships anchor and use the time to check their rigging. I noticed that the *Henrietta Marie's* cordage seemed somewhat frayed in spots as they passed us coming in. They can use this rest to check it and reave in any replacements needed. You can return ashore when that's done and eat then."

Jack Hudson had followed the conversation with interest. "I see a Captain's work is never done. We'll have to swap stories while we eat. I'm curious to know what brings such a large group this far into the unknown and I'm sure you want to know more about the full story on what happened aboard the Discovery."

"That I do! But first, show me this wherry you built. Your ingenuity in fashioning the sail is amazing." Svend followed behind, after pausing to pull out a sketch pad and pencil to record the scene.

* * *

Luke sat back, savoring the heat from the whale oil fire. "That was an excellent meal! Who knew you could do so much with just whale, caribou and fish!" He looked toward Svend, who'd been very quiet during the meal. "What do you think of it son?"

Svend nodded and then quickly mumbled, "I'll be back in a few minutes." He looked very distressed and slightly green. He started to head beyond the light of the fire, but paused and picked up his rifle first. Heinrich was about to say something, but just nodded to himself when Svend remembered the gun. His pupil had learned the hard way about safety in a strange location and had remembered his lesson.

204

Joseph didn't even notice Svend's departure. He'd been fascinated to find out that one of the Inuit party was female. She was Jack Hudson's daughter, Kirima. He'd sat next to her throughout the meal and practiced his language skills.

Luke noticed the byplay and turned to his host. "I see my interpreter is putting his skills to good use. Just before we arrived, he was saying that he hoped he wouldn't misspeak and I'd end up with another wife." The comment had been loud enough for Joseph to hear and he started to blush. Evidently, Kirima understood enough English because she started to laugh at Joseph's discomfort. She whispered something to him that that caused him to choke on the bite he'd just taken.

Jack was quick to take up the joke. "It seems my daughter is honing her hunting skills. I hope your interpreter knows what he's in for. He may have been right about *someone* ending up with a wife!" The smile on Jack's face was the first that Luke had seen since they met. "I have a request to make that concerns my daughter."

They were interrupted when a loud scream brought everyone to their feet. It came from the direction of the whale carcass. Two of the Inuit had gone off to finish loading the wherry with the last of the meat and boil. A second scream was cut short, but the sounds of a struggle were clearly heard on the night air. A final moan and the tearing of flesh were followed by a bubbling sound. Something large had attacked the two men. Heavy footsteps could be heard coming from beyond the shallow hummock. Beyond the circle of the firelight, only the nearby hummocks were dimly visible in the Arctic twilight. A shadow was moving just beyond the nearest rise. Suddenly, a frenzied polar bear was revealed by the firelight as he stopped at the crest of the slope, covered in blood. In his jaws he held the feebly struggling body of one of the Inuit hunters. Seeing new prey, he flung the body aside and stood on his hind feet, bellowing a challenge. Jack Hudson was closest. He reached back and grabbed the spear lying there. He then charged the bear, alone. This wasn't the first polar bear he'd faced. He knew he couldn't kill it alone, but he could slow it down. He stopped short and jabbed at the bear, trying to distract it so that the others could seize some type of weapon before the bear reached the campfire.

The bear lunged and his claws raked Jack's left arm from the shoulder to the elbow, knocking him aside. The spear fell from his hands as he landed face down on the moss. Kirima screamed at the sight of her father's injury, but stood transfixed, too shocked to move.

Her scream drew the bear's attention. He dropped to all fours and started down the slope toward her. The short delay gave Joseph just enough time to grab his gun, cock it, and aim. When he pulled the trigger, the priming misfired and there was no time to reprime. He shoved Kirima aside with the gun's butt and continued with a pirouette to use the gun as a club to stop the bear. He struck a solid blow to the bear's head. All it accomplished was to shatter the gun stock and turn the bear's attention toward him. The bear's return swipe caught Joseph on the back as he stumbled from his swing. It launched him through the fire to the other side of the circle of light. He lay there trying to beat out the flames on his trousers with his one good arm. His other shoulder was drenched with his blood.

The bear's delay wasn't wasted by the rest of the party. Heinrich had an extra second to check his priming, before firing. The bear was broadside to him. His only reliable shot was for the heart. He took it, knowing that it would still take some time before the bear died. He prayed it would slow him down so that someone else could finish him before it killed again.

In the meantime, Svend was just returning from using the privy pit. When he heard the screams, he yanked his belt tight and ran back toward the fire, repriming his rifle as he went. As he crested the hummock outside camp, he arrived in time to see Heinrich's shot. His father and Heinrich were now squarely in the bear's sights for its next attack. As the bear reared up, it seemed to realize it was mortally injured as blood frothed from its mouth. That realization just enraged it more. It let out a bubbling moan and turned to face the source of its pain. Svend remembered Heinrich's advice from the last bear attack he faced. A brain shot was his only hope to stop the bear before it killed more of the party. When the bear roared again as it started to charge, Svend calmly sighted on the mouth and fired. The crack of the rifle was immediately followed by a spray of blood and brains as the ball entered the brain from the mouth and blew out a section of skull as it exited. The bear stiffened and then fell over dead at Heinrich's feet. Captain Foxe reached over with the sword he'd drawn and prodded the bear to make sure it was dead.

Heinrich turned toward Svend. "About time you showed up! I'm *really* glad you remembered your lesson." Moans from around the fire quickly drew their attention back to the wounded.

With the detached calm of someone who had just faced imminent death, Luke noted that Kirima was not attending to her father. Kirima was examining Joseph, so Luke glanced over to Jack Hudson. The quick look was all he needed and he ran over to the pile of trade goods by the boats. Rifling through the stack, he found the bolt of cloth he knew was there and threw it to one of the two Inuit who were already seeing to Jack's wounds. The shorter hunter immediately started to tear strips for bandaging the wounds.

A brief examination of the hunter the bear had dragged into the camp was enough for Luke to ascertain he was dead. The bear had crushed the chest in his jaws, puncturing the aorta. The pool of blood around the corpse was almost the entire blood supply a body could hold. The other victim was somewhere beyond the whale carcass. *Time enough to search for him after the nearby wounded were treated.* Luke took the flask from his hip and shooed the two Inuit away before they could smear grease on the wound. The books he'd seen in Grantville said alcohol was good for keeping wounds from suppurating. It *was a shame to use such good rum for such a mundane purpose, but needs must*! He pulled the cork on the flask. Once the rum had liberally bathed the site, he took the bandages and bound up the wound. Luckily, the sealskin garments Jack had been wearing had kept the claws from digging in too far. The flesh was torn badly, but the muscle and tendons were still attached. If infection could be contained, there was a good chance of recovery.

Svend stood nearby, reloading his rifle, along with Heinrich. Luke motioned toward the whale carcass. "There's still one victim out there. Go see if you can find him, and see if he needs tending."

Heinrich interrupted, "Let us finish reloading. We don't know that there isn't a mate out there. We'll go as soon as we're loaded." A final thrust with a ramrod seated the shot. Five seconds later, both rifles were primed and Svend and Heinrich walked slowly into the dark. Each scanned the quadrant to their front as they fanned out, rifles at the ready. Two minutes later, Heinrich called out. "We've found the other, but there's no need to hurry. He's definitely dead!"

One of the Inuit helping Luke with Jack Hudson seemed to get the gist of Heinrich's call. He let out a wail. It surprised Luke and he turned to Kirima, "What's wrong?"

Kirima said flatly, "That was his brother, Yutu! This was his first whaling trip. He came because his brother kept asking my father to bring him. Now he's dead." She turned back to Joseph. His coat sleeve was drenched in his own blood. "I'm not going to lose you too! You saved my life when you could have fled. She pleaded with Luke, "Pass me more bandages! I've just about got his bleeding stopped. Please use your medicine on him too!"

Luke finished binding up Jack's wound and hurried over to see what he could do for Joseph. The wounds were more bloody than dangerous. Like Jack, Joseph's clothing and his stumble, had avoided the major blow. There were five furrows across his shoulder that would hurt like the blazes for the next few weeks, but a quick job with a sail needle and thread would have him as good as new. As he poured rum on the gashes, Luke told Kirima, "Just bind him up. We'll take him and your father to the ship and have the surgeon sew them up properly. Joseph's not in any danger from those cuts. I'm more concerned for your father. His wounds are much deeper." The concern in her eyes told Luke all he needed to know about Kirima's affections. Joseph definitely had made an impression in a short time! A hail from the shore caught Luke's attention. The longboat party was back, just in time!

Chapter 27

It was some time before the surgeon was able to break away and report to Captain Foxe on the status on his patients. He found Luke standing with John Barrow at the ship's wheel discussing what further delays might result from the attack. "Excuse me Captain; I've finished with the patients." He then stood there silently, waiting for the Captain to reply.

Luke looked at him, "And?"

Mordecai continued, "They both should recover. As you suspected, Joseph just needed some stitches to close the surface wounds. Barring any infection, Jack Hudson will recover too, but his arm will be stiff from the scar tissue. I had to leave a small area open to make sure any pus could drain properly. I bathed the wound again in rum, just as you ordered. Hopefully that will keep the infection to a minimum. He won't be able to travel in an open boat for some time."

"That's what Mr. Barrow and I were just discussing. We'll escort his party back to their village. It's on our way and will give us a few days to talk further with him. Is he awake now?"

"Yes, but his daughter is with both of them. She sure seems concerned about Joseph." His leer almost made Luke chuckle.

"You know Mordecai, you're just a dirty old man. The young man saved her life. She's a right to be concerned."

The leer just got bigger. "I may be old Captain, but that was no *chaste maiden* kiss I saw her give him when I finished with him. I don't know what went on there at the meal, but that boy sure is a fast worker!" He smiled like a father that saw many grandchildren in his future. "You go see if I'm mistaken!"

Luke motioned for him to precede him down the ladder. "Lead on! I want to see this warrior's maiden." When they reached the cabin the surgeon had set up as a temporary recovery area, Kirima was seated on Joseph's cot holding his good hand while she held a heated discussion with her father. She stopped abruptly when Luke poked his head in through the doorway.

Jack Hudson looked like a schoolboy who'd just been caught by his teacher hiding a frog in the teacher's desk. His eyes tried to focus on Luke, and after a second he mumbled, "Thank you very much for saving my people. I don't know how I repay this debt." He looked over to Kirima who gave a nod, "My daughter's life is yours. She agrees." He sighed and sank back, face down on the cot.

Luke wasn't quite sure what had just transpired, until he saw the look on Kirima's face. She was smiling like someone who had just won a valuable prize. As she looked at Joseph, Luke realized *who* the prize was. *I just hope he's in agreement and doesn't upset my plans!*

Luke turned around in the cramped cabin and shooed Mordecai out ahead of him. "Your patients seem to be doing fine! I'll come back in the morning and speak to Jack then. I think their nurse will be able to handle any nonemergency needs until then." He turned back to Jack and added, "I'll see to your people and their boat. We'll pass them a line and tow them back to your village so you won't have to risk an open boat with your wounds." Jack gave a weak wave with his good hand and fell quickly to sleep, his pain deadened by the rum he'd been given.

Svend arrived just then to check on his friend Joseph, but Luke turned him back with reassurances that all was well and that they really needed to rest. He gave Svend an errand to occupy his mind. "Go find the red headed native. I think he understands enough English that you can let him know that Jack Hudson should recover. Tell him we'll help them finish their loading of the meat, if they need us, and we'll tow them back to their village. Jack's going to need rest and warmth for a while and we can give that to him aboard our ship. If he needs anything, he should ask you for it."

When Svend arrived at the camp, the remaining hunters were holding an animated discussion. After some false starts, Svend was able to piece together enough English and Cree that Adam understood to convey the sense of his father's instructions. The red head pointed to the wherry and indicated all was ready for departure. If the *Köbenhavn* would pass them a line, to tow the wherry, they would paddle the two remaining kayaks. When Svend tried to stammer out that it would be a long trip, implying they might not be able to keep up, Adam informed him not to worry, they would keep their speed down to where the sailing ships could keep up! When Svend finally realized what Adam had said, he started laughing and nodded agreement. He then gave the two an update on Jack's condition and assured them they could visit whenever they needed. Adam quickly asked if he could see him now and offered to take Svend back to the ship in his boat. Eyeing the light-weight craft, Svend diplomatically declined the offer, saying he needed to make sure his sailors returned promptly to their duties. Adam smiled and then pushed his craft off from the beach.

* * *

The next two days were touch and go for Jack Hudson. Despite the surgeon's care, he developed an infection. On the third morning, he woke up and asked what was for breakfast. Mordecai was summoned and after a brief examination he announced, "It appears the fever has passed. If the patient can restrain himself from overdoing, he should recover. Just broth and biscuit for breakfast."

212

Jack scowled at the announced menu, but eventually acknowledged after he'd finished that it was all he could handle. Luke arrived shortly before the meal was finished and sat down on the one chair in the crowded cabin. Kirima sat on Joseph's cot, helping her father eat while he lay on his stomach, so as not to disturb the dressings on his back. After Jack finished the last of the broth and gave a contented belch, Luke asked, "So now that you're back amongst the land of the living, what are your plans?"

Jack tried to fix Luke with a stare but failed. "I don't know. I assume we're heading toward our clan's summer camp, so how soon until we arrive?"

Luke smiled, "As fate would have it, your recovery is well timed. We should be there within a few hours." He pointed toward the stern. "We have the wherry in tow and the rest of your party is keeping ahead of us in their own boats. Adam was very helpful during your recovery. If you're up to it, I have something we do need to discuss before you leave our hospitality."

Jack tried to turn over but thought better after the bandages started to pull. "You're right. We never did finish our discussion of the other night. What do you have on your mind?"

"You asked once why we were here and then left me with the impression you don't want to go back to civilization. Is that your intention?"

Jack lay there, not answering for a few minutes and Luke began to wonder if he'd fallen off to sleep. Jack finally cleared his throat and replied, "I dreamt for many years about returning to England. I still miss many of the comforts; books, plays, foods." A wistful smile came to his face, "Warm weather!" He gave a shiver to emphasize the point, but then continued in a graver tone. "But in the last few years, I've come to realize I've taken on responsibilities here. I've become a leader to my adopted people. Bringing the benefits of civilization to them, while protecting them from the uglier side of it, means more to me. I've tried to teach my people but I am no teacher. Kirima is very bright and deserves to have the chance to get an education and have a bright future. You said you wanted to trade with us and I agree, on two condition. You take Kirima with you and provide her an education and send us teachers in the future. She's already agreed and just needs your blessing."

Luke was surprised that Hudson's request coincided with the plans he had intended to discuss. "I will be more than willing to assist in educating your daughter. We already have one teacher with us and I can send for another to arrive next spring. Kirima can start as soon as we get settled at our new home. With your permission, we'll build a small trading house at your summer camp to house a trader when our next group arrives. It can have a school room included. That way, you can prepare your people for the new opportunities they'll face."

Jack smiled wanly, "That's fine. I'm sure I'll see some resistance to change. Waiting 'til next spring is a good idea. The more gradual the change, the more likely the changes will be accepted and used." He closed his eyes and drifted off to sleep.

Luke turned to Kirima and spoke quietly, so not to wake Jack. "Are you in full agreement with your father's request? If not, I'm sure I can work something out with him."

The look that Luke got was one normally reserved for half-wits. "I've heard stories all my life about my father's native land. I thought most were just stories. Now I see that the truth was *more* than he had told me. You'd have to tie me up to stop me from going, that's why he asked you. Besides, you have *other* incentives to entice me along." She looked toward Joseph with a faint smile.

Joseph took Kirima's hand. "I'm sure my father will welcome her to our village. Our peoples have lived in peace for many years. Besides, the reason he sent me with Captain James was to bring knowledge of the new

214

ways back to my people too. A school will help show your peaceful intent better than any words you could say."

It suddenly struck Luke that Joseph had been evaluating their intentions ever since he had sailed with Captain James. Thankfully, his intentions had always matched his actions. Hopefully, his father would listen to his proposal when they arrived. In the meantime, he had preparations to make for landing Jack and setting up the trading post. A hail from the masthead announced the village was in sight. He nodded, "If you'll excuse me, I'll leave you to seeing to Jack's needs for the transfer ashore. I have some tasks of my own if we're to sail by the morrow."

The entire clan crowded the beach as the small fleet approached. Luke watched through his glass as the small boats beached and told the news of the attack and deaths. Jack was already on deck, lying in a makeshift stretcher that could fit in the longboat for the transfer ashore. In a muted voice he asked Luke, "How are they taking the news?"

Luke walked over from the rail so he could answer without the entire crew hearing. "I think our presence has overwhelmed most of the crowd. It's evident who the families are, though. Yutu is comforting an older couple and a young woman appears to be devastated.

Jack shook his head, "That would be Yotimo's wife. She's expecting later in the summer."

"Would a gift of blankets and a lantern help her? We have some extras in our trade goods."

Jack looked at Luke in surprise. "I should say they would. I don't know whether you're clairvoyant or just lucky, but a lamp is highly prized by my people. It will go far in helping her find a husband to raise her child."

Luke motioned to a nearby seaman and whispered some instructions to him. Within minutes, three blankets, a lamp, and an iron cooking pot were added to the supplies going ashore.

The ships hove to without dropping their anchors. It took some time to safely hoist Jack's stretcher over the side into the longboat. John Barrow made sure the stretcher was lashed down securely and even called the stroke as the boat made the short journey ashore. When they reached the beach, seven men splashed out into the surf to manhandle the stretcher ashore. They took Jack directly to his caribou hide tent and made him comfortable. Kirima stopped by briefly with Joseph and returned to the longboat with a small bundle of her personal treasures. Luke spent a longer time with Jack, reiterating his commitment toward Kirima's schooling and making arrangements to have the lumber delivered in the spring to build the trading post and schoolroom. When the landing party returned to the ship, Jack Barrow was still hoisting the longboat aboard when Luke gave the order to make sail. His anxiety to reach the final destination was evident to Svend as he watched his father. He quickly finished his sketch of the landing site, making sure that it was detailed enough for the ship that would return in the spring would recognize the spot.

Chapter 28

Late July 1634 Copenhagen

The *Bluefin* sailed into Copenhagen harbor weighed down with her cargo of cod. Captain Nielsen contemplated the three linen packets and the pouch he had to deliver, wondering whose should be delivered first. A nearby argument between two sailors over whether they would go home first or stop at a tavern first made up his mind. Mette Foxe would get her letter first. The King and the Abrabanels would have to wait! As the ship tacked to reach the fishmongers pier, Captain Nielsen noticed that a number of changes had occurred since they had left. Out in the harbor, what could only be salvage operations were underway on a strange vessel. It looked like some type of raft with walls. Ashore, there were distinct signs of damage from cannon fire. *So the tales we heard were true! The Swede had attacked!* Danish flags were flying from the palace and there were more strange ships anchored off the naval piers. Everything appeared peaceful and normal. A stop at Mette's tavern seemed even more urgent now. He needed to find out what had been happening and who the other letters needed to go to now.

As he entered the tavern, Jan's eyes took a moment to adjust to the dimmer light. Before he took two steps a cry of "Jan Nielsen, you're back!" caught his attention as a pregnant Mette Foxe rushed to meet him.

"What news do you have? Are Luke and Svend alright? Is the new settlement safe?" Mette's questions would have kept pouring out but Jan gave her a quick hug and then held her at arm's length, studying her figure.

"Yes, to all your questions. And it looks like I'll have to send the word to Luke that you're doing well to. It appears your new marriage suits you well!" He laughed as she blushed. "I came here as soon as we landed to get Luke's letter to you. The King will have to wait his turn." He held up the other packets. Mette blushed at the implied compliment. "Now tell me what's been happening since we left. From the harbor, it looks like someone attacked, but who won?"

Mette grabbed his arm and guide Jan to an empty table, at the same time motioning to the barkeep to send over drinks. "Sit down and I'll tell you. It's a long story!"

An hour later, as Mette finished the tale of Bundgaard's arrest and escape during the bombardment, Jan grew pensive. "If he's still loose, I think Luke would definitely want you to join him. The new settlement is growing fast and houses are already being built." He pointed toward her belly. "How soon are you due? Even with the baby, you'd probably be safer sailing with the next supply ship."

Mette interrupted before he could go further. "Plans are already underway to do just that. I have someone that's ready to buy the tavern, as soon as he receive the funds. The ships want to clear well in advance of the fall storm that's forecast. All you hear are complaints on how slow the work is going and how the Company's offering land for those that want to relocate. I'm getting thoroughly tired of it all! Now, finish your beer and see to delivering your other packets. *I* have a letter from my husband I want to read and I don't need you reading over my shoulder!" She gave Jan a friendly slap on the back and retired upstairs with the letter.

* * *

As he approached the palace to deliver the King's packet, Jan withdrew both packets from his jacket. For the first time, he realized the packet for the King was *substantially thinner* than the Abrabanels'. He shoved the thicker packet back in his jacket. *No need to let the King know he's not getting all the news!*

It took two hours of waiting and explaining before Jan got an audience with the Prime Minister's secretary. He was told in no uncertain terms that he could turn over the packet and then be about his business. Luke had told him this might happen and that as long as the packet got that far, he was safe to turn it over. It was getting late, so Jan handed the secretary the packet and then returned to the tavern for a meal and a room. He would deliver the Abrabanels' packet in the morning. Luke had warned him that he might have to spend a lot of time answering their questions.

* * *

Jan got directions from Mette, before he turned in, on the location of the Company's new offices, and then set out early the next morning on foot. His rolling gait marked him as just back from a long voyage and the few doxies still trying to make one last mark for the night halfheartedly propositioned him as he passed. Jan just smiled and shook his head. Best not to antagonize them, in case their pimp was nearby. He hurried on, trying to look down on his luck and broke. He tried to ignore the heavy pouch inside his shirt. As he neared the office's address, he realized things must be looking up. The neighborhood was bustling with new buildings going up where he remembered that old warehouses had stood. When he rounded the last corner, Jan was surprised to see a line of people waiting outside a new office with a sign proudly proclaiming, 'Hudson's Bay Company, Land Office for the Gold Fields of the New World!' In smaller letters it added, 'Official office for all relocation transportees. Next ship sails August 1st'. For as earlier as it was, some must have spent the night waiting outside the office. Packs, children, and small carts clogged the sidewalk all the way around the far corner. As he bypassed the line, a younger tough, who was keeping order, called out, "Wait your turn like the rest!" Jan held up the packet with the Abrabanels' names on it. "This says I go right in! I've worked for the Company a lot longer than you have. This is news fresh from the colony!" As soon as he said that, Jan realized it probably wasn't the smartest thing he'd ever done. The crowd lost all order and crowded around, pelting him with questions. As the tough tried to restore order, Jan slowly pushed through the crowd and finally reached the door. Another guard checked the packet before quickly unlocking the door and letting Jan slip inside.

Reuben Abrabanel was sitting at a raised desk at the rear of the room and instantly recognized Jan. He broke into a broad grin and rushed to meet his visitor. "Captain Nielsen, I'm delighted to see you! I had heard that your ship docked late yesterday and that you'd been to the Castle. What news do you have for me?

Jan pointed to the chaos outside. "I think we need to go someplace a little quieter."

Reuben laughed, "Nonsense, that happens all the time. Ever since the King announced that there was going to be a flood this fall, we've been swamped with applicants. Half the buildings you see around here are temporary housing for the emigrants that will be leaving next month. I just hope Captain Foxe is ready for them."

Jan insisted. "I think you *really* don't want me making a full report right here. I have some substantial examples of the mining results to deliver to you for safe keeping."

As the implications of what Jan was hinting at sunk in, Reuben glanced at the crowd outside and the two guards and turned white. "I think I understand. Follow me to the back room. You can *give* me the full report there.' He turned to a young clerk who was trying hard to look occupied. "Aaron, go quickly to Factor Bamberg and request he drop whatever he is doing and come here as quickly as possible. Tell him there is news from the New World." The young man nodded and slipped out the back door.

Brave New World

by Eric Flint

Magdeburg, capital of the United States of Europe

August, 1634

Francisco Nasi leaned forward and placed a thin folder on Mike Stearns' desk. Then, sat back with an odd little smile on his face. If Mike didn't know the man better, he'd think Francisco was a bit embarrassed.

Impossible, of course. The Sephardic Jew served Mike as his chief of espionage, security, and whatever other sundry and divers matters he wanted kept privy. Francisco had some official title, which Mike tended to forget, but that was the gist of his position. Despite his relative youth—he was still shy of thirty---Nasi was a veteran of the Ottoman court. A *surviving* veteran, more to the point, in a court which was probably the most powerful and almost certainly the most dangerous in the world.

The point being that embarrassment was no more possible for him than it would be for a python who had mastered the jungle.

Still, he *looked* embarrassed.

"I'm afraid," Nasi said, "that some members of my extended family—very extended family, you understand —have been up to some mischief."

He cleared his throat. Mike decided to make it a little easier for him. "Francisco, I'm well aware that the Nasi 'family' bears far more resemblance to a clan—you might even say, a tribe—than anything Americans usually mean by the term. That means there's no way, of course—not given Abrabanel resources—that you or anyone else could stay on top of everything members of your family are up to anywhere in the world."

He grinned. "So just come right out with it and give me the bad news."

Francisco gave him a thankful look. "It's not exactly 'bad' news. More in the way of complicated news."

Mike made a face. "If there's a distinction between the two, when it comes to foreign affairs, I have yet to encounter it."

"True enough, I suppose." Francisco poked the file with a forefinger, edging it perhaps two inches closer to Mike. Who, for his part, made no motion to pick it up.

"Summarize for me, if you would."

"The gist of the matter is that two of my cousins—very distant cousins, you understand—took it upon themselves to help finance an expedition to the New World."

Mike folded his hands before him and assumed a placid expression. "There are, have been, and will be many expeditions to the New World."

"True. Not many of them, however, are well-financed, led by a capable and very experienced explorer and commander—that would be Captain Luke Foxe—backed by the English ambassador to Denmark—that would be Sir Thomas Roe—and given discreet but significant support by Christian IV, the King of Denmark." He paused to take a breath. "Which support seems to have included providing Foxe and Roe with a large number of colonists. Much larger than such expeditions normally consist of—and much better equipped."

"How many colonists are we talking about?"

Nasi cleared his throat again. Wonder of wonders.

"Close to four hundred. Along with a great deal of equipment, including mining gear and the wherewithal for a sawmill. That's to be expected, since they include a sizeable number of miners and lumbermen. They also have enough provisions to get through at least half a year with no difficulty. Finally, they seem to be quite well armed. Not just with hand weapons but possibly some cannons as well."

"In other words, Christian's backing is extensive. Whatever he's up to, he's serious about it."

"So it would seem."

Mike rubbed his face with his hand. "And what *is* he up to, do you think?"

Nasi looked out the window pensively. "I'm not certain, if course. And in any event, there are a number of possible answers to that question. They range from 'he's just looking to make some money' to 'he's developing a long-term plan to secretly build up Denmark's naval power.'"

"And your best estimate is..."

"Somewhere closer to the second, but still short of it. I don't think Christian, even at his drunkest, is irrational enough to think that he could offset Gustav Adolf's advantage in having up-time technical advice and assistance, when it comes to developing a navy. Simply having access to the naval supplies provided by a large New World settlement wouldn't be enough."

"But it would be enough—might be enough, let's say —to keep Denmark from becoming completely overshadowed by Sweden in naval terms."

"Yes. And I think—"

Mike waved his hand. "Yeah, yeah, I know. Christian's read the same books and encyclopedia articles Richelieu has, and come to the same conclusion." His voice assumed a slight sing-song pitch. 'The future is in the New World. Whoever controls North America will dominate the world, yadda yadda yadda.'"

Nasi gave him a quizzical look. "I've noticed before that you don't seem unduly concerned about that. Why?"

"Because I don't believe in voodoo. There isn't any magic power emanating from the soil of North America,

Francisco. The pre-eminence of the United States in the universe I came from stemmed from a lot of historical factors, very few of which can be duplicated in this universe by people like Cardinal Richelieu—much less the king of Denmark."

Nasi leaned forward in his chair. "Such as?" His tone was curious, not challenging.

"Start with the fact that by the year 2000, when the Ring of Fire happened, the United States was the world's third largest nation in terms of population. We're talking about *three hundred million* people. That's a lot of economic muscle—not to mention a lot of battalions, when you need them. And how did the country get so big? By drawing people from all over the world because we had a loosy-goosy attitude toward immigration and we were willing to give people a lot of personal, political, religious and economic leeway once they arrived. You think a French absolute monarchy—which is what Richelieu is trying to build—could possibly duplicate that? Much less the Danish junior varsity?"

"I'm not sure what a 'varsity' is, of either the senior or junior variety, but I see your point." Francisco leaned back. "I take it, then, that your main concern with this development is how it will affect relations between Christian and Gustav Adolf. When Gustav Adolf finds out."

"Which he's bound to soon enough. There's no way you can keep something like this hidden for very long."

Mike rose from his chair and went over to the office window. He gazed out at nothing in particular for perhaps half a minute before speaking again. Then said: "That being the case, I'd rather he heard it from me. Build trust, etc. etc.—and I might be able to have an effect on his reaction. Set it up for me, will you?"

"Certainly."

* * *

Gustav Adolf didn't keep him waiting. He saw Mike the next day and listened to his explanation patiently and without interruption. When he was done, the king hefted the folder Mike had given him.

"Quite slender," he said. "You are thinking we should let this folder continue to thicken, yes?"

Mike couldn't help but smile. There were ways in which he and his sovereign, despite being born three and half centuries apart, were very much alike.

"I don't see where there's any harm being done, and it would be interesting to see what happens."

Gustav Adolf studied the—still unopened—folder for a few seconds. Then tossed it onto his desk and rose from his chair.

"I agree. And it will help keep Christian from mischief. Or perhaps I should say, mischief that really matters to me. You will keep me informed, I trust."

"Certainly."

It was the king's turn to smile. "I've seen some of Shakespeare's plays, you know. I was particular taken with *The Tempest*. Oh brave new world, that hath such schemes in it."

226

More about Eric Flint's 1632 universe.

In April of the year 2000, a six-mile sphere centered on Grantville, West Virginia was displaced in space and time to Germany and May, 1631. The inhabitants of Grantville decided to start the American revolution early; the nobility of Europe were not amused.

This story, by Eric Flint, is the basis for a great deal of lively discussion on Baen's Bar. The conference is entitled "1632 Tech Manual" and has been in operation for almost thirteen years now, during which time over five hundred thousand posts have been made by hundreds of participants. You can join in the discussion at **http://bar.baen.com**.

As of mid 2013, the 1632 universe has spawned sequels including two anthologies: *Ring of Fire 1 and 2* and ten novels: *1633, 1634: The Galileo Affair, 1634: The Ram Rebellion, 1634: The Baltic War, 1634: The Bavarian Crisis, 1635: The Dreeson Incident, 1635: The Eastern Front, 1636: The Saxon Uprising, 1636: The Kremlin Games, and 1636: The Papal Stakes.* Three of these have been on the New York Times extended best seller list.

In addition, the conversation on *"the bar"* began generating so-called "fanfic," stories written in the setting by fans of the series. So much of it was written, and of such quality that in consultation with Jim Baen, Eric began producing an online magazine of stories and non-fiction articles set in the 1632. Originally sold through Baen's Webscription service, the magazine is now bi-monthly and is sold at **baenebooks.com**, through **Amazon.com, BN.com** and by subscription at the magazine's own web site: **HTTP://www.grantvillegazette.com** The Gazette pays professional rates for stories and non-Fiction and is an SFWA qualifying market. To date, more than 120 authors have been published in the Gazette. As of mid 2013, forty-eight issues have been released making the 1632 universe the largest single shared-universe in publishing history with over *seven million* words in print. In addition, a "best of the Grantville Gazette" volume is published annually by Baen.

Even more (as if that wasn't enough)

Any series needs a bible. The bible for the 1632 web site is at **http://www.1632.org**. This site collects in one place, all the technical information, archives, and files of interest to the happy habitants of the Baen's Bar 1632 Group. You are invited to browse this site, get involved in the discussion groups and even read the free e-book versions of the stories that started it all - 1632 and 1633.

You can see files and pages of interest to fans in general and those who would like to write in the 1632 Universe. Potential authors need to check out the Author's Manual files and peruse Rick Boatright's "Dead Horses" article to see if your idea has been flogged to a pile of dog food.

Science Fiction fandom has spawned many conventions, and 1632 is no different. Each year the 1632 writers, including Eric, Paula and the principle members of the 1632 Editorial Board get together with fans at a convention chosen in various places around the world. There is usually a link to the next such gathering at 1632.org. In 2013 the 1632 folks will be gathering at

Contraflow III, October 18-20, 2013, New Orleans, Louisiana.

In the past, 1632 minicons have been in locations as diverse as Chicago, Tulsa, and Germany (including visits to the location where Grantville landed, near Jena, south of Magdeburg.)

Thanks for participating as a reader. Feel free to join in further. We're always looking for new readers, writers, artists and fans. You will be more than welcome.

Eric Flint - Founder and Senior Writer
Paula Goodlett - Editor

and the members of the 1632 Editorial Board

Rick Boatright, Laura Runkle, Walt Boyes, Iver Cooper, and Kim Mackey

Important links to the 1632 Universe:

The main 1632 "encyclopedia" site:
http://www.1632.org

The Grantville Gazette:
http://www.grantvillegazette.com

Baen's Bar:
http://bar.baen.com

Baen Ebooks:
http://www.baenebooks.com

Other titles available from

Ring of Fire Press

Eric Flint's
Ring of Fire
Essen Steel
Kim Mackey

Eric Flint's
Ring of Fire
Joseph Hanauer
Douglas W. Jones

Eric Flint's
Ring of Fire
No Ship For Tranquebar
Kevin H. and Karen C. Evans

Eric Flint's
Ring of Fire
Second Chance Bird
Garrett W. Vance

Eric Flint's
Ring of Fire
Turn Your Radio On
Wood Hughes

Eric Flint's
Ring of Fire
Medicine and Disease
Various Authors